PRAISE FOR
How to Be a Grown-Up

"McLaughlin and Kraus have done something much more interesting by making Rory funny, self-aware, and supremely competent: a fully realized human being. The joy of this book is not wondering whether she will succeed, but watching her do it. Rory is a modern damsel in distress who doesn't wait for a prince to rescue her but pulls on her boots and strides out to slay the dragon herself."

—Eliza Kennedy, *The New York Times Book Review*

"Such a cupcake of a book, it feels like you're doing something more self-indulgent than reading."

—*Kirkus Reviews*

"Humorous and rewarding . . . smart and lively."

—*Booklist*

"A super-fun romp of a generational collision and a marital breakdown, starring a flustered but steel-strong leading lady."

—*Library Journal*

"The book never fails to set a course for adventure and make it hilarious, with the occasional moment of quiet reflection on modern times."

—Bookreporter.com

"This book is LOL funny."

—*Ft. Worth Star-Telegram*

"McLaughlin and Kraus have given us late thirtysomethings a little summertime indulgence. As *The Nanny Diaries* did for readers in their twenties, *How to Be a Grown-Up* hits the midlife sweet spot."

—*BookPage*

HOW TO BE
A GROWN-UP

A Novel

EMMA McLAUGHLIN
and
NICOLA KRAUS

WASHINGTON SQUARE PRESS
New York   London   Toronto   Sydney   New Delhi

WASHINGTON SQUARE PRESS
An Imprint of Simon & Schuster, Inc.
1230 Avenue of the Americas
New York, NY 10020

First Washington Square Press trade paperback edition July 2016

WASHINGTON SQUARE PRESS and colophon are trademarks of Simon & Schuster, Inc.

For information about special discounts for bulk purchases, please contact Simon & Schuster Special Sales at 1-866-506-1949 or business@simonandschuster.com.

The Simon & Schuster Speakers Bureau can bring authors to your live event. For more information or to book an event, contact the Simon & Schuster Speakers Bureau at 1-866-248-3049 or visit our website at www.simonspeakers.com.

Manufactured in the United States of America

10 9 8 7 6 5 4 3 2 1

Library of Congress Cataloging-in-Publication Data is available.

ISBN 978-1-4516-4345-9
ISBN 978-1-4516-4347-3 (pbk)
ISBN 978-1-4516-4346-6 (ebook)

To Sophie, Theo, and Luke,
the ones, the answer, and the reason

"I think if I make it to 40, I can be pretty amazing."

—Wendy Wasserstein
Uncommon Women and Others

Part I

Chapter One

Although Labor Day was late that year, the heat still sat on the back of my neck like a wet towel. I stood on the porch with my three-year-old, Maya, and watched through the trees for a car kicking up dust on the road. After two weeks at my mother-in-law's place outside Woodstock, NY, with no air-conditioning and no WiFi, we were both Ready To Go.

"Rory, honey!" she called from inside. I cringed. Terms of endearment were never a good omen.

"Yes, Val?"

"Did Maya touch my dream catcher?"

Maya shook her head, her ponytail, still wet from the swimming hole, swiping back and forth across my thigh. "I don't think so, Val," I replied. "You were really clear with her about what not to touch!"

"If you say so."

I liked Val, more than most other women like their mother-in-laws, but one more hour of trying to be polite in that humidity and something Edward Albee was going to break out between us.

The original plan had been that my husband, Blake, would be with us for the whole trip. We'd hike the Catskill Mountains with our ten-year-old, Wynn, and take both kids to the man-made beaches along the Esopus Creek. But then Blake got yet another callback for this Netflix series he'd been auditioning for and had to jump on a plane to LA at the last minute. I was deeply rooting for him to get this part, rooting from the subatomic particles that flurried in my atoms. He needed it. *We* needed it.

Blake was that rare animal, a professional working actor, and he had been since he was a kid. But after Maya was born, the flow of residuals slowed to a trickle, revealing our income's instability like a cracked riverbed. Our whole summer, our whole lives, were now coming down to his landing this role, which was as within his power as winning the lottery.

"Mommy, listen!" Maya started jumping and pointing. The screen door squeaked open, and Wynn ran out to join us on the porch just as we glimpsed the rental car coming up the drive.

"Yay!" I joined in their happy dance before bending to grab a duffel. The car cleared the maples and there he was. Blake Turner. Sitting at the wheel of a red convertible.

I looked down at our two weeks' worth of clothes and toys and sports equipment. Even if Maya sat on my shoulders we wouldn't fit.

I was about to open my mouth and ask some variation on, *What the what, Blake?!*

But then I caught his face. Despite seeing his kids for the first time in weeks, something that would normally make him literally do cartwheels, he was struggling to smile.

"Well?" Val came out. "Did you get it?"

Marrying an actor was not something I'd set out to do.

It was, in fact, the embodiment of my parents' worst fears—any parent's, probably. Right up there with your child joining a cult—or having no sense of humor. Certainly for Sheryl and Randy McGovern of Oneonta, New York, this was nowhere in the plan. My parents had met at accounting school, and I'd like to be able to tell you they're not exactly what you're picturing—that they have a leather fetish or even high cholesterol. But they are exactly, endearingly, the people you would trust to keep you out of trouble with the IRS. So I lose a lot of time imagining what it was like for them the first day I came downstairs in the sparkly beret I salvaged from the YMCA lost-and-found and forced them to sit through my third-grade rendition of "Hey, Big Spender."

Amazingly, they were supportive. Mystified. But supportive. Even when I decided I wanted to forgo a traditional college education to attend the performing arts conservatory at SUNY Purchase, where I discovered two unexpected things: first, set design. Second: Blake Turner.

The first time I saw him on campus, I thought I was hallucinating. I thought some potent combination of homesickness and paint thinner had conjured my teen crush, as if he were a genie sprung from the well-kissed pages of *Tiger Beat* magazine. I could not believe Blake Turner, *the* Blake Turner, was at my college.

As he slipped into his cafeteria chair in his ripped plaid shirt, dirty wool hat pulled low over his painfully beautiful features, only one sentence blared in my head: *I will die if I don't touch him.* I immediately ran back to my room and called my seventh-grade best friend. Because it was 1992 and no one had e-mail yet.

We knew his story by heart. How he was nine when he was scouted to be in *Cooties*. Then, once that was a blockbuster, and he played Harrison Ford's son in that drama about the horse farm, before you knew it he was a bona fide heartthrob. But then he just kind of . . . disappeared.

Campus rumor had it that, as he coasted into puberty, with his aquamarine eyes and floppy brown hair, he started losing every part to these real-life buddies his age named Leo and Toby. So his agent told him to bide his time, that once he reached his twenties, with his looks, the number of parts would blow wide open and he'd be steadily employed again.

So he walked among us at Purchase where I, and everyone else who liked boys, swooned for his Hamlet and his Ernest, his Jean Valjean and his Equus. Especially his Equus.

Toiling in the nerdy set design department, spattered in paint, dusted with plaster, hair knotted with a pencil, tool belt dragging down the waistband of my (what would now be considered mom) jeans, I didn't stand a chance.

"Of course, you stand a chance!" my best friend, Jessica, would yell at me as I stared longingly at him across some God-awful house party. "Lots of famous people are married to normals." Blake was famous-in-waiting—about that there was no question. The only silver lining in the looming black sky of graduation was Blake's inevitable success and that we'd always be able to say we went to college with him.

"They like being the hot one," Claire, our third roommate, agreed.

In hindsight, it's hilarious that this was their argument: famous men marry average women. Not, "Hey, he's a college guy with a penis who's had a few drinks. I bet with very little prompting, he would agree to put it in you somewhere." We were young, steeped in the romance of our undergraduate studies, and playing the long game.

Of course, after graduation, the further I got into my twenties, when marriageability *should* have been the criterion, the vaguer my objectives became. I got excited about a guy because he was excited about me. Dating in New York felt like I was constantly, breathlessly trying to capture vapor with a butterfly net. Whether the vapor was poisonous was a let's-cross-that-bridge question.

Then, occasionally, on the nights Jessica and Claire were out of our tiny East Village apartment, and I'd catch Blake on TV, in an old movie or doing a guest spot on *ER*, I'd feel that heat pulse through my skin like I was thirteen again. Every time, I had the instinct to lift my hair from behind my ears, as if he could see me through the screen.

Then one autumn night, shortly after my thirtieth birthday, Jessica and I ducked into a bar on Avenue B we hadn't planned to go to, but the temperature was doing one of those abrupt plummets and we were both underdressed. Jessica's boyfriend, Miles, was in Chicago for his master's in fine arts, and they were trying on a separation that never stuck. Most likely due to dispiriting nights like that one.

I was about to wriggle ahead to get us drinks when Jessica grabbed my arm, throwing me off balance in my Sexy Shoes—the ones I pointlessly wore to bars that were so crowded I could've been wearing bunny slippers and no one would've known. "It's Blake!"

"Oh my God, where?" I ducked my head, untucking my blond hair and checking my teeth with my tongue at the same time as my feet started backing toward the exit.

"By the bar. *Say hi*," she said forcefully in a way that would eventually serve her well with two sons.

"No! *He has no idea who I am.*"

"Then introduce yourself and say you went to a college the size of a public bus with him."

"I *can't*." I dared to gopher my head over the crowd and she was right. Blake Turner. At the bar. Gone was the plaid shirt, the Dinosaur Junior tee, the hat that could have walked down the aisle at graduation by itself. He was wearing a tight-fitting dress shirt and good jeans. He had a Wall Street haircut. But the face was just the same. I was all hot static in an instant.

"What is wrong with you?" Jessica demanded. "You're thirty! You just negotiated a raise from the biggest bitch in your department."

"I don't know," I groaned. "When I look at him, I think I still have braces."

"You are hot, Ror. Hot." It was impossible for me to metabolize that. I think some part of our brains freeze in puberty, and where you were in the social hierarchy is the image you carry around for the rest of your life. This goes both ways. When I see class president Cindi Sherwood working at the gas station down the road from my parents', she still smiles at all the male customers like they'd be lucky to get one minute of her broken-tooth time. In my mind's eye, I was waiting for my growth spurt, for my boobs, for my Clearasil pads to finally *do* something. While I never crept past 5'3", the fact that when my boobs finally arrived, they left me with an admittedly enviable figure was something I just could not hold in my head.

"But what about my sloping eyebrow?"

"You crazy fucking nutcase. No one can see that but you." She took my shoulders. "I will give you twenty dollars to go over there right now."

"But I didn't shave." And that's thirty. He won't remember my name, but if he does, the only logical next step is sex.

"If you don't do this and he marries Jennifer Garner, you will re-gret it for the rest of your life."

"Okay." I was about to nut up. In my version of the story, I was seconds away from breathtaking bravery. But . . .

"Rory McGovern!" It was like Bono knew my name. I spun slowly to face—

"Blake? Wow."

He threw his arms out and hugged me. Really hugged me. "This is so awesome." He turned to the guy he was with, a shorter blond with a weak chin. "I went to college with these guys!" he said, meaning us. "This is my friend, Chester. We're doing *True West* at the Cherry Lane. Can I buy you a drink?"

"Sure!"

"I'm so stoked to see you guys. They were both super talented in school," he explained to Chester, who didn't seem to care, while I got jostled by people trying to find space where there was none, and searched for the perfect pithy anecdote to sum up my life. "Hey." He smiled at Jessica. "Still writing?"

Drum roll to the: "Yes, but" . . .

"Yes," she answered, bracing her smile, "but not creatively." The nauseating "yes, but" had become the refrain when running into anyone from school where we'd been dancers and painters and poets. Now we were Pilates instructors and makeup artists and tutors. "I work at a website," Jessica added. "It's a news aggregate. I'm editing."

"Cool." He nodded. "What about you, Rory? Still wielding that nail gun?"

I couldn't believe he remembered that. Me crawling around the set during tech for *Private Lives*, him with his shirt off making out with Condra (moon in Sanskrit). And I got so distracted by the way he held her face that I nearly nailed him to a flat. "I am now fully licensed. I also have a black belt in power sanding, and in several states I'm allowed to carry a concealed awl."

He laughed. In my mind, I threw my fists up overhead like a triumphant boxer. "So you're still doing set design?"

"Actually Jessica rescued me." I put my arm around her waist. While waiting for her Big Idea for the next Great American Something, Jessica had started writing for women's magazines. When she burned out on reporting "20 Ways to Make Him Wild" and "I Was a Child Bride," she eventually got a job at Domino magazine, reasoning, "We all need something to sit on. You can masturbate on your couch, you can menstruate on your couch, I don't care. It's no longer my problem. I'm just telling you about the couch." When her editors needed someone to make a $500 coffee table look like a $5,000 table, she called me. When I realized it paid better than trying to build an entire set out of toilet paper rolls for some shithole black box on Twelfth Avenue, I stayed.

Then the editor from *Domino* moved to *Elle Décor*, where I met a photographer who recommended me to an art director at *Architectural Digest,* and eventually I was freelance styling for photo shoots all over the city and able to move down from Morningside Heights and rent my own tiny studio in a brownstone on West Eightieth Street. I had made it.

You know, except for the my-cross-eyed-assistant-is-engaged-so-what's-wrong-with-me thing.

"I'm a stylist for shelter magazines," I told him.

"That sounds like fun." He smiled kindly.

"Oh, who cares. You're in *True West!*" I gushed. "And we saw you on *Desperate Housewives.*"

"And *CSI,*" Jessica chimed in.

"And that movie with Vincent Gallo about the hustler."

"It's a living," he demurred.

"No, you're *famous,*" I rebutted him. I mean, not famous how we'd thought he'd be famous. Maybe famous only to us, but the real kind was clearly only minutes away. All you had to do was look at him.

He leaned down, the tips of his fingers in the small of my back, his lips grazing my ear. "Want to find a table in the back?"

"Let's get another drink," Jessica prompted us.

One drink turned into three. A natural raconteur, Blake regaled us with behind-the-scenes stories from the sets he'd been on, until Jessica and I were holding our stomachs from laughing so hard.

Chester looked peevish. "You want to get out of here?" He abruptly stood and addressed Jessica.

"Okay."

I knew she was being the Pan Am stewardess of wingwomen, but I let her go, feeling instantly nervous to be alone with Blake. "I'm sorry," I said, apologizing that he'd inadvertently gotten stuck on a date with me.

"You like crepes?" he asked.

We walked across Tompkins Square Park to the all-night stand on Avenue A while he told me how rehearsals were going, how Chester was holding back. We shared a Nutella banana, and I couldn't feel the cold anymore.

"You have whipped cream on your lip," he said.

"What?" *Kill me.*

"No," he said, when I failed to get it. And he leaned in and swept it away with the tip of his tongue before pulling back.

It's hard to believe that fairy tales weren't written by single women, that it wasn't really Hannah Christian Andersen. Because there are hours, nights, when we are suspended in such exquisite perfection that we are aware, even as they are happening, that only clogs and soot can await us in the morning.

I took his hand and pulled him toward the curb, my other arm hailing a taxi. "Eightieth and Amsterdam, please."

I rested my head back on the seat next to his and he looked in my eyes. He placed his hand on my thigh (thankfully skipping my prickly calves) and slowly moved it up. Not speaking. Until his fingers grazed the lace trim of my thong. Which he edged aside and slipped a finger inside me.

He hadn't even kissed me yet.

As the sun rose, I girded myself for him to be on the sidewalk with the morning edition, but he held me until my alarm. And we had sex again while I should have been at spin class with Claire. I called the calorie expenditure even.

I had never felt anything like what it was with Blake. And it wasn't just that I'd had eighteen years to build it up in my mind. Blake knew how to touch me—my insteps, the soft skin on the underside of my forearms, behind my ears. And what he didn't know, he asked, and in a way that dissipated any shyness. Then he wanted to know where I liked to have brunch. We walked through the park, and that night he cooked me dinner. He was just . . . there. Blake Turner, in my butterfly net, in my studio apartment—in me.

≡

"Well?" Val prompted him again as we stood on her dusty driveway under the blazing sun. "Did you get the Netflix thing?"

He shook his head.

"Oh, Blake," I said, an ache rippling out from my breastbone, "I'm so sorry."

He picked up his phone from the passenger seat of the convertible. "My agent left the message while I was in the air. Fucking coward." Blake had started swearing again, having decided that Wynn was ten and had heard it all by now and that Maya was still small enough not to be paying attention. I did not agree, but this didn't feel like the moment to bring it up.

"Oh, honey, you'll get the next one," Val said, her gaze already off him as she pointlessly started moving the luggage around the porch. "You want a frozen banana?"

Ignoring her, he picked up his smile, got out of the car, threw his arm around Wynn's neck, and pulled him to his side. "You guys have fun?"

"We caught a frog," Wynn said. "I looked it up. It's a Northern Leopard." They told him all about our short-lived adventures in amphibious pet ownership while Blake scooped up Maya and tickled her tummy with his nose, making her squeal.

"Last bathroom visit, guys," I announced. They ran into the house, and I expected Blake to take me in his arms and squeeze me as he always did after being away. But he just walked past me to open the trunk.

Okay . . .

"So, we'll talk tonight?" I couldn't help but seek confirmation.

"Let's just pack up."

I nodded, unsure what to do. Step back and let him realize this exercise defied the law of physics? Or try to manage it.

"Wow, we sure have a lot of shit," he said angrily as he struggled to close the trunk with half our luggage and Wynn's bike still on the ground.

"Well, we thought we'd have an SUV like we rented to drive up,"

I said, stuffing what I could in all the floor spaces. Wynn and I would have to ride with our legs crisscrossed.

"Yeah, it was all they had left."

"When you made the reservation?" I prompted him.

"I forgot, okay. Look, some of this crap will just have to stay here until next time."

"No!" Maya burst into tears as she returned to find him unloading one of her Hello Kitty bags filled with stuffed animals. "Not my fwiends!"

"Not that one, Blake. It's okay, Maya, we won't leave your friends."

He scowled and I reopened the trunk. "Let's just go through everything and figure out what we can leave here."

"You're leaving stuff here?" Val asked, coming outside again as if she'd been listening for her cue.

"Yes, is that okay?" I asked, because her son had absented himself from the conversation as he always did when we needed anything of her. Even staying for two weeks to cover the gap between camp and school and not one, as would have been her first choice, had been completely negotiated between Val and myself.

"Well." She pursed her lips. "I'm having friends up to stay when the leaves change."

When Blake's grandparents died, Val had come into a little money; she bought a farmhouse and moved up to Woodstock. Gone were her shoulder pads, her broker's license, her struggles as a single mother. Instead she studied Reiki, wrote iffy poetry, and threw pots. Everything she'd wished she'd embraced as a teen in the sixties and a big f-you to what Scarsdale had raised her to want: the dentist she landed at Boston College, whom she dutifully supported through his DDS, until he left them for—wait for it—his big-breasted dental hygienist *and* screwed her out of alimony.

Hence the wind chimes. The Don't Frack with Me bumper stickers. And a deep unwillingness to do anything asked of her.

"That's not until late October, Val. We'll get it before then," I assured her.

"Well, sure." She looked away, trying to be casual. Subtle. "If you have to."

I was ready to get in that clown car, hold my husband's hand over the gearshift, and put a hundred miles between me and Woodstock. "Okay, guys, let's get going!"

It's hard to pinpoint on a long, hot family ride in creeping holiday traffic that someone is actively not talking to you, as opposed to just trying to survive, but I started to suspect, sometime around the George Washington Bridge, that Blake was not talking to me.

And we needed to talk. Had needed to talk for months. To keep our Screen Actors Guild health insurance, Blake needed to book $30,000 worth of union jobs each calendar year. His theater work didn't count toward it, and neither did all the nonunion film stuff he did for friends, but between residuals and Something Always Coming Through, we had squeaked by. I should clarify that none of this would have been possible without The Apartment.

Blake had inherited the rent-controlled lease to the classic six on West Fifty-Sixth Street where Val had decamped with him after the divorce. It was supposed to be transitional, but after Rudy Giuliani came into office and the city went from being a place families fled to to a place you donated sperm, blood, organs, *anything!* to stay—a rent-controlled apartment just blocks from gentrifying Columbus Circle was something no one would give up.

So with our low rent, our union health coverage, our ability to jointly cover child care until our kids started public pre-K, we had just made it, without any financial cushion, from month to month. For ten years. One hundred and twenty months. With any injury, strike, or root canal threatening to submerge us.

So when this year started and he failed to book a single pilot, I began suggesting that we might want to have The Talk. What was the plan? Would we keep doing this until the kids left for the college we couldn't help pay for? Zeroing out our bank account every month? Waiting for the euphoria when he got a job? The euphoria that was feeling more and more like we were just junkies living from fix to fix.

But then he went up for this new Netflix series. It was a leading part, the game changer, his Don Draper. The closer Blake got to forty, Jon Hamm, who was still waiting tables when he auditioned for *Mad Men*, was referenced in our house with the frequency some families talk about Jesus.

The studio flew Blake to LA, put him on camera, tested him with Maria Bello, tested him with Katherine Delaney, although he couldn't get a handle from the dialogue if they were supposed to be his wife— or his mother. Back and forth through the spring and into the summer. He didn't want to take another job in case he had to "jump." I took as much freelance work as I could scrounge up, but things were getting very, very scary. I leaped for the mail every day like a teenager, looking for the residual checks that were getting us through.

"Blake, I'm so sorry," I said as we pulled up at our building. "But as soon as the kids are down, we really need to start to figure this out." He was dropping us off with all the gear before going to return the car.

"Sure," he said, without looking at me as he left.

While he was gone the kids and I unpacked, then started laundry and had dinner. Then went to the park to enjoy one of the last summer evenings. I was laying out their school clothes for the next day when a text finally came from Blake: "Ran into Jack. Grabbing a drink."

It seemed that I'd been asleep for hours when I felt him slide in next to me. I didn't want to fight. I wanted to curl into him, feel his fingers in my hair, his heartbeat under my cheek that told me I wasn't alone, that we would figure this out. Team Turner.

But he didn't move any closer. He was sweating whiskey.

"Did you have fun?" I whispered.

"Got a call from Pete. Someone dropped out of that short he's directing in Rhode Island," he said groggily. Outside, the late-night traffic made a soft whir, a stop/go in time with our conversation. "Ten-day shoot."

"Okay?" I said it like a question. "When?"

"Tomorrow."

"But you haven't seen the kids in two weeks."

"We'll FaceTime. I'll catch the train in the morning after we drop them off." He wasn't asking; he was telling.

Ten more days. As a solo parent. I could do it. If this was what he needed.

"But when you get back, Blake, we're going to talk."

Chapter Two

"Jesus, are you okay?" Jessica asked the next morning as I knelt on the floor of Maya's room brushing her hair for her first day of pre-K. Jessica was already at her office at the Time Warner Center, just a few blocks away. I could picture her chewing on a pen to give her nails a break. Now the editor of the parenting vertical of the *Huffington Post,* she worked hours that should have completely precluded parenting, only her sons, Henry and Gus, were seven and five.

"I'm bummed for him—for us. This really seemed like it was finally The Thing. Maya, stop wriggling," I said through teeth clenching a Hello Kitty rubber band. "But at least now Blake can't fight me on finding a full-time job."

"Oh, Rory," Jessica said, which was shorthand for, *Full-time job? Where? Doing what?*

"How's it going on your end?" I asked.

"Well, we started the day with Henry down on the living room floor with Minecraft saying, 'Mom, I'm trying to figure out how to kill the most people.' And I said, 'Honey, let's not call the dweebils or weebils or whatever they are "people," because it sounds bad.' And in a way it's so sweet because he can't even process why that would be. Death has no cognitive underpinning for him. Kill probably doesn't even have anything to do with death. So Henry and Gus tried to leap into an explanation of the game, but of course, I was already late for work. I have to try to make it home before they're asleep so they can teach me." Jessica had so made the right move when she decided to get back together with Miles after his MFA. He ran a successful graphic design company from their brownstone and did the drop-offs, the pick-ups, the sick days, the grocery runs—everything Blake should also have been in charge of and yet, mysteriously, wasn't.

"Ooh, there's Claire on the other line," I said. "Let me get this."

"Tell her I love her and I want my blouse back. Bye!"

"How's my girl doing?" Claire asked, huffing on the Stairmaster. Claire was an abstract painter whose "yes, but" was now working in the planning department of the Museum of Modern Art.

"She's getting pigtails for her big day."

"Mommy's making me!"

"Put me on speaker. Hi, Maya. It's your Godmama."

"Hi, Claire!" Maya adored Claire, who, at forty-one, was convinced she would never have children of her own and lavished her with everything Sanrio could dream up.

"I'm just calling to say, rock it hard. Keep an eye out for anyone who looks nervous and offer them some Play-Doh. You could have a friend for life. Then call me tonight and let me know how it went."

"Okay!"

"What are you wearing?"

"The gween dress you gave me with the heart shoes and my pwincess undies."

"Princess undies, nice. You're not worried you'll anger the Upper West Side progressives?" Claire asked me as I took her off speaker.

"I have zero objection to the whole princess thing. As far as I'm concerned, it's the last hurrah of being the center of the story. After Disney, it's just a fast downhill slope to being Dead Stripper 3 on *Special Victims Unit*."

"Oops, here comes the next incline. She'll do great. Call me later." And she was gone. That was quintessential Claire. Remembering it was a big day, calling to pump Maya up, knowing that I was nervous because she is a December birthday and would always be the youngest in her class, and then—poof—back to her glamorous life of shaking down the rich and famous for cash.

"Okay, guys, go kiss Daddy good-bye and we'll meet by the door." Despite his promise of a family drop-off, he was still sleeping it off.

I grabbed my purse from the front hall bench and checked my reflection. This had been an aging week. In my opinion, aging hap-

pens in bursts, like how presidents go gray overnight. I'd been tread-
ing water for about eighteen months, but suddenly the lines around
my mouth were deeper. This is when Jessica would say, *Because you
smiled so much with the kids all summer.* She was an optimist.

I did a quick spin to check my profile. While I, like pretty much
all other New York moms, had kept my figure through a steady program of stroller pushing and subway-stair navigating, I knew if I
lifted my blouse, the ravages of two pregnancies were memorialized
around my belly button. Some days I'd like to grab my thirty-year-
old self and scream, *Do not eat a single salad, do not waste a second worrying about your butt or your imaginary cellulite! You are firm! Your nipples
face upward, and your vagina is like a vise! Go forth and be naked in confidence!*

I sighed and put my bag on my shoulder.

"Daddy, Daddy, look, I have pwincess undies!" From the hall I
could hear Blake laughing.

"Let's not let everybody at school know about how cool your undies are—not on the first day."

"Okay."

He chatted effortlessly with the kids for a few minutes, reassuring
Maya and pumping up Wynn, while I stared at the pinstripe wallpaper we had hung together when Wynn was still in his bouncer. I was
about to call out to keep them moving when Wynn asked, "You want
to say good-bye to Mom?"

"Already did, buddy. You guys get going." *Huh.*

"Okay, it's eight o'clock," I shouted. "Everyone grab your backpacks!"

We could never tell anyone at school that we had trouble with the
bus—or waited for the train—because technically we were supposed
to live within walking distance.

While the area around Columbus Circle had been populated with
oligarchs, none of them were sending their kids to the Hell's Kitchen
public schools, which remained sketchy at best. So I held onto and
sublet the lease to my old studio to secure them spots in the coveted

zone for PS 87. A major no-no. But with private school tuition hovering around the $40,000 a year mark, so worth the risk.

And if I ever told my parents those numbers, they would have driven down and forcibly taken me home to Oneonta—where my brother and his wife were happily sprawled in 3,000 square feet, a decent school was a given, and having a car wasn't more work than having a dog.

Wynn, who'd been very quiet on the walk, suddenly clutched my hand. "This is my last first day."

"Here, yes, but I promise you have so many firsts coming up in your life, buddy."

"But I like it here. I don't want to leave." We were about to run the middle school admissions gauntlet, which was supposedly more confusing and stressful than applying to college. "But you're a fifth-grade senior! You're gonna rule the school!"

Wynn spotted his best friend, and they ran in together, leaving me to focus on getting Maya situated. I kissed the top of her lovely head and then had to extricate myself. Not from Maya, who was already ambitiously building a Hello Kitty out of blocks, but from the other mothers.

The mom scene at PS 87 was sharply divided into two factions—and I knew what they said about each other because I'd been on both sides. When Wynn was born, I tried to keep working, but the challenge of being freelance was that jobs would come up at the last minute, or change dates, or be in Miami and just when Blake would say, "No sweat, I've got you covered," he'd get an audition and we'd fight over which was more important: my paltry day rate or the chance of Blake booking a show that could pay our rent for months.

Meanwhile, I risked being called the worst name in the business: unreliable. So I slowed down, figuring that when Wynn started school I could ramp back up. Which I did for three years.

Then a particularly rigorous bout of makeup sex knocked my Mirena loose and—oops!—Maya.

So I've done those post-drop-off coffees. I've heard the smug tut-tuts about what the harried office moms are missing, and why did they bother having kids? And I've dashed to the subway, overhearing the condescending dismissals of the moms with "nothing to do all day."

But I look at it this way: imagine there are no working moms. Suddenly we're plunged back two hundred years. Now imagine there are no stay-at-home moms. Who the hell is keeping my kids' school running? Who am I going to for advice? So the world needs all of us, and we should stop writing shit about each other on the bathroom wall that is UrbanBaby.

That day, I was the harried one with twenty minutes to get back down to midtown. I nabbed a cab, stared at my phone, took a deep breath, and dialed.

"Hello, gorgeous."

"Hello, Clive," I said to my agent. He had been my booker for fifteen years and still liked me, despite the many times Blake's schedule had interfered with my taking an assignment.

"Aren't you supposed to be at the shoot?"

"First day of school, but don't worry. I already prepped the site, and Zoe is there." Zoe was my assistant. She'd been with me since she'd graduated Parsons because she Figures Shit Out. The story's about wallpaper, and the apartment doesn't have any? She would never sidle up to me and whine, "But they took down the wallpaper." She'd buy some wrapping paper and invisible tape. She was a solution rolled in an answer stuffed inside a miracle—a turducken of efficacy.

"What can I do for you?"

"I need a job." I'd been planning that I'd work more frequently now that Maya would be in school from nine until six, but freelance. "A full-time job. As soon as possible." I felt like one of those grizzled farmers in disaster movies who stare at the cloudless sky and abruptly say, "Get in the basement."

"I don't know of any staff positions coming up, but you know you're front of mind for freelance." I was hearing daily about editorial staffs being cut like snowflakes from copy paper, leaving teams most notable for their holes. And the more experienced (read: old) the employee, the more glaring her cost on the payroll. With women my age the first to go, competition in the freelancing sector was quadrupling while opportunities disappeared. Right as our confidence ripened—right as our children were finally loading the dishwasher—we were being reduced to low-hanging fruit.

"Thank you, Clive."

"You okay, kid?"

"The older I get, the more I love that you still call me that. Bye."

The cab pulled up outside the high rise and, one ear-popping elevator ride to the edge of our atmosphere later, I was greeted at the penthouse by the same sight as always: some pristine backdrop of sumptuous serenity being crisscrossed by manic twentysomethings wearing surgical booties over their shoes. These homes would never have so much—energy—in them again.

Splash! "Shit."

Among this abode's many thrilling attributes, the entrance gallery had been built over a water feature, like a lily pond, and you had to leapfrog across alabaster squares to get to the living room. According to the interview these photographs would accompany, the owners wanted guests to "slow down," forcing them to "take in the view." Because otherwise they might miss the three-story-high windows looking all the way out to the Atlantic.

Splash. "Shit."

"Can you all *please* stop falling in the Zen gateway! You are all so fucking gormless." That was Glen, our photographer from South London. He talked like a Guy Ritchie film and was permanently angry.

Zoe slipped beside me and wordlessly handed me my coffee, which was somehow always still hot because Zoe was magic. "How's it going?" I whispered.

"Glen is having a hard time with the light."

"I see." Actually I couldn't because I was squinting. The day I had come to plan the shoot, there'd been one of those hard August rains where the sidewalk smells like earth. Now the sun was shining and the all-white living room was blinding. Literally. Beams banked off the high-gloss walls, the polished floors, the metal furniture—it was relentless. I slipped on my sunglasses.

"What is that in your mouth?!"

I spun around, about to spit out my gum, only to discover the owner of the house, in white platform shoes and white harem knickerbockers, glaring down at her toddler. The child gamely shrugged as her Filipino nanny came running down the floating Plexiglas staircase. "Mrs., I so sorry. She got out while I was changing the twins."

"Open!"

The child dropped her lower jaw and the mother reached in and extracted a small black lump. A raisin?

"Po, take her upstairs." The mother deposited the item on the aluminum mantel. That's when I saw the pile on the floor of identical lumps. Before I could introduce myself to her, she dialed her white phone. "Hello, this is Mrs. Heller. I bought the sunflower seed installation. Yes, well, my daughter put one in her mouth. Well, there was a problem with toxic ceramic dust at the Tate, right? So do I need to do anything? Well, should I have my nanny take her to the pediatrician? . . . Okay, I'll tell my nanny to keep an eye out for that. So how does this work? Will Mr. Weiwei send me a replacement? Should I put the broken one in the mail? . . . You're joking! They just arrived and there's no warranty? That's outrageous! I bought—well I don't remember the number, but it has Taoist significance and I don't want to be one short! Put Mary on the phone!"

I tiptoed away so I could adjust the final compositions for Glen and keep my mind off Blake. I'm sure you're wondering what there could be left to do to a house that's had millions of dollars of attention lavished on it. Well, for one thing the flower arrangements that make the homes seem alive—those were always brought by us. I remember a shoot we did in a town house off Fifth. Five stories of authentic art deco no expense spared: gym, wine cellar, floor flown in from Italy, ceiling from France, but the wife had a standing order for a fishbowl of pink roses for the front hall. Roses from the deli. There was no other pink in the house; it made no aesthetic sense whatsoever, but there you go—

Splash!

Then we heard, "Oh fuckety fuck fuck." Even sight unseen, the clipped vowels were instantly recognizable. So now we all knew what it took to make the great Kathryn Stossel swear: falling in standing water up to her calves. She rounded the corner, her sopping sling-backs dangling off her fingers. "Can someone get my assistant up here with some shoes? Tell her I'm wearing the navy Balenciaga." She said it to no one in particular, but within the hour, her assistant would blow through the door. If Kathryn gave orders to an empty room, I'm sure the furniture would strive to fulfill them.

Kathryn was the editor in chief of *World of Decor*, our boss, and official New York tastemaker when it came to all things aesthetic. *Kathryn Stossel thinks the new Bergdorf's tearoom is "charming,"* and suddenly reservations were harder to get than any actual service once you were seated. From Farrow and Ball to Crate and Barrel, nobody would dare put anything on the $10 billion home goods market without consulting her.

"Well, that'll teach me to rush." She kissed our apologetic hostess, who, I could tell, could not quite believe Kathryn was in her apartment. It had to be the culmination of everything she'd been hoping for since she was shown the first floor plan.

Kathryn visited sets in person only when the decorator was a big name because a certain dance had to be performed: *We love your design* so much *we want it in the magazine, but Rory here is going to re-arrange it. No reason.* That was because what looked stunning in person frequently did not photograph well. Subtle layers of deepening gray looked monochromatically flat and needed the fuchsia bedspread from the guest room hung behind the couch like a wall covering. Or sometimes for texture, I needed to grab a fluffy pillow from a kid's—or a maid's—room. Also, people frequently got so excited about being selected that they'd run out to make their homes *even better.* So we'd arrive on the day to a host of horrors. I've switched out drapes, moved couches, rehung art, all under the watchful eye of a decorator who'd like to hit me over the head with the nearest Cycladic bust.

"Ah, Kathryn, darling, there you are." Kevin Kliborne, the de-signer, did a sort of glissade over to her. Rumor had it that he changed his last name from Cliborne for his insignia. And, before that, from Pinkus—for obvious reasons.

"Kevin." Tight smile. Kathryn detested being called darling. In addition to it being the Twinkie of greetings, as she put it, it was also the endearment of choice from her ex-husband. "How is it going?"

"We're having a little trouble with the light," Glen piped in as she put her sunglasses on. "We could do the exterior rooms at night?"

"No."

"At dusk?"

"No."

"Come back when it rains?"

"Glen," she said crisply, "our brand is sumptuous homes captured in sumptuous morning sun." He scurried away to strategize, and possibly find a bathroom to get stoned in, and that's when I noticed her hands were shaking.

"Kathryn, could I get you some juice?"

She let out a puff of a laugh. "I can't remember the last time I had juice." Behind her oversized glasses, the corners of her eyes were watering. Which, technically, is crying. But that was not a verb one could hitch to Kathryn. She put a hand on the back of my arm. "I didn't know we had you today."

"And every day if you want me," I told her. "Maya started pre-K this morning, and I'm ready to dive back in."

"Hmmm," she hummed and looked away, inspecting Clive's choices. "Mrs. Heller?" she called out. "Can I use your powder room?"

"Absolutely! In the hallway just off the gallery!"

Kathryn casually led me in that direction, while chatting without pause about how the epoxy floors had been bonded and sanded so it would seem like one continuous white surface without seams, not a single seam, until we were the only two people in the hallway and then she yanked me into the bathroom with her.

It was a small space paneled in mirrors, so that we were reflected every which way into infinity. There was no imaginable scenario where I would ever pull my pants down—it was like a dressing room on steroids.

"This was so designed by a man," Kathryn observed.

"Kathryn, what's going on?"

"Asher is trying to fuck me."

I looked at her quizzically, not least because this was now only the second time since we'd known each other that I'd heard her swear.

"Not literally. Oh, dear God, how disgusting." As the editor in chief of *Narcissus*, the glamorous final word on all things Hollywood, Asher Hummel was essentially a professional sibling to Kathryn. Each presided over one of Stellar Media's most profitable assets, under the cross-eyed paternal gaze of Mort Studecker, the octogenarian media mogul. "He's gunning to get me out."

"But how could he? You *are* Stellar."

Kathryn picked up a linen towel from a stack and twisted it, the veins in the back of her tennis hands popping. "If it were still the nineties, we'd have just noodled along with me thinking he's a buffoon and him thinking I'm a bitch. We could have kept exchanging Christmas presents and gotten on with our lives. But this is not the nineties, we need a deft hand, and he is not a deft hand; he's a monkey."

"What happened?" I felt like I was hiding out between classes with the captain of the cheerleading squad. I wanted to offer her my hair spray.

"I have kept our ad pages up with garters, suspenders, bubble gum, and safety pins."

"You have a phenomenal track record," I agreed.

"But Asher's ad pages are neck and neck with mine. What Mort doesn't take into account is that you can sell ads next to celebrity portraits in your sleep." The towel started to fray.

"Has Asher done something?"

"I should not be telling you this." She blew out. "God, there is no place for my eyes to land in here! What was this room built for? Tiny orgies?" She snapped her head hard to the right, her neck going pop pop pop. "A few months ago Asher suggested that Stellar invest in this new website, called JeuneBug, founded by these twelve-year-olds straight out of B-school. The whole thing was untested, and I recommended against it. *Today* I find out that Asher talked Mort into investing five million dollars. Five million! So I go into this JeuneBug and ask to see the mechanicals for the launch, and I am politely rebuffed."

"They *rebuffed* you?" I was aghast.

"I was told these girls only answer to Asher—and he's not think-ing with his head." She raised her eyebrow. "I hate this apartment. It feels like we're trapped in someone's bonded teeth." Then she peered at me, a thought forming as she lifted her glasses into her chin-length bob. "They need someone in interiors. Now, I can't put you up for it, can't endorse you, or even let them know we're friends. But a job like this could change the playing field for you."

"Well, I could use a change, that's for sure. But working for twelve-year-olds who rebuff *you*? I don't know."

Her green eyes were like jewels in her tan face. "I have a deep gut feeling you could be perfect. And I am never wrong."

I had to laugh. "See, that's why you're you," I said.

"Hm?" She dropped the towel in the mirrored basket.

"I'm wrong all the time."

Chapter Three

Sophomore year I scored a pair of green cowboy boots at the Salvation Army that were the epitome of Sheryl Crow prairie chic. I wore them with one of my grandpa's old suit vests and other accessories you'd find in a Wild West photo-stand.

Hoping my "artistic phase" was coming to a close, my parents had optimistically gotten me a summer job as a bank teller, a position that required a week's training in a windowless room in the bowels of an office park. For eight hours a day, under the scrutiny of a po-faced woman, I processed bank slips that had been filled in with the names of Disney characters. Minnie Mouse wanted to withdraw eighteen dollars and put five into a certified check for Donald Duck. Goofy wished to make a transfer to his savings account. Daisy was trying to make a penalized withdrawal from her retirement account, perhaps having gotten hooked on methadone. It was the giggles that got me fired.

My parents were mutely distressed in a way that only makes sense now that I'm a mom—and wife.

After spending the night smoking behind the garage while listening to the Smashing Pumpkins on my Walkman, I got up, pulled on those boots, and went door to door on Main Street. By the end of the day, I'd landed a waitressing gig, which suited me much better, and a boyfriend, who didn't suit me at all. But he kept me deliciously distracted for eight weeks and, according to Facebook, eventually got married in Vegas wearing a cape. That was the last time I lived at home.

The morning after Blake left for Pete's shoot, I woke knowing it was time for me to take the reins. While he was regrouping—and by *regrouping,* I mean having his ego reinflated by a production that remunerated in compliments and beer—me and my cowboy boots needed to figure this out.

Before the doormen had even hosed the sidewalk, I got Clive to make the call to this JeuneBug and set the interview. If they were in desperate need of "shepherding," as Kathryn put it, then I aimed to Little Bo Peep their asses off.

The next day, the city was still on broil, and by the time I got the kids to school and myself to Herald Square, I was making one of those Faustian bargains: I would wear any amount of heavy down, slog through any amount of snow, just please, God, let it get cold. I couldn't remember what freezing felt like, but it had to be better than this.

I got off the elevator on the tenth floor to an orgasmic blast of air-conditioning and a hot pink Lucite wall. The receptionist who buzzed me in was wearing a blazer over a chevron-patterned romper. Due to the Lena Dunham effect, thighs in the office had become commonplace. Girls of all sizes were now wearing things I once would have called panties to answer phones and populate spreadsheets. "I'm here to see Taylor and Kim—they're expecting me."

She nodded as if she might have heard me—or might not. "At nine," I added, taking a seat beside a life-sized My Little Pony encrusted with crystals. The fact that I'd met its creator, a Dutchman as drab as his art was flamboyant, put me at ease. Then I heard something that sounded like ballerinas slapping their toe shoes against a wall to soften them. And around the corner came . . .

"Hi. Taylor," she introduced herself brusquely. Tan, prepubescently thin, with waist-length dark brown hair, she was easily five foot ten *before* she put her heels on. If I'd passed her on the street, in her skintight sleeveless dress, its hem a fraction of an inch past her ass, I would have guessed she was a floor girl at Bebe. On her way to a club.

"And I'm Kimmy." Her pale blond hair was parted down the middle and pulled in a low bun, accentuating large milk-blue eyes.

"Rory." I pivoted to her, but she didn't extend a hand; they were tucked up under her chin, holding her black sleeves in place. Only the tips of her toes and the backs of her hands were visible. I tried to determine what exactly she was wearing, but my best guess was a large bolt of black jersey held in place with angst.

These two were not at all what I'd been expecting. They looked as if they hadn't paused for so much as a menstrual cycle between degrees. Were they geniuses? Was this what Mark Zuckerberg would look like if he were a girl? A hooker, or Yoda?

Wordlessly the two women turned away, clip-clopping in unison—Taylor atop her fear-me shoes and Kimmy on her geisha clogs. On the far side of the sparsely populated bullpen, glass partitions created two offices. "Come in. Have a seat," Taylor instructed, gesturing to the canvas chair across from her python-print leather desk. Kimmy carefully deflated onto a Moroccan pouf so she was level with my knees while Taylor opened the lid of her thermal mug that said PUSSY across the front in blocky silver font, and poured in her Starbucks.

"These are great offices," I said, looking into the airshaft as if it was a view of the Louvre.

"My mom loaned us her designer," Kimmy answered, her voice hoarse.

Taylor shot Kimmy a silencing look, making her shrink further into herself like something on *National Geographic* under attack. "So you want to work at JeuneBug," she challenged.

"I think you're onto something brilliant here." Although they hadn't gone live yet, so I was basing that on their landing page: *Wait for it!* "I'd love to hear a bit about JeuneBug's journey."

Taylor sat back, flared her ribs, and cupped her armrests. "JeuneBug grew out of our final MBA project: 'Old Media: Who Cares?' The giants are trying to adapt, but it's like trying to make faster horses instead of inventing the car. We're inventing the car."

I tried to keep my smile from wavering. "That's so interesting," I murmured.

Taylor crossed her shaved arms. "We're a digitally native business, a technology company that produces media instead of a media company that uses technology. Everything we're doing is optimized."

"Everything," Kimmy echoed, then started to cough.

"Of course. So smart." Not a word. "Well, perhaps I should talk you through my portfolio?" I reached into my bag.

"I'm Googling you." Taylor flicked a finger at her obscured computer screen and Kimmy roused herself to go around the desk to join her.

I sat with my knees together while they scrolled through whatever the Internet dragged up with my name attached. *How had I never Googled myself?*

"You've been doing this a long time," Kimmy observed astutely.

"I've worked with pretty much every major designer, yes. I came to it from theater, so I know how to achieve drama and have an eye for editorial."

"And you had a perm."

"Sorry?"

"You had a perm?" Kimmy asked.

"Yes . . . in sixth grade. Sorry, are you looking at—"

"Facebook." Taylor peered at the screen. Mortified, I mentally ran through the photos posted by my family. "Oh that's cute how you don't care how you look in a swimsuit. Very Dove. So you graduated in . . . ?"

"1995."

Taylor and Kimmy caught eyes.

"Rory." Taylor paused, presumably to let my own identity sink in. "We raised a significant capitalization—"

"Significant." I was starting to think Kimmy was actually on Taylor's personal payroll as her gospel chorus.

"—on the premise that we are building this from the ground up with no preconceptions. We haven't been steeped in ways that, frankly, no longer work. We don't want to start bringing in *old* thinkers."

My aunt, watching her daily VHS recording of the last remaining soap opera, was an old thinker. I rooted for Katniss and had sex dreams about Adam Levine.

Then Kimmy's palm landed hard on Taylor's arm. "Is that North West's nursery?"

"Oh," I answered. "Yes."

"You worked with Kanye?" I had Taylor's attention.

"Y-yes?" I helped photograph the nursery his decorator styled that his nanny raised his child in, but—technically—yes.

"So you've styled for celebrities?"

"Oh, yes," I said.

"Celebrities with kids?"

"Sure. Elton John, Pink, Gwen Stefani." I wasn't sure they understood what a photo stylist actually *did*. "A rock and roll chic that would lend itself well to JeuneBug." Whatever the fuck JeuneBug was.

"We don't have a curator for the design vertical," Kimmy said to her cuticles.

I sat forward. "That's where I can add value." I handed her my résumé, which, following their Googling of me, seemed like inviting her to an ice cream social after we'd 69'd.

Taylor held my gaze. "JeuneBug is about to fill a *massive* hole in the marketplace. Massive. Walk Madison from Eighty-Sixth Street to Ninety-Sixth Street and what do you see?"

I mentally called it up. Armani Kids, Bonpoint, Crewcuts, Magic Windows, Jacadi, Rosie Pope, that British store with the titanium pram in the window. A four-year-old could blow her clothing allowance in a few blocks, maybe even in a single store. "Kids' shops."

"These boutiques are moving $500 dresses so fast they can't keep them in stock, yet no one is directly tapping this consumer where he likes to eat, where she likes to have her hair done, where he wants to vacation."

"And by 'consumer' you mean—?"

"JeuneBug is the first lifestyle site for kids," Taylor answered triumphantly.

"For their lifestyle?" I coughed.

"Yes." She squared her arms while Kimmy cracked a hint of a smile and I tried to imagine Wynn's lifestyle. Was Ninjago a lifestyle?

Taylor's eyes sparkled under the awning of false lashes, like diamonds under a straw hut. "It's a no-brainer, right? And that's before we even talk about proprietary software. The site will function as a catalogue. For too long, magazines have been relying on featuring brands in their editorial pages in the pathetic hopes of getting an ad buy—but that's a dwindling revenue model. You click on any item in our stories, it's an instant purchase. *And* we get a fee."

"So the pages are gridded like InStyle spreads?" I asked.

"Ugh, no," she snapped. She spun her monitor to show a photo of a toddler running through Central Park in something nicer than my wedding dress. "Looks like any page in any magazine, right?" *Vogue for the toothless,* I thought. "But when our consumer clicks on the dress, or the shoes, or the tiara, they buy it."

"The children?"

"The moms. But we will have a function on the app where kids can swipe and tap. But everything they pick is held with the concierge . . ."

"We hate the word *shopping cart*. It's so—" Kimmy shuddered.

". . . until Mommy can approve."

"Wow." It was all I could say. "How enterprising. And the position?"

"Running our Be vertical," Kimmy answered.

"A vertical is what print media calls a 'department,'" Taylor added as if I was a foreign exchange student.

"Yes, I'm familiar. My best friend runs Huffpo's parenting vertical. So . . . *Be*?" I asked.

"Interiors," Taylor clarified.

"Because kids should have a place where they can just . . . be," Kimmy explained.

My phone buzzed, and I glanced down as I silenced it: *Incoming call from Husband Blake.* "Sorry," I apologized. "Gaga's people. Look, here's the truth." They needed me to shepherd them as much as they needed me to teach them needlepoint (which I could have done). "You can poach someone from Refinery 29 who can style antlers in Williamsburg, but I know luxury. I know glamour. Heart-stopping glamour. And I can translate that for any age demographic you want. And, I should mention, I have two little sophisticates at home." And if this paid off my credit card and helped me put a down payment on their sophisticated orthodontics, well, it was a win-win.

"Huh," Taylor said thoughtfully.

Having worked around my share of flaming egos, I knew my only currency here was status and my only hope for that was to leave. Not beg. Begging would have been bad. "It was a pleasure, Taylor. Kimmy. I actually have the first PTA meeting of the season today so I have to . . ."

"That kind of thing wouldn't be a problem?" Taylor asked as I picked up my bag.

"Which kind of thing?" I stood.

"Needing to leave early for . . . kids."

"No more so than anyone else here who has kids," I reassured them.

"Oh, no one does." She crossed her arms like I had suggested her employees had VD. "No, no."

"Got it." For kids—by kids. Jesus.

"We'll be in touch."

When Blake traveled for work, FaceTime was an iMiracle for connecting with Wynn and Maya. And even when he and I couldn't talk during the day, we always managed to kiss our good-nights before nodding off.

"Sorry I couldn't pick up earlier," I said into my earpiece as I turned down the light and dropped onto our bed. "How's it going?" I asked, realizing that Wynn's science book, which I'd intended hours ago to deposit in his backpack, was on my pillow.

"Fine. Hot."

"I know. I'm so over it." I forced myself to get back up and put the book away. "So, guess what? I have some potentially amazing news."

"Yeah?"

"I think I may have found a full-time job." I closed myself back into the cooling bedroom. "It's a young company called JeuneBug. The hours might be crazy, but Stellar seems to really believe in it."

"I've been gone for a day," he said.

"It all happened really fast, but this could be the answer—"

"Because you don't think I can turn this around?"

"No, Blake. I just think one of us needs to—"

His audible exhale cut me off.

I scratched off a glob of candle wax from his night table. A remnant from more romantic evenings. "The girls who run it are such pieces of work." I tried to lighten the conversation. "I mean I'm sure they're smart as hell, but the attitude—"

"What if I have a job? What's the plan for picking up the kids?" *Oh, that we should be so lucky that we were both simultaneously employed.*

"Well, they're in aftercare at school 'til six. So we'd get a sitter." I wiped the shavings into my palm. "But if you're ready to talk logistics . . . I mean," I proceeded carefully. "What are you thinking?"

"I'm not, Rory. This shoot's intense. Pete's got a lot of ground to cover. I should jump, actually. He needs me."

"I need you." I was surprised by the smallness of my voice.

"Do you?" He was really asking.

"Seriously?"

"I've got to go—"

"Wait. So do you not want me to take this job?" I asked. "If they offer it to me?"

"Well, it's not like I have an alternative to rescue you."

"I'm not expecting that. I have never been expecting that." Even when I imagined myself as the not-famous half of our couple, I wasn't thinking in terms of rescuing. "Have you talked to your agent? What's Richard's sense of things?"

"They're calling places. I'll try you back." He hung up, leaving me holding a handful of clumped wax—and pretty much everything else.

Chapter Four

I awoke to Maya kneeling over me, pressing the horn button on the toy car keys Blake and I both swore we did not buy, yet somehow lived with us anyway. "It's morning, Mommy!"

"Hey, Mayabear!" I volleyed with a perkiness betrayed by my closed eyes.

"Ith today a thchool day or a home day?"

"School day."

"Aw."

"But I'll make pancakes." I stiffly pushed up to sit and checked my phone. Blake hadn't even tried to reach me. But a job offer from Taylor had arrived in my inbox a little after midnight. I shuffled into the hot hallway as the attachment uploaded.

Wow.

The package they were offering was better than I'd imagined from a start-up—and definitely more than I'd make if I booked a freelance job every day for the next year. I forwarded it to Jessica.

"They are giving you a point, Rory!"

"A point?"

"Equity, baby. Done and done."

And to Claire.

"So you hate them, big deal. This oil tycoon loaning us a Rothko thinks 'the gays' are responsible for hurricanes."

And finally, to Blake. Subject line: *What should I do?*

His response came in before the griddle was even smoking: *Whatever you want.* I couldn't decide if he was being supportive or snarky. And then I couldn't believe that I was standing over a hot griddle in a Sep-

39

tember heat wave trying to make Mickey Mouse pancakes for the children of a man whose texts I was trying to interpret like I was twenty.

Monday morning was Maya and Wynn's chance to give me their version of first-day pep talks before I dropped them off. "Athk thomeone if they wike Play-Doh," Maya advised me, parroting Claire. "You could have a fwiend for wife."

"Don't ask questions when people are chewing," advised Wynn. "Don't wipe your nose on your T-shirt. And don't be a dork."

"In my defense," I told them, "I only do that when I'm about to throw the shirt in the hamper."

"It's still gross."

"Thanks, Wynn."

As I stared into the impassive face of Ginger, JeuneBug's receptionist, I was glad I had availed myself of the kids' wisdom because I did not sense any forthcoming here. She waved in the general direction of the long white tables that filled the JeuneBug bullpen, like a library reading room by Ikea: "So you're over there." About thirty people working, but twice as many stations were sitting vacant. The staff typed and browsed with old-school Cinnabon-sized headphones tamped over half-shaved heads.

Ginger walked me to a vacant seat. "And there's a director meeting in ten in Capri, 'kay?"

"Capri?"

"The conference room."

"Thank you." I pulled back my pink chair, looking for—anything. A trash bin, a phone, a drawer.

"Oh, do you need—?"

"Somewhere to put my things? Yes, that'd be great, thanks."

"Right. Your power switch is on the floor." My orientation complete, she walked off.

One could see why Capri was in need of romance. It was just a side of the room cordoned off with a glass divider that framed a beige pushpin wall, an incongruous backdrop to my flamboyant colleagues, who were all sporting a look I'd named Aggressively Unflattering. Tented, cropped, backless, speckled with zippers and revealing odd swaths of skin, their outfits represented the worst of what the last three decades had to offer. And then there was me in a pencil skirt and blouse. A stranger might have assumed I'd rounded up club kids for questioning.

Taylor stood at the front with Kimmy, who embraced her coffee as if midway through a kabuki ode to the bean. "Updates." Taylor rubbed her bare arms. *God, she'd be so much happier if she just put on a cardigan.* "We're going beta in thirty, so we expect decks for Halloween coverage from you guys pronto. Obviously, these should be force-ranked by potential ad rev clicks. And the latest branding op is Cushbars. Here's the swag." She ripped the top off a box of energy bars and slid them down the Formica table. "Ping feedback on placement ops to Kimmy. And the big get is our new Be Vertical director, Rory McGovern. Rory has legged stints for spreads that have over a million uniques. And she did the Kimye nursery. Rory?"

Recognizing my name among the lingo like a dog, I stood from the group, who alternately tore into and apprehensively sniffed their Cushbars. "Hey, everyone." I waved. "Thank you, Taylor. I'm excited to be onboard and look forward to leading Be to phenomenal ad rev." Ad rev I knew. And monetize. I could monetize with the best of them.

"Yay!" Taylor clapped. Everyone clapped, the sound oddly muffled by sleeves pulled over palms. "Okay," Taylor continued. "Pitches in my office Wednesday. And I'm saying this now: don't backload your appendixes. I'm talking to you, Merrill."

A woman in a liberally safety-pinned RISD sweatshirt shrank further into it.

"That's fucking B-school copout bullshit. Kimmy, anything else?"

"Just, whoever is spitting their gum into the bathroom trash, you need to stop. Just . . . stop."

I followed Taylor as she returned to her office while I quickly pulled up "deck" on Wikipedia—Taylor was most likely *not* asking for a skateboard or a roof system. "Thank you for the welcome," I said to her.

She nodded acknowledgment as she slipped in her Bluetooth. Kimmy joined her at her desk, similarly wired and dialing her phone.

"Okay, we're both on. Is it cold there?" Taylor asked. "Oh, it's hot as balls here. Summer just has to let go already. It's disgusting."

"Disgusting," Kimmy echoed.

"I'll let you have your call." I spun to leave.

"Now's fine," Taylor instructed.

"You have a question?" Kimmy asked me—possibly.

"Yes," I jumped in. "I'll catch up quickly with your approach, but I just wanted to clarify about this deck."

"We have a lot of confidence in people. A lot," Kimmy emphatically informed the floor.

"Definitely," Taylor agreed. "Hi, John, Taylor's here. Is Greg on yet?"

"You know," I whispered, "I really think I should come back when you're done with your call."

"Rory, we give everyone *huge* responsibility." Taylor poured her Starbucks into her PUSSY mug. "Sometimes they mess it up, but seven times out of ten, they get it right."

"That's great." I'd taught two human beings to stand upright, shit in a toilet, and not, you know, die. "I was just hoping for a quick translation, but you're obviously busy—"

"I'm listening. I told you I was listening. This is Taylor."

"Are you talking to me?" I was so confused.

"Hi, Greg," they said in unison. "We can hear you." Impatiently Taylor waved for me to keep talking.

I tried again. "A deck is a . . . ?"

"Oh!" Kimmy said with relief. "Funny. That's really funny. You're funny."

"Me?" I asked.

Taylor's hand slowed into a you-were-just-putting-us-on wave. "Yes, Greg, that's better. We're still waiting for Kip."

I pulled the door shut behind me, circled back through the conference room, grabbed my Cushbar, and returned to my desk. I was startled to find that my colleagues, the drowsy-eyed web browsers, had been transformed into frenzied contestants in a Project Runway workroom. A few people even stood over their desks as they sketched, typed, and scribbled notes on electronic tablets. I eyed the RISD girl. "Merrill? Rory." I extended my hand. "Good to meet you. So, what's your vertical?"

"I'm Catch."

"Catch?"

"As in throw and. Games? Um, I kind of really need to get back to this?"

"Sorry. Yes. I was wondering if you just could translate for me. A deck is a . . . what?"

"Your idea? How you present your idea?" She slipped her head-phones back on.

"Right. Of course. Thank you." My *idea*. One word down, forty more to clarify.

Within hours I was on a roll. (Or, as I read on the side of the wrapper a few minutes too late, on "double the rush of Redbull" that "differentiates the Cush brand.") I knew how to present an idea. I knew Halloween. And "space" and I were like this. My ideas for Halloween space: go!

I'd attended enough kids' parties with budgets that dwarfed our wedding's to know if I could dream it up someone out there was not only making it, but commanding some exorbitant price. Combing notes I'd saved from the more eccentric designers I'd worked with, I called the Austrian woman who specialized in crystal skulls and the craftsman in Italy who made leather bats. While less emotive than the guy to my left, who periodically pulled his hat to his chin and dropped to the floor as if shot, I made progress.

Actually hours flew by, and before I knew it, I was unlocking the front door with kids in tow. Despite the heat, and possibly synthetically buoyed by Cushbar, I was feeling better than I had in days. I was going to rock this job, and Blake was going to rebound.

Wynn and Maya dropped their backpacks and beelined for the

kitchen while I scanned the mail and discovered, as if to validate my recovered optimism, an envelope from Blake's agency. I tore into it. Five thousand dollars from NBC Universal for the three-episode arc on *Charmed* in permanent syndication. *Yes, yes, yes!* I kicked off my heels.

But wait. The last two times he'd been paid for the same job it was $6,000. I dialed his agency as I flipped on the AC and went to the fridge.

"Richard Blankfein's office."

"Hey, Angela, it's Rory, Blake's wife."

"Hi," his assistant said with as much awkwardness as you can infuse in one syllable.

"Hey, I'm sorry to bother you with this, but we just got a check for five thousand, so I think the fees were taken out twice." I handed Maya a carrot stick.

"Sure, let me pull it up." Tap, tap, tap. "Yeah, I think you're right. I'll have them send you the balance. Oh, and Rory?"

"Yes?" I shook my head at Wynn, reached for the cookies, and traded him the bag of carrots.

"I'm happy to help you with this, but moving forward you should call accounting directly."

"New policy?" I asked conspiratorially. It was a race to see who was more annoyed by Blake's agency: its clients or its employees.

"Oh." There was a pause. "Um. You should ask Blake."

"Ask Blake what?" There was another stupidly long pause. "Angela?"

"Blake's left the agency." Her words detonated in my face.

"Oh. He's—he's—" I stammered. Wynn peered up at me, and I pivoted to the wall. "Been on set—doing this short for a friend—we've been like ships passing, so, yeah, um, thank you." I hung up.

"I'm *starving*," Wynn groaned.

"Take out the chicken, okay? I just need two minutes. Thank you." I went to our bedroom, pulled the door shut behind me, and called Blake. It went straight to voice mail. I called again. And again. I could just see it. Blake losing his temper when that Netflix job fell through, taking it out on the messenger.

"It's me." I gripped the phone. "Look, I know you fired Richard. I don't know why you didn't just—we have to talk about this, Blake, we *have* to. Whatever you said to him, you guys have history. If you apologize, I'm sure he'll understand. Please call me. *Please.*"

"Momm-mmy."

"Starr-ving!"

I splashed cold water on my face, stripped down to a tank top, and executed a 75 percent microwaved dinner, concurrent hair washes, two hours of homework, three bedtime books, and a debate over powering down Wynn's iPad that left me questioning life itself. The kids finally passed out, and I stood in the dark kitchen snarfing chocolate chips like a stoned burglar.

Blake would've used a British accent to quip about us being the staff from *Downton Abbey,* waiting on the kids' every quixotic request. Or done the one where we're their roadies, but instead of getting them onstage to perform in front of thousands, we're just getting them to bed.

Washing down the chocolate with the last of the sauvignon blanc, I walked through the dining room, passing the narrow shelves where I'd made a project of family photographs. Slowing, I realized there was a blank spot between the shot of Blake and me feeding each other cake and one of my favorites, a production picture Jessica had found in the Purchase archives and given to us for our fifth anniversary. It had been taken backstage when Blake was starring in *Equus.* In it, he's about to go on, and I happened to be standing just behind him in the wings, holding a wire horse head. I remembered the moment as soon as I unwrapped it because Blake had been about to strip naked in the play's climax. My cells were lifting toward him through that sundress like metal shavings to a magnet.

But now the photo that lived beside it, of the two children we would go on to make together sharing their first bath, was missing. The one in which Wynn, wearing a suds beard, grinned next to a tiny Maya as she splashed in my forearms. Had Blake taken it with him?

The blinking light from the answering machine that predated my life in the apartment caught my eye. Oh, thank God, he must have left a message while I'd been getting Wynn a washcloth. I hit Play.

"Hi. This is Emily. Emily Strang. I just wanted to tell Wynn that I heard we're doing wind sprints at practice tomorrow so he should bring an extra bottle of water. He can call me at 858-346-6430 if he has questions or to talk or whatever. Okay, so . . . thank you. Bye." The young girl's voice waivered among the hope, feigned purpose, and cards-on-the-table that is calling boys. I knew, because a woman does, that Emily Strang had rehearsed those sentences, most likely with friends, possibly before the bathroom mirror.

How was I old enough to have a son being called by a Girl and yet still be a Girl waiting for her call? It was like getting acne when I was pregnant. One of those trials should surely age-out the other. Fuck, what wisdom had aging earned me?

The answer came from the glow of the DVR clock, the worn Persian under my feet, the windowsill plants rustling in the breeze, from the same mundane, terribly hard-wrought world that was the farthest thing from a rock concert.

It told me: step away from the phones. Check the lock on the front door. Wipe down the counters, pick up the toys, turn on the dishwasher, turn off the lamps, plug in the chargers, and pull out the cleats. Check, collect, and distribute until the house had been shut down for the night.

I slipped on the Victoria's Secret nightshirt I'd had since high school that was worn to a deeply comforting nub, and which Blake had declared a bummer, and crawled diagonally into our bed. Our bed. *Because I'm not some girl on the soccer team, for fuck's sake. I'm his wife.*

Chapter Five

"You cannot just *not* call me," I hissed into Blake's voice mail the next morning as I paced the vacant Capri.

"Every day he doesn't apologize to his agent," I said to Jessica a few seconds later, "is one more day that he's not getting put up for shows. Even *with* this job, I can't float the four of us alone."

"Ror, you can't eat his shit for him so you have to sit on your hands. Hang strong or stay tough, or whatever people say who've already had their coffee."

"Are you okay?"

"Nosebleed," she answered succinctly, mother shorthand for "while the rest of the world was asleep, I was changing sheets."

"Oh, God, so sorry." My phone beeped. "Shit, that's Kathryn. Keep me posted." I clicked over. "Hello?"

"Rory. I got your message. I'm glad they had the wisdom to hire you. It speaks well of them, frankly. It almost calms me down. So how's it going?"

I looked back to my desk where my Halloween deck was taking shape.

"Actually, I really think they might be onto something. I mean no one ever went broke handing a lighter to people with money to burn."

She let out three quick syllables of laughter. "I'm going to suggest fire as the theme of the next Design Fair."

"Thank you again for this, Kathryn. I really appreciate the opportunity." *Lifeline,* I wanted to say as we hung up, *thank you for the lifeline.*

≡

By five Blake still hadn't called me back. He had sent Wynn a video cheering for the soccer practice he was missing, so I knew he wasn't dead. Which was bringing up conflicted feelings. *"How is this happening?"* I texted Claire, mostly to check that my cell still worked.

"Are you worried?" she asked.

I was. But Blake was an actor, epic histrionics were not unheard of in our house, and time management had never been his strong suit. He could easily call in an hour thinking it was still this morning. *"When he gets over himself and moves on to the embarrassed part, there will be no dinner nice enough."*

"No oral sex tender enough," Claire texted back.

"No kitchen floor clean enough."

Thankfully unaware that I was sitting on the sidelines plotting revenge, Wynn joined the other kids in the warm-up. I was glad not to be missing this, even if I had to imply I was meeting the production designer of *Saw* for a consult to walk out of the office early.

"Stella!" Maya shouted before abandoning her scooter to join the girl spinning like she was auditioning for *Hair*.

"Rory." Stella's mother, whose name I hadn't committed to memory (and it was seasons too late to ask), greeted me. "I haven't seen you in forever. Did the Turners have a good summer?"

"Yeah, back-to-school craziness. Thank God the heat broke, huh?" Would she notice that was not an answer? Because I did not want to start talking about how the Turners had been because what might come spewing out was how we were.

"Ugh, yes. Blake's night off?" she asked, looking over my shoulder down the length of the field as I realized palpable disappointment was rippling over the moms. Everyone stopped standing up straight, what was left of our collective boobs retreating back into the caves between hunched shoulder blades.

I have never minded the mom crushes that followed Blake like

steam from a locomotive. I imagined this was what it was like wherever the David Beckhams and Will Smiths of the world were doing
pickups or helping at the school fairs. Blake wasn't that famous, but
he was that good looking.

"He's working, actually. Are you guys going anywhere over the
October break?" Years of watching Claire make small talk with
MoMA patrons had taught me to (a) cover the weather and (b) follow up with vacation plans. People always have vacations planned,
maybe not imminent ones but someday. If nothing else, they wish
they did. Once the location is disclosed, there're endless travel logistics to mine for follow-up, making it inopportune to grab your con-
versational partner by the elbows, say your husband fired his one
professional advocate, and ask, *What is he going to do now? NO RE-
ALLY, WHAT?!*

Tuning back in, I realized she was telling me about a business trip.
I tried to piece together what it was that she did. Something about a
site visit. Social work?

". . . in the desert . . ."

Archaeology? Did people still do that? I mentally scanned my
"Stella's Mom" file: husband had a thing for boat shoes, needed
someone to stay with her dog last spring, loved *Gone Girl*, got her
oranges only at Fairway. That was it. I was ashamed that I didn't know
her and every other parent there the way I thought I would when we
signed up. My sister-in-law's neighbors met every Sunday at each
other's houses to talk while preparing family meals for the week. I
didn't even know where Stella lived. Apparently somewhere that allowed dogs.

"How about you guys? You and Blake have anything fun coming
up?"

I caught sight of Maya's face going Sweeney Todd. "Sorry, have to
triage," I excused myself.

"He thays we're bad guys. I'm not bad guys," Maya shouted, tears
springing laterally out of her eyes. "I'm not!"

Unfazed, a boy Maya's size wielded a bubble wand like an AK-47
at us both.

"Dylan, how about asking the ladies what game *they* want to play?" The boy's father jogged over to grab the wand.

"I'm not a bad guy," Maya restated emphatically.

"Oh, me neither," the dad clarified. "I swear. So sorry. We'd agreed on bubbles," he apologized to us.

Dylan looked like a can being stepped on. "I don't want to do bubbles. I want her to be bad guys." Bubbles were nowhere in Dylan's vision.

"Even huge ones?" his dad enticed. "I mean, I was going to make megabubbles, but if you're not into it . . ."

"I want megabubbles!" Maya declared, eyes brightening through the flood.

"Let me try just one, okay, Dylan?" His dad gently took the wand from him and, after a pump, arced it toward the clouds. The oily rainbows floated tauntingly, bringing Stella running over. Even Dylan couldn't resist. His dad gave the wand back and the girls chased Dylan's creations with delight. "Like it never happened," he observed. "Dylan is bad guy obsessed. He turned half a grapefruit into a gun this morning. It was kind of impressive, honestly."

"Maya would trade me in to be a Princess Twilight Sparkle Pony in a heartbeat. I read it's something about needing archetypes who have more power than us."

He grinned. "Well, it's good to know that if you want to upstage me, you have to be able to fly."

"Lucky you. All that's required to take me down is a tiara and some cheap heels."

"He's actually our third little guy so I've been to this ego-crushing rodeo. My second, Matt, is on the field there."

I followed where he pointed to a smaller version of himself gathering around the coach with Wynn. Then my gaze went to a wiry girl in shin guards furtively watching my son. Strapped into a bra supporting nothing. She was *ten*.

"Josh Rosen." He extended a hand. "Dylan and Matt's dad."

"Rory Turner." I shook it. "Wynn's mom."

"Days like this make the city feel . . ." He shrugged, peering up through his Ray Bans at the sky, "deceptively gentle."

I was relieved to be back to discussing the weather with a certified stranger. "I remember trying to keep my daughter entertained at the playground during one of Wynn's practices two years ago, and it was that first day of fall where the air turns abruptly bitter. All she wanted was to leave the padded rubber play area and climb around those rocks with the rat poison and broken beer bottles. Time slowed to a crawl."

"That makes me feel better. I thought it was just my boys who want to be wherever they're not supposed to." From the heft of his watch, I placed him from one of the limestone buildings nearby.

"Is Matt new to the league?" I asked, as I didn't recall having met Josh.

"He didn't want to do soccer. But there was no way I was schlepping him down to the rink at Chelsea Piers just to stand in a parka and watch him get his teeth knocked out."

"You can totally do that right here," I assured him. "I'm sure someone on the opposing team would oblige."

"I say this like it's all me," he demurred. "But the truth is, I wouldn't be here if I hadn't just gotten in from Geneva an hour ago."

"Long hours?" I asked.

"I'm a banking cliché. How about you?"

"I work for a site. It's—" I still couldn't say "kids' lifestyle" without cringing.

"A secret?" he asked.

"Only to me. A new media company. Can I ask you, actually, I've been in search of a translator for some of the . . ."

"Jargon?"

"Yes."

"Bring it."

"Okay." I tugged my phone from my jeans and read the notes I'd made from the meeting. "What does 'force-ranked' mean?"

"Hmm, depends on the noun it's modifying. Use it in a sentence?"

"I'm presenting a deck tomorrow and I've been asked to force-rank it based on 'potential for revenue.' Wikipedia said it's a 'leadership construct.'"

He laughed. "It's just fancy speak for highest to lowest."

"So plain old-fashioned ranking?" I confirmed.

"Every new generation needs our language to submit wholly to their awesomeness," he said as his phone rang.

"That they do," I murmured in agreement. "That they do."

He pushed his sunglasses up into his thinning hair as he answered the call. He had one of those faces that was probably not knee-weakening in college but was getting handsome with age. "Hey, babe, yeah, we're on the field . . . Yup, he has his cleats . . . I know, I found them in the hamper . . . I took a guess . . . Because if I was looking to torment my little brother, that's where I would have hidden them . . . Don't bother with defrosting at this hour. Let's just order in. Whatever you want. Sushi?"

I just stood there, listening to a guy who knew that defrosting was a pain in the ass, ready to walk over to the nearest tree and knock my forehead against it. Because in my twenties, Josh was not the kind of guy I ever would have gone for. *Finance? Law student? Where's the mystery? Where's the magic? Where's the passion?* I'd wanted David Beckham without any of the endorsement deals. And I got it.

Boy, did I get it.

The next afternoon, holding my completed deck, I took a spot in the line forming outside Taylor's office behind the guy who directed the Savor vertical. I'd assumed it was about artisanal PB&J until I saw him compiling Deepak meditations. How *were* toddlers remembering their spirits?

I texted with Jessica while the other directors and I shuffled forward in DMV-like increments.

"There was a time I'd have brought in doughnuts to make everyone here love me."

"There was a time when my boss asking me to get 'noisier' would have given me a panic attack," she texted back. *"Now I just ignore him."*

I checked to see if I'd somehow missed something from Blake. I hadn't. I was restraining myself from jumping up and down like Yosemite Sam.

"I'm wai-ting," I heard Taylor.

"You guys are fast," I said as I tucked my phone in my pocket.

"Our viewers are faster." Taylor was perched on the front of her desk, a stripe of purple panties visible between her legs. She crossed them, leaving a patent heel dangling. Kimmy sat in Taylor's desk chair like a king who'd just lost the war. The combined tableaux conjured that iconic photo of Larry Flynt and his stripper girlfriend—the one played by Courtney Love—back in the hot minute we wanted to look like her.

"How are you feeling?" I asked Kimmy.

"It's moved into my ears."

"I'm so sorry to hear that." I looked for somewhere to prop my Halloween storyboard, but my only option was Taylor's desk.

"What's that?" she asked, jumping up as if it'd bitten her.

"My deck." I flipped back the velum to show them the spread. "Ranked as requested. The numbers next to each item show the uniques it's getting at its current points of sale."

"Where's the final?"

"The final?"

"First of all." Taylor slapped her palm on the board. "No. This format is just—no. Second, JeuneBug is not about decorations. Decorations flag 'temporary.' We want the consumer who's going to commit. And, third, anyone can go to Party City."

I took a breath. "This is an $8,000 skeleton made from Tahitian lava. They don't sell those at Party City, Taylor. They don't even sell them in North America."

Taylor flared her surgically adjusted nostrils and stared hard at me. "Your vertical is *Be*. How is our JeuneBug consumer going to *live* Halloween in its most luxurious, exclusive, unprecedented incarnation?" I still had no idea what she wanted. I suspected she didn't entirely either. "I think we just need to decide this never happened. I mean, we're seeing a lot of shit, but this is—"

"Yeah," Kimmy summarized.

I was speechless. The worst? Really? Worse than the guy who sucked a lollipop ring? "I'm sorry you're disappointed, but I'm just not following."

"No, that's *exactly* what you're doing. You know who she is?" Taylor asked Kimmy.

Kimmy nodded. "The gopher."

"Excuse me?" I asked.

"In school, on the project. Everyone has their role, the skill they bring to the assignment. But there's always the gopher. That guy who lies low, makes all the coffee runs, and then shares the grade."

"Let me be clear," I strained. "I am not phoning this in. If you want my proposal in a different format, or would prefer not to use a party setup, both are easily addressed."

"We're going live in a week, Rory. We don't have the bandwidth to babysit. And let *me* be clear: I'm not putting to market what's already fucking out there. If that's all you know how to do, I feel sorry for you. I seriously do. Next!"

Stunned, I walked back to my desk, eyes going to Merrill, who had her windbreaker tented over her head. Making sad kitten sounds, she felt for a napkin to blow her nose, then took the flash drive sitting by her laptop and flung it across the room.

No one else had presented a board. No one else had even gone in with paper.

I made it seem as if I was stepping out for coffee, which turned into walking the twenty blocks home. I needed to think—away from the low din of everyone's headphones. I didn't know which was making my heart pound more: the fact that they'd talked to me like I was an asshole—or feeling like one.

But I also knew what I fucking knew. Successful interiors, even in editorial, are perfectly calibrated advancements on the current aesthetic. Who on earth would want to live Halloween? But then I'd been in enough homes to realize that somewhere out there was someone who wanted to live just about everything.

I just needed to lie on my bathroom floor and hyperventilate. Really quick, then I'd get right back out there. I turned onto our block—and that's when I spotted Blake walking out of our building.

The first time we'd ever spoken, I'd been sent behind the theater to paint props and unexpectedly rounded into him running lines by himself. Despite the frigid November temperature, all I had on was a rayon sack dress and come-hither Doc Martens. He offered me his down vest.

He was one of the first guys from New York City I'd met, so I couldn't have known that his bundling was not unique. I'd come from a town where teenagers denied the interminable winters, where local boys postured in open jackets and sleet-filled Jordans. Their ears tingeing purple, they looked as comfortable as pop stars lip-synching through chattering teeth in the Macy's Thanksgiving Day Parade.

Not only do City Boys zip up their coats; they own hats, plural. They pull up hoods. They layer. They even wear their backpacks strapped onto both shoulders. I mistook this preparedness as confidence, an ability to face things as they were. In truth, it was just a necessity from growing up without a car. As with the other cool things I assumed Blake invented (e.g., the Urban Outfitters Look Book), I wouldn't be able to contextualize that aspect of his appeal for years.

Now there he was, under our awning, hooking his Oakleys, a souvenir from *The Bourne Ultimatum*, into his collar. He slung a bulging duffel over his shoulder and turned his prized ten-speed in the opposite direction.

"Blake?" I called and then, "Blake?!"

He stopped but didn't turn around. I ran after him, my mules slapping the pavement. "What the fuck?" I panted, catching up. "When did you get home? Where are you going? Why haven't you called me back?!"

"They wrapped my part early." He regripped his handlebars, his hair in his eyes. "I'm going to crash at Jack's."

"Crash?" I was shaking. "This isn't college, Blake. Real shit is going down. You need to call Richard and apologize—"

"No," he said with such force it propelled me back. "I didn't fire Richard, Rory. He fired me."

"What?"

"He just doesn't see it picking up." He brushed the sidewalk with the tow of his Converse. In his absence, Blake had become a caricature of himself, his feelings oafish. But now I saw he was as terrified as I was.

"Oh, God, I'm so sorry. Why didn't you tell me?"

He pursed his lips, looking away. From five floors above, our home seemed to be watching us. I imagined the rooms slipping into a Havisham-esque decay as we failed them, the idea of us that I cherished receding. Suddenly Living Halloween clicked. "Blake, please. I don't want you to feel like you can't deal with this in front of me. This is *our* problem, *our* life. What if we got someone to help us sort this out?"

His head dipped in a concessionary nod.

"Really?" I leaned forward to catch his eyes. "You'd be up for that?" I loved those eyes, had loved them since I taped them over my bed in seventh grade.

"Sure."

I took a few steps closer. Our faces almost touching. "Please, Blake, just come upstairs. The kids miss you so much." I reached out, my fingertips touching his bare arm, making contact for all of a second before he withdrew.

"I'm trying to get a lot of things straight in my head. I'm no good for them to be around right now, Rory. I'm sorry." And he kicked his leg over the bike and propelled himself down the block. Away from me.

Chapter Six

I called Jessica the second I got up to the apartment.

"Oh, God, are you separating?" she asked.

"No!" I said vehemently. I took a breath. It was a fair question. "No," I added, my conviction returning. "He's just—he's put himself in Think Time."

"Oh."

"It's so painful for him to face that—wow—I guess . . . his acting career is over." I slid against the cabinets down to the kitchen floor. I knew that my wanting him to repair the relationship with his agent was inconsistent, but right now he had one way to make money— one—and maybe I was as scared as he was to let go. "I think he needs the conversation to be facilitated by a professional."

"So he's going to see a therapist? That's great."

I held the can of coffee beans I could no longer figure out how to turn into a beverage. "No, we are. I have to find someone who can help us talk about this transition productively. Or, you know, at all."

"Good for you."

"And in the meantime, I'm just going to keep telling myself he's away on location."

"Right."

"Jess?" I asked quietly.

"Yes?"

"Someday we'll look back on this and laugh?"

"I'm sneaking out to come hug you right now, Rory."

"Right now I have to find a therapist who takes insurance and figure out if the Children of the Corn took a nap, what their crib would look like. Rain check on that hug, but thank you."

"You're my hero," she said. "Okay, going to post more pictures of puppies spooning with babies."

By the end of the afternoon, therapists had quoted me enough three-figure hourly rates that I had to actively restrain myself from calling Blake and saying, *"Really? You can't sit down with me and have this conversation like a normal person? Because for the same price we could fly to Europe."* Forget the other Grown-Up Careers I fantasized my kids would pursue; it was now couples counseling or bust.

And back to The Hills Have Eyelet coverlets.

When I got into work the next morning I stopped by Taylor's office to find her with her chin resting on her desk like my parents' retriever begging for scraps. Her arms extended in a diamond shape, she held her phone in front of her while she typed.

"Taylor?"

"Yep." She didn't look up.

"My first shoot is Thursday and I wanted to ask about the invoicing procedure for the staff?"

"Staff?" she echoed.

"The photographer and assistants."

"Rory," she huffed my name. "No assistants."

"Sorry?"

"Those are the calories we cut," she stated.

My eyebrows furrowed. "But I need an assistant."

She let the phone flop down but stayed prone. "You think you need an assistant because you've always had an assistant."

"Right." Hookah-smoking Caterpillar. "I've always had an assistant. Glen, the photographer who is already making time in his schedule as a favor to me, has always had an assistant since he *was* an assistant."

"My guru says anything that comes after the words 'I need' the universe is going to give you the opportunity to let go of."

"On Thursday?"

She resumed typing. "That's what your app package is for. Didn't Ginger hook you up?" she asked.

"I'll check with her."

At reception I approached Ginger, who was wearing a T-shirt that said, "Boys (heart) BJs."

"I almost wore my shirt that says, 'Duh.'"

"Sorry?" Ginger asked.

"Never mind. Who do I speak to about my app package?"

She made a sound like gargling. "Tim." She pointed me back to the bullpen.

"Tim?" I called hesitantly over the heads of the other vertical directors.

A halo of dark red frizz rose into view and then dipped back down behind a massive screen. "Tim?" I asked again as I approached. He glanced up fearfully, small eyes blinking behind thick spectacles. His hair blended into a scraggle of a beard, which, coupled with his general roundness, gave the impression of a mole or badger, like he was the programmer from *Wind and the Willows*.

"Yes?"

"Apparently, I need an app package."

He held out his hand.

"Oh, hi, I'm Rory." I shook it.

"No." He yanked away like I had warts. "Your phone."

"Oh, sorry." I tugged it out of my blazer pocket and handed it to him. He swiped across the screen. "It's already on here."

"It is?" I looked down with him.

"It clouds with your computer. You want me to enable everything?"

"Just me. Just enable me. Thank you."

You are . . . late. You are . . . late.

"Guys!" I shouted for the kids from the front hall the next morning as I grabbed my keys. "My phone says we're late."

"How does it know?" Wynn asked, lugging his french horn to the door. His auditions for performance-based middle schools were coming up. I guiltily realized that with all that was going on, I hadn't been as on him as I should have about practicing. I didn't honestly care if he was a french horn prodigy. Except he kind of was. And maybe all ten-year-olds were just incapable of making themselves do anything but play World of Warcraft. I was the opposite of a Tiger Mother—a hamster. I was a Hamster Mother.

"I don't know," I confessed. "It clouds with my computer. Maya, why did you change?" She had removed the outfit we'd agreed on and put on a party dress. With her Miss Piggy pajama bottoms.

"I wathn't feewing it."

"I see."

You are . . . late, the voice said louder. I would have to name it. "Maya, we can't wear pajamas to school."

"I want the piggy pants!"

Before I had children, I wondered why little girls were dressed like Fruit Loops, as if we all had cataracts and it was the responsibility of children's clothing manufacturers to make sure we could discern form. Even after Wynn, the mystery lingered. To this day, he is relatively fine to throw on whatever, barring that summer he wouldn't take off his Thomas the Tank Engine rain boots and we had to sneak into his room while he slept to spray antifungal on his little feet.

Then I had a daughter whose opinions are violent and quixotic. When she was a baby, she would burst into tears for no reason. Dry, fed, burped, rested, she would wail at me like I was an imbecile. I now know that she will not wear anything with a tag, discernible seam, or reverse stitching—like polka dots. Any kind of texture against her skin is unbearable to her. And she *loves* purple. With pink and turquoise and banana yellow. Loves it.

So until Blake got back, she would be that kid. The one in the tutu and the rash guard. And I could not give a fuck.

You are . . . late.

"Okay, fine. Let's go!"

We were halfway to the train when the rain that wasn't supposed to start until lunchtime broke. "My thandals! My thandals are getting wet!" Maya screamed as if lava were falling from the sky. I heaved her onto one hip, feeling my vertebrae do something that looked like an accordion midperformance.

Blake had been away for weeks at a stretch before, but always with an end date. Now, not knowing when I was going to be able to tag myself out and catch my breath was unnerving. I realized that I depended on his returns as if they were finish lines. I used them to determine when to flat-out parent (impromptu giant art projects) and when to conserve my energy to go the mothering distance (Dora).

You are moving in the wrong direction!

"Mommy, are we?" Maya asked as Wynn and I ran with our jackets raised over our heads. My phone rang. We tried not to slip down the subway stairs.

"Hello?" I answered breathlessly as I pulled out my Metrocard.

"Rory," Kathryn said, sounding like she was dry in a town car. "Listen, I'd be curious to see the mechanicals for the launch pages as soon as they're compiled."

"Uh, sure," I said, unsure if it was actually an "uh, sure" situation. Guessing that if Taylor wasn't allowed to know I knew Kathryn, it probably wasn't.

"Thank you." She hung up, and I tapped at the settings as we waited for the subway but couldn't figure out how to disable it. Wynn even gave it a try. When we turned off the sound, my phone shook without stopping like a vibrator going for a Christmas bonus.

"Mom," Wynn said sharply as we approached school. "Turn that *off*. You look *weird*." What, with the Cuisinart in my purse?

I set it on a low volume. *You are moving in the wrong direction,* she whispered urgently from my bag. It was starting to feel that way.

By the time I got to the therapist's office, I had to take off my ballet flats and tip the water out. The bottoms of my pants were dripping.

Blake smiled at me as he opened the door to the waiting room, his hoodie sweatshirt similarly sodden. *Aren't we a pair?* he seemed to say as we glanced around at the other couples sensibly covered in Burberry.

This was the kind of thing I had loved about us when I moved in with him, two creatives on the edge of the old Hell's Kitchen, ordering off the early-bird menus, buying the day-old bread. When we carried the buckets of paint and sanders into the apartment, our neighbors kept complaining that a "crew" was coming and going after-hours. They couldn't imagine anyone doing the work themselves. We sat on the floor and ate $5 pad thai and Blake listened for Wynn's heartbeat and we felt special. Our own little Bohemia in the Bergdorf's triangle.

But now I was forty-one and suddenly felt like an asshole for trusting the forecast and being married to someone who also trusted the forecast. One of us should have an umbrella! We didn't both need to have one. I didn't have a penis. There was a differentiation of responsibilities, but someone should have an umbrella.

"Mr. and Mrs. Turner?" a woman beckoned from a doorway. Behind her I could see pickled floors and white walls, like a beach house. "I'm Dr. Brompton." She looked like a former dancer in an oatmeal-colored wrap sweater over white jeans, her gray blond hair twisted up with a pencil. "Please have a seat."

Blake did his actor thing of sitting with his legs crossed under him, which he did when he was getting down to work on something. *Great. Let's get down to work.*

"Okay." Her voice was syrupy yet breathy as she placed her notepad in her lap. "What we're going to do today is root out whose fault the problems in your marriage are. We're going to dig into the blame. Who wants to go first?" Wait—what??

"I will, I guess," Blake said as I tried to process what the hell had just come out of her mouth. He exhaled. "Okay. Rory's really judgmental."

"Wait," I interrupted before I could even let that land. "I'm sorry, I thought we were going to have to use 'I' statements and own our feelings."

"See, there you are, judgmental," he said in a tone that indicated he was just warming up.

"You think I'm judgmental?" I asked. How long had he been festering about this? About me?

He addressed Dr. Brompton: "Part of what attracted me to Rory at the beginning was that we were both artists, but really, deep down, she's just like her parents."

"Mommy, I hate you!" I saw myself standing over four-year-old Wynn at the playground, tears streaming down his face because I wouldn't let him stay and play in the thunderstorm. *"I hate you!"*

Blake's just angry at life right now, I told myself. *He doesn't mean this; he's hurt and he just wants to strike at something and I'm the safest thing.*

"I don't know if she's changed or that's who she's really always been, but it's definitely not the kind of person I would have been attracted to, wanted to build a life with."

"Wait," I said again, swallowing my reaction, trying to get this back on track. "We're supposed to be coming up with a blueprint for moving forward. For your career change."

"See, just like them."

"Um . . . we should be so lucky." I swiveled to Dr. Brompton, stunned smile on my face. "My parents own their home outright. Have no debt. Have a retirement account. Long-term care insurance. And living wills. And nobody ever forgot to pick me up from school."

"I did not forget," he said through gritted teeth. "I was late."

"Because you forgot." Why was this relevant? I didn't want to sound like this.

"Losing track of time is not the same as forgetting!" He was baiting me.

"You want to know the last time I 'lost track of time'?" My heart sped. "I was in labor. *That* is not a luxury I have. I do not go grab a beer with my friends after an audition and then look up and realize my eight-year-old— I'm sorry." I appealed to Dr. Brompton, trying to steady myself. "How is this productive?"

She squinted behind her glasses. "Someone is to blame. We're here to figure out who."

I struggled to think clearly. "But your book is called *No More Blame.*"

"Oh. You haven't read it." She sat back. "Couples therapy is traditionally a gateway drug to divorce. Why? Because people pay hundreds of dollars to have these polite *useless* conversations. Then they go home where I can't help them and tear each other apart. So in my process we dive *into* the blame." She arced her pressed palms. "We become blame warriors. So, Blake, continue."

"It's gotten to the point where nothing I do is good enough. Seriously, nothing."

What? "That's not true, Blake."

"It is."

"Can you be specific?" she prompted him.

"You don't let me flow with the kids. Every morning, you're just go, go, go."

I was dumbfounded. "When we're trying to get out the door and you stand there like you've never seen them before, when they don't have shoes on, which is a pretty obvious place to start, I get angry."

"I was never on time for school. I skipped out on whole years. You're so focused on what's not happening. The important thing is that they're not just being hustled from one place to the next. That they love to learn. That they read."

"Well, that's what they're learning right now. In school."

"Let him finish," Dr. Brompton interrupted me.

He pressed his palms together. "You always have to control what I say, me, the whole process."

"Blake, I don't want to control you, or the process! It's just that" —at $250 an hour —"I think we should focus on the plan."

"Fuck the plan. You're not hearing me. I'm not happy, Rory."

"Of course you're not happy; your agent fired you."

"No." He twisted to face me, his eyes grabbing mine. "I'm not happy with you. With us. How we are, how we've been. I'm not happy."

I was hearing him. Hearing him so hard I felt like I was being flung from a car accident. "Um . . . so, I'm sensing you're not coming home after this."

He shook his head.

"Okay." *It's just a tantrum, just a tantrum, just a tantrum.* "Well, while we continue working this out . . ." I was biting my tongue, which was clamping on my throat, which was squeezing my larynx, which was compressing my stomach, which was gripping my intestines, which were hanging onto my colon. ". . . we have kids who need to see their dad. Every day."

"I—"

"Every day." I could speak for them. Speaking for them was all I could do. "You will pick them up from the extended day program. You will bring them home. We will tell them you're in a show. And leaving early every morning before they get up. Okay?"

Stewing silence.

"Blake, *okay*?"

"Okay!"

Dr. Brompton leaned forward. "This was very productive. Shall I put you down for next week?"

"I'm so sorry," Jessica said for the tenth time as she sat on my kitchen counter eating out of a bag of Skinny Pop that night. "Dr. Brompton came so highly recommended."

"It's not your fault," I said as I stirred the leftover meatloaf into the leftover crushed tomatoes for what was hopefully going to morph into bolognese sauce.

"But do you *blame* me?"

"I do." I laughed. Then, in a burst of magical culinary thinking, I switched spatulas as if that might do the trick. "The thing is I know what's running him. He's mad at himself, mad at his agent, mad at the world, but the only person in the room is me, so he's decided I'm the problem."

"You're suddenly a stranger," Jessica added.

"Exactly. Only that knowledge does me a fat fuck of good because I'm not the one who has to get it. He does."

Without moving, she opened the door to the fridge and grabbed a Fresca. "So he just trashed you for an hour?" She popped it open.

"Please. Forty-five minutes. I shudder to think what a whole hour would cost."

"I am coming back as a high-class therapist," she said, flexing her feet, and we both saw the heel of her shoe coming away from the sole.

"You want to borrow a pair to wear home?" I offered.

"Nah. It's been like this for weeks. I keep thinking elves are going to repair them while I sleep, but no luck."

"Miles isn't also a cobbler?" I asked of her husband.

She didn't answer, but sat on the granite absentmindedly stroking the lip of the can. "I'm never going to make out in the back of a cab again."

I looked over at her. "Go on."

"I mean, just, speaking of strangers, no one tells you. No one slows you down that night you first hook up with the person you're going to be with for the rest of your life and says, 'sign here if you're willing to never make out in the back of a cab again.'"

"Or in the rain."

"Now I'd be too worried about getting sick."

"When I first moved in here, we'd go on the roof and fuck whenever it poured," I said wistfully as I stirred.

"On the ground?"

"No. It's landscaped. They have benches. I'd sit facing him in a long sundress."

"See! You will never do that again. And we are not old."

"But, Jess, we did it. We crossed the finish line without AIDS or crabs or chlamydia. And those guys, those make-out-in-the-back-of-cabs guys, they sucked for the most part." I poured the spaghetti out over the sink, jerking back from the steam.

"Okay, yes, well, there's that. It's just sometimes, when Miles wants to have morning sex when we had garlic the night before, I just wish I could go back to being unknown. To being someone he'd brush for."

"Hel-oh-ho!" Blake called jovially from the front hall. Having picked the kids up as agreed, he was in Dad mode. I would not be surprised if they both had Starbursts tucked away somewhere on their persons.

"Mom!" We heard the kids stampede to find me.

"I'll be going." Jess hopped to the terra-cotta tile and slipped out the back door, whispering, "Keep me posted."

Blake stuck his head in the kitchen. "So, I'm gonna go."

I blew out, realizing that I had been hoping he'd stay for dinner, that if I could just plug him back into our lives this would be over. "Okay— Blake?" I stopped him.

"Yeah?"

"I'm sorry." I stepped forward. He was standing next to Wynn's faded Spider-Man collage. "If I've done something to make you feel like you can't be here, I'm sorry. We love you." It was the opposite of what I felt, but it was my Hail Mary.

"Rory . . ." His eyes lifted to the ceiling. "I don't think we should see her again. That, uh, got a little out of hand."

"Right?" I said, relief drenching me like a hydrant had been opened. "That was nuts." The kids bounded in as I moved to set a place for him at the dining table.

"Dad, Dad, Dad, look at my new baseball card/headband/slime/ dance move!"

"Guys, guys, guys," I said. "Dinner's ready. Wash your hands and clear the floor before I step on a calico critter. I made spaghetti." We would eat like a family and then we would talk this through like people who've been married for ten years—

"Sorry, you two, but I've got to hit the road." Blake turned for the door. "Night shoot."

"Aw." They stomped out to follow him to the vestibule while I stood there alone.

"Bye, Rory," he called out.

"Bye," I said, his words from this afternoon lacerating me afresh, making me think we had a bad marriage. I ladled out the pasta.

We did *not* have a bad marriage. Of course it didn't help that I'd gotten pregnant right after we got engaged, that we didn't have a lot of memories of prechild days to draw on, but we would get through it. I mean, yes, the last year had been tough. Blake was crabby a lot of the time. He was impatient with the kids in the morning, withdrawn from me at night. But this was just a phase; I knew that.

Every couple has a Fight. When Jessica made the mistake, once every few months, of asking Miles if he had, say, taken the boys to get their flu shots, Miles would blow up and say something to the effect of, *You do not get to breeze in and out of here and then fucking backseat-drive how I get all the shit done.* And she would scream back, *Keeping our health insurance and 401k is not fucking breezy, and do you think I wouldn't trade it all in a heartbeat if you made more fucking money?* Every few months, same fight. *Every couple we knew had one,* I re-assured myself when Blake inevitably forgot something pertaining to the kids, like Friday is early pickup, and I lost it, then he called me a controlling bitch and I called him an irresponsible human being. We had to take ourselves in context.

I ladled the pasta into three bowls, the fourth sitting empty on the counter. And suddenly a thought made my stomach go cold. *What if he didn't know we were in a context?*

Chapter Seven

You are going the wrong way! Someone needed to show me how to turn off my virtual assistant or I was going to throw my phone in a mailbox. It was my first photo shoot for JeuneBug and, without Blake, I wasn't able to get to the flower market at five and on set by six, as Zoe would have. So as soon as I got the kids to school, I settled for a bale of branches from the local florist at ten times the price. *See, Taylor, an assistant pays for herself.*

When I raised the gate on the industrial elevator, I found Glen lying on the cement floor of the studio I had rented. I stood over him with the branches in my arms, ready to make a Blair Witch crib. "Rough night?"

"My . . . back," he grunted, "is out."

"No."

"I am not supposed to be loading in cases of equipment like a fucking twenty-three-year-old. I love you, Ror, but I'm not doing this shit again."

"Don't move. I'll call someone."

"Just leave me be. Set the whole thing up, and I'll talk you through it."

"Me?"

"Do you have a better idea?"

I looked at the clock. I had three hours to turn ten cartons of unassembled designer furniture, a chandelier that necessitated its own guard, and five bolts of black silk into something Rosemary's Baby would sleep-train in. "Let me know if you need a pillow."

I started by pulling out my power drill and assembling the most ornately carved single bed I could get my hands on. It was sent over from the Tribeca showroom and cost more than everything in my apartment combined. I didn't have the time to install the brackets so no one could sit on it or breathe too hard in its direction, but it would do for pictures. Painter's mask in place (following much negotiating with the designer's publicist), I sprayed the whole thing black, then hung the Tim Burton images I'd downloaded and blown up myself. Getting the chandelier hung was kind of like the first time we flew with the kids: I just left myself and made it happen.

Hours behind schedule, the touch I was most proud of was the $600 Wednesday Addams getup from the Jaeyoon Jeong Collection that I laid out on the custom rocking chair, as if this were her room.

"Glen, how are you doing?"

"I really need to take a piss."

I heard Taylor's shoes come off the elevator. "Okay!" Clop-clop. "How's it going?"

"I need to pee," Glen reiterated from the floor. "And some oxycontin wouldn't go amiss."

"Can I see my money?" She peered around.

"Tah-dah." I gestured to the set.

"In the laptop."

"We haven't shot anything yet."

"Rory." The bare arms crossed. "We only have the space 'til six. There is no budget for overtime."

"I know, but without assistants, it takes a full day to put this together."

She scowled. "Honestly, Rory, what about your app package?"

I walked over to the next furniture box to be unpacked and lay my phone atop it. "Go," I commanded the device. "Nope." I turned back to Taylor. "My phone cannot assemble a bureau, hang fabric, or paint a set. All it can do is keep prompting me to order coffee and lunch, but I don't have time to stop and, you know, physically do that."

"What's that?" She pointed disdainfully to the bundle of twigs.

"The next setup—the nursery, but I planned to be assembling that while Glen shot the first space and—"

"Rory." She held her palm up, which had a faded doodle of a dollar sign on it. "You *have* to be more efficient. You know what we learned in B-school?" She tilted her head in pity for everyone who would never make it to B-school. "Things will take as long as you decide they're going to take."

I wanted to see her assemble a single Ikea dresser. "Taylor, my goal is to walk out of here tonight with three setups in the can." She winced at my old-school vernacular. "I'm doing as much as humanly possible with two hands. So either pay for the overtime or pay for an assistant."

"Why did you log in from Stellar?" she asked bluntly.

"Pardon?"

"Tim noticed you logged in last night from 525 Madison Avenue." I what? *Wait—could Kathryn do that?* My password was WynnMaya so, yes, very likely she could. "What were you doing at Stellar?"

"Waiting for a friend to have dinner." I didn't blink.

She didn't blink back. "Fine. Get your assistant here. But tomorrow we'll have a postmortem to review why you failed." She tried to stride out regally, but her heels were so high it was more like a newborn camel. I dialed Zoe, the first useful thing my phone had done all day. Calling Kathryn would have to wait until I got home. I wasn't exactly sure what my app package did, but transmitting a phone log to Taylor did not seem out of the question.

"Oh, Ror, I would've loved to," Zoe said, "but I'm assisting on a shoot in Milwaukee. Some bottling magnate. His pool is tinted yellow to look like beer—I *cannot* convey how gross it is."

"Zoe, that's great, I'm so excited for you." Shit.

"Do you want me to send my roommate? She's in a carpal tunnel brace, but she means well."

I declined, wished her a safe flight home, and hung up. "Okay, overtime it is."

I called Blake. He answered. Progress. "Hey, Blake, thank you for picking up." *I am not the problem.* "I'm so sorry, but I'm stuck here. I probably won't be home until after midnight. Can you stay?"

"Oh." He bristled.

"What?" I asked tentatively.

"It's just that Robbie texted—he has house seats to *Long Day's Journey* and he wants to introduce me to the director after."

"Oh." NottheproblemNottheproblemNottheproblem. "Okay."

"I really think I should go," he said firmly.

"I hear that."

"You're managing me."

"You want to go, great, just get a sitter." At twenty-five dollars an hour to see the longest play ever.

"Who should I call?" he asked.

"Just go down the list."

There was a pause. We both knew he had to ask. "The list?"

I took a breath. "In our shared iCal. It's ranked from their fave to least fave." Now I sounded like Taylor.

"When did you do that?"

"I don't know, last spring. Can you just look?"

"Yes, I can look, Rory. I'm not retarded."

"Blake!" My back ached, my eyes burned, and my restraint snapped like a released rubber band. "You *have* to stop using that word. The kids will copy you."

He hung up.

When I got home in the early hours of the next morning, the sitter was asleep on the couch. Though she hadn't wanted to say it, it was obvious that Blake had come back after the play and packed up. His underwear drawer was barren, his T-shirts gone. The flip travel clock that had been his grandfather's was missing from his night table, as was his complete collection of Jerzy Kosinski. All that was left in the medicine cabinet were his old eyedrops.

To the sound of the running bath, I dug one of his tees out of the bag destined for the Salvation Army—the Beastie Boys one that said No Sleep Til, the one he wore almost daily when Wynn was a baby. I gingerly lowered myself into the steaming Epsom brew, my whole body hurting. I lay my head back on the cold porcelain rim, covered my face with the worn blue cotton, breathed him in. And sobbed.

≡

"That's it," Claire said over the phone the next morning as I sat down at my desk, looking at the reply from Kathryn to my clandestine voice mail about the login incident: *"I'd never do anything to get you fired."* Not sure if we had the same interpretation of what that could encompass, I went ahead and sent her the mechanical. "You're coming out with me."

This had been Claire's standard line since freshman year at Purchase. F in statistics? "That's it, you're coming out with me." Olaf Knufnagel told me he could be into me if I lost some weight? "That's it, you're coming out with me."

Which implied that Claire was like one of those princesses who walked through a door in the back of her closet into an alternative college where the beer was always cold, the guys always showered, the floor loogie-free. But somehow in her presence, we did find the witty foreign exchange student, the twenty on the sidewalk, the dorm room with the good vodka.

Maybe that's why she'd never gotten married. How could anyone want to trade all that for loose pants and takeout in front of the DVR because you have to, not because you want to?

"Claire, I am too old to go 'out.'" And I was exhausted. And sad. And unsure of myself.

"Nonsense. Halloween. After the kids succumb to their sugar crashes, I'm picking you up for a huge costume party at the museum. Big design theme, totally you."

"Actually, they're both sleeping at friends' places."

"See, the universe wants you to misbehave." Or that.

JeuneBug went into beta and, despite Taylor using my shoot as an excuse for every scrimp in spending ("Oh, the water cooler's empty? Sorry, we used the money paying Rory's location overtime."), the Be vertical got the most traction that first week. Even I had to admit the pictures came out amazingly. Any parent with $20,000 and a love of the macabre could not find a better blueprint for a nursery. And apparently several had clicked through to buy the bed, only to be disappointed when they found out it didn't come in black.

By Friday it did.

Over the next few weeks, Blake and I got into the uncomfortable rhythm of our strange estrangement. He picked the kids up from school; I texted when I was approaching home; he left. I sent him the information for one couples' counselor after the next, but he kept finding fault with their bios. When we were finally recommended one he was enthusiastic about, there was a three-week wait for an appointment.

And suddenly October had flown by, and I was standing next to Maya at Ricky's staring forlornly at the racks of prosti-tot costumes. What happened to just being a strawberry? Why was she supposed to be a sexy strawberry? Why was I? I was alarmed.

"Mommy?"

"Yes?"

"Who's taking me twick-or-tweating?"

"Me."

"I want Daddy."

Me too.

"We'll just have to see if he's free with his show. I hope he is. I want him to be." I knew our excuses to the kids were starting to sound flimsy.

"I want to be Batman."

But Wynn was Batman. Would he see this as endearing? Or be enraged that she was diluting his brand?

"Are you sure, honey?" The first time I found myself transforming a cardboard box into Plex well into the wee hours while Blake watched *Lost,* I almost moved *him* in time and space. Thereafter I vowed that, despite my love of a hot glue gun, it was worth my mental health to fork over twenty-five bucks for some cheap piece of Chinese shit that made them so *so* happy.

"Batman. I am, wike, tho thure." Since starting pre-K, Maya had developed the habit of talking like a teenager from the 1980s. Via Elmer Fudd.

"Mom!" he said. "She *can't*."

I turned to Wynn, braced to intercede, before I realized the jumpsuit she was holding was red. For Robin. Oh, this was too perfect. I was actually going to be able to post pictures on Facebook that made me look like I had it together. A can of green hair spray for me and I'd be golden.

"Wynn, you're *both* going to be Batman," I said purposefully, using my eyebrows to guide his eye to her red jumpsuit. *"Okay?"*

"But that's not—"

"Okay?" I interrupted him.

"Yay!" Maya shouted. Now I just had to hope no one else burst her bubble.

We made it through two whole hours of the bizarre ritual that is Halloween in New York. We urbanites give it our all, but tromping up and down fluorescent-lit back staircases doesn't hold a Diptyque candle to shuffling through dry leaves.

As we waited in the vestibule for the host of Wynn's sleepover, the sugar my kids had consumed was reaching its peak; Maya was doing something that looked like that running move from *Flashdance* and Wynn was pretending to be a broken robot. I couldn't drop them off fast enough.

"Hi!" The Buzz Lightyear dad who greeted us seemed happy to see me.

"Oh—hi!" I did a double-take. "Josh, right?" Even in a white plastic jumpsuit, he was handsome. Ten years in, I had yet to tip over to a place where I did not care if the attractive dads found me attractive. I never flirted or engaged with them as anything other than Wynn's mom, but even with Maya in a front-pack and chalk all over my butt, I was not ready to be invisible. So why was I wearing a large overcoat and a green wig? Would it have killed me to be Catwoman? "Or should I say, Buzz?"

"Yes, I, uh, I've been wearing this costume since the first one came out." He winged his elbow at me to show a rip.

"That's dedication." Wynn had already wriggled past Josh and disappeared into the apartment. "Uh, good-bye!" I called after him. "Sorry, I'm confused. Is this your party?"

"Oh, no," Josh said. "Just some of the parents from the soccer team volunteering to stand by in case anyone codes."

"Give them the *Pulp Fiction*?"

"Exactly."

"Twick or tweat," Maya said to the wall, her eyes already rolling back in her head.

"Stay for some wine?" he asked.

"Oh, thank you," I said, scooping her into my arms. "But I should get this one to her sleepover before she turns the corner into some kind of succubus."

"It is a horrible holiday." He smiled.

"And you've done it times three."

"Enjoy this part. My oldest is heading to a club downtown dressed like a pimp."

"See, that will never happen to me because we are moving to Amish country."

"Josh," a woman called from inside. "Matt's claws aren't retracting!"

"I'm needed. Well, see you on the field."

"Now that it's miserably cold? I wouldn't miss it!"

And, trying to figure out if there was such a thing as a smile under a Joker mouth that looked at all appealing, I got us on the elevator.

Once home, I had only forty-five minutes to wash the green out of my hair and transform myself into celebrity decorator, Kelly Wearstler, which I hoped met Claire's mandate: "It's a big design scene so do *not* look like a mom, for fuck's sake." I gave myself Swiss Miss braids and pinned a vintage gold ashtray to them. I made earrings out of two midcentury chandelier tubes, worn with a metallic jacquard miniskirt and hot pink suede shoes. And to gild the lily, I had downloaded the *Playboy* spread she did in the 1980s and decoupaged it onto an old bustier.

"You look a-mazing," Claire said delightedly when she picked me up in a cab. She was dressed as a Magritte in a black bodysuit, bowler hat, a Granny Smith apple in one hand, a pipe in the other. She still had a bangin' bod. *Maybe another reason not to have kids,* I thought as I sucked in against the corset that had fit me rather well in my twenties.

We pulled up outside the MoMA, bypassing the line for their annual Halloween fund-raiser. Inside the ground floor was packed. Pale blue lights flashed in the marble atrium in concert with the throbbing base. The DJ (a Ronson, I think) was lapping the crowd into a frenzy.

"Drink?" Claire offered.

"Yes, please."

I was enthralled. And overwhelmed. And tired. I couldn't imagine doing this all again. Pretending my feet weren't hurting when they were. Pretending the music didn't grate when it did. Pretending my bare shoulders were impervious to the draft when they weren't.

I wanted to call Blake to tell him we needed to cut through his anger—and blame—and figure this out. For Wynn and Maya. For me. We *had* to. As I stood there getting jostled, I vowed to find a couples' therapist he couldn't resist, make him feel in control, blow him nightly—anything to never have to do this all again.

"Fabulous, right?" Claire asked, handing me a cocktail. "Oh, hello!" she waylaid a stranger to introduce me. "This is Bucky Thorton." The little bespectacled man blinked in gratitude that Claire knew his name. "He has just helped us acquire the most *fabulous* collection of Russell Wright, very rare stuff."

Bucky blushed. "Oh, well, now really, I just—"

"Nonsense." She touched his chest. "You're a generous spirit with a keen eye. This is my friend, Rory. She loves midcentury modern."

"I l-love your hat," he stammered.

"Thank you." I looked around, taking bets on what would bleed first, my feet or my ears. I had hoped the costumes would be incredibly creative, but the twentysomethings were wearing the inevitable variations on a theme of undies. I felt my phone vibrate and hoped someone's sleepover had gone pear-shaped so I could excuse myself with dignity. Instead it was a push notification that lamb647 liked my picture on Instagram. I opened it to see which of the portraits of my dynamic duo had won praise.

Only it was Blake. Standing next to boobs. Big boobs. The nipples were hidden behind two half jack-o'-lanterns, but still. Boobs. Big ones. Where was he? What could he be at now, at our age, that looked like a college party? What was happening to us? Oh God, what if I was wrong—what if he wasn't just taking his professional frustration out on me?

"Is this guy botherin' you?" A man in his fifties with the build of a defensive lineman stepped between Bucky and Claire.

"Grant, I didn't expect you tonight." Claire's smile stiffened.

"Daughter wanted to come, asked me to buy a table." He pointed to the Moulin Rouge posse resting their boas over the backs of their chairs. The joke was that any of them would get with Blake in a heartbeat. Two pregnancies weren't writ large on his body. I shuddered to think what would happen if I wandered over to a table of twentysomething guys and tried to ply my wares.

"This is Rory," Claire said, her voice getting tighter.

"So, Rory." He sized me up. "Nice ass. The one pasted on your top—haven't seen yours. Yet." He chuckled like Beavis. "How you like my atrium?"

"Um, it's very open—and tall. Very atrium-like."

"Claire, I like this one, she's a pistol." Just then a server passed with a tray of lemon-drop shots and I downed two. "We on for lunch Thursday? I want to discuss the grout in the sculpture garden. It feels all wrong to me."

"Of course. Oh, they're playing my song! Would you excuse us?" Claire pulled me onto the dance floor.

"You missed your calling," I shouted in her ear, trying to put Blake and his boobs out of my head.

"Oh? This wasn't it?"

"How much have you parted from Grant?" I asked.

"Twenty-five million."

"God damn. And you don't have a dime to show for it."

"But I *love* the sculpture garden's new grout." She raised her hands over her head, and I felt the shots make my edges hot and fuzzy like warm angora.

I thought back to the second half of junior year. I did an exchange program in Florence, where I found a club to go at night. Super-cheesy: you took a slide to get down into it, the whole bit. And they had these red shiny cubes anyone could climb on to dance. And if the men watching liked what you did, they threw money at you—as I discovered one night rocking out to, of all things, "Smells like Teen Spirit." After that, I went every night like it was my job and ended up paying for a whole backpacking trip through Greece. I was always industrious.

Dancing. That's what life had been missing. Not the silly, slide-around-the-kitchen-with-Maya kind, but the dirty, deep, out-of-myself kind.

Suddenly the crowd parted a little, and I saw this guy—tall, lanky, wearing a bright green turtleneck and leggings, a vine wrapped around one leg. He bounced over to me in his green Converse.

"Kelly Wearstler?" he asked.

"Jolly Green Giant?" I responded.

And then his hands were on my hips and his lips were brushing my bare shoulder and we were dancing like the MoMA was the staff quarters at Kellerman's. With thick blond hair and pale blue eyes, he was like Eric Stolz. A young Eric Stolz. God, he was young. And his hands were *everywhere*. Almost. An hour passed, maybe more. "Let's find a bathroom," he whispered in my ear, his fingers grazing my bustier. "I want to be inside you."

Could it be that simple? We hadn't even kissed. "Wait here." I stumbled away through the crowd to find Claire.

She was standing by the sushi table talking to a woman dressed as a Mondrian. I strode up to her, hugged her tight—and then tumbled past for the revolving door. "Thank you!" I called as it sprung me onto the deserted red carpet. I slipped off my shoes and ran the six blocks home as if he was chasing me.

Dropping my clothes to the bedroom floor, I let the ashtray clatter on top. Naked, I jumped into bed and flipped the duvet over me—holding myself still, waiting for the lust to abate like the spins. I wanted it to stop.

Stop, stop, "Stop."

From my tiny clutch bag I heard a buzz.

"You up?" the text asked.

I immediately dialed him back.

"Hey," Blake said softly, "you're awake." He sounded surprised. Good. He'd had me in a near-constant state of surprise for two months.

"Just got in. Those were some amazing boobs."

"What?"

"We share an Instagram, Blake."

"Oh—right—sorry, that was Charlie's girlfriend—that was a goof." Oh. "How was your night?"

"I went out with Claire. It was Claire-iffic. You?"

"Jack and I went over to Charlie's for a little bit, but then I came back here. It wasn't my scene."

I rolled over on my elbow. "What's your scene?"

"Watching Maya and Wynn divide their candy. How she tries to hide the Jolly Ranchers from us." Us.

"I miss you," I whispered.

"I miss you too." There was a long pause and I wasn't sure if he was still there. "I'm sorry I'm so fucked up," he said. "I don't know what I'm doing."

"Neither do I, Blake. None of us do."

"But I—I don't know if I can be there right now. You make me so mad—"

"Shhh, not tonight," I soothed like I was rocking one of the kids.

"I can't sleep."
"Let's just stay on the line."
"Okay."

We drifted off like that, to the sound of each other's breath. In the morning the call was disconnected, but I don't know which of us hung up.

Chapter Eight

The first time I encountered the New York City marathon I'd been living in Manhattan all of four months and was attempting to find my way back to my apartment from a hookup. Waking up in the Bronx, I might as well have been in Shanghai. When I finally spotted the entrance to a subway I was cut off from getting there by a police barricade. Fighting tears, I noticed the tradition of runners writing on their shirts so that bystanders can yell motivation.

"Do it for Aunt Mary!"

"Continua, José!"

"Go, Sammy's Daddy!"

At a time when I was professionally and personally out of the game, the interaction was a revelation. The runners' bloodshot eyes flittered to mine and they picked up steam from my encouragement. "Home stretch!" I added. How often do you get to say that and have it be true? And couldn't we all write the motivation we craved on our shirts? *"Do it for your kids' tuition, Tom!" "Those heels'll be off soon, Cheryl!" "He's going to call, Jane!"*

The following fall when Jessica announced that the three of us were doing it she got no resistance from me. In the absence of a direction on any front we would become People Training for the Marathon. Living on a primary diet of Tasti De-Lite, about as hydrated as POWs, with Skechers standing in for gear, we faced an admittedly steep fitness curve. But when that training binder showed up from the New York Road Runners it was like getting a message from God. Pages of guidance! Seemingly achievable goals! A plan with an end date! We labored over workout charts and workout mixes, mused as to what we would write on our shirts, and bought armbands to hold our Sony Sportsmans.

It was a disaster. Jessica had a complete meltdown in a spring snowstorm. I immediately booked a show and could only train sporadically. Claire made it the farthest. Six qualifying races before she broke a bone in her foot.

But what I remember most about the ill-fated endeavor is the extremity of each mental phase of a race. Tedium. Despair. Euphoria. Repeat. It was all about finding that flow. And holding on to the belief that no matter what your body told you, you would make it to the end.

In the days following Halloween, Blake's silence deepened and the tiny flame of hope I had cupped in my hands against the wind was dying. My lungs were screaming and my feet ached. When was he coming home?

Val became a runner after the divorce and attending the race to support her had always been one of my favorite Turner family traditions. I'd pack a thermos of hot chocolate, and together with the kids we'd head out to cheer on the world.

But this year . . . this year there would be no "together." Blake would not, he specified in an e-mail, be there on Friday to receive his mother when she arrived at the apartment.

This year, in which I was becoming increasingly desperate, I would be vulnerable.

"Talk to me," Val instructed, following closely, despite my retreat to the kitchen under the pretense of brewing her tea. I had spent ten years trying to avoid the joint overshare about Blake, but now every molecule was dying for it, like the Dixie cup of water at mile sixteen that would only give me a cramp. *What did she know, why was he like this, where had I failed, when would it be OVER?* Dropping her jacket on a stool, she listened for the sounds of the kids in the living room, politely tearing into the gifts she'd brought them. What child doesn't thrill for local honey? "Rory?"

"Didn't Blake tell you?" I asked obliquely.

"He was never a voluble kid," she said, raising her hands, her mandala beads clacking. "He's retreating, it's what he does. When he didn't get the Six Flags commercial, he didn't say a word for an entire week. Dr. Weinstein, down the hall, finally had to look at him," she summarized dismissively, like she'd called in pest control.

"Blake stopped talking?" I asked, thrown. Riveted. "How old was he?"

"Oh, I don't know—seven or eight the first time."

"The first time?" I looked out to where our son was reading sheet music, his cheeks full of bagel, his sweatshirt streaked with mud.

"I mean, he wasn't catatonic, just, you know, glum. He's an artist. But unlike his shithead father, his kids are his heart. He knows the best thing for him is to be with you."

"He said that? Recently?"

She patted my back as I blinked back tears. "Focus on gratitude, Rory."

I blew my nose in a paper towel. "Sorry. The indefiniteness of him being gone is making me nuts."

"He gets embarrassed, doesn't know how to return to the party. I mean, that's what Weinstein said. So how are you doing?" She gave me her most supportive expression. "Talk to me."

"Well, it's hard." Dixie cup, Dixie cup. "Two kids, two schedules, Wynn applying to middle school, Maya gets frustrated that the older kids can do more so I've had to meet with her teachers, and this new job—"

"Think who you're talking to," she abruptly cut me off. "I mean, at least you have a community." She pulled a baggie of acupuncture herbs out of her canvas tote, which she yanked open, causing a puff of brown dust to settle on the counter. "We didn't have blogs or meet-ups. Being a single mother was embarrassing. We had failed."

"No, I know." I stepped back. "I'm hardly a single mother, not even close." I poured the boiling water over the brown powder, which instantly gave off the scent of monkey.

"Our generation got turfed out of our apartments, our social standing. We didn't know to lawyer-up yet. We didn't know to fight. I looked at the divorces in Blake's class as he hit high school—those women came out swinging. You want to fuck the girl at the Porsche showroom? It's gonna cost you, buddy. Not that I'm carrying regret. Regret's cancer. No." She shimmied her shoulders and dropped her head back to exhale a yogic breath.

"I don't . . . this is not that," I said, feeling, as I frequently did with Val, like I had to apologize on behalf of the 1980s.

"Now that I'm here we'll talk. He'll take his mom for a cannoli from Roccos and get it all out in the open." She tilted her head conspiratorially. "What do you want me to ask?"

I hated having to depend on Val as my go-between. Her opinions were strong but quixotic, and inconsistencies were embraced with equal fervor. She could tell Blake to cut the shit—or that sabbaticals are a vital part of the life journey. And she'd consider both pieces of advice helpful.

But I didn't want to be like that parable where the guy's lost at sea and God sends help via dolphins and driftwood, but the guy drowns because he's so fixated on getting a rescue ship. We just needed out of the water. Were the means that important?

"Just find out when he's coming home," I asked what I vowed I wouldn't.

"Rory, just trust. Trust he will return when he is meant to return. So kids," she called, turning her back to me, "do you love the honey? I know the beekeeper personally. Great guy."

But, with far more skill than I had shown, Blake evaded Val all weekend, so I was teetering from tedium to full-on despair by the time she left Sunday morning to catch the ferry to the starting line. Then, because the universe decided I was never going to be allowed to stew in my pajamas like a normal wife in crisis, I received an unexpected call to bring the kids to a Marathon viewing brunch at Kathryn's. Much frantic lint-rolling ensued. "Of course I'll meet you there!" Claire said over the phone. "Don't be nervous."

"Kathryn is Editor in Chief. While friendly, she does not invite the likes of me to her home." Which meant that metaphorically I was either about to be hit with a headwind, or a tailwind, and there was no way to tell which.

On the eighteenth floor we were greeted by a server offering champagne.

"Do you have chocolate milk?" Maya inquired as Claire helped her off with her coat.

"Can you imagine?" I asked Claire, having been unable to let go of it all weekend. "Your kid not talking for *a month*? And she takes him to see the guy down the hall—who grows his own pot?"

"The seventies." Claire shuddered. "I'm amazed he didn't advise her to roll Blake in a rug and rebirth him."

"Rory." Kathryn emerged from the cluster of guests. There had to be at least a hundred people there.

"Your home is gorgeous," I said as she kissed my cheeks. The gallery stepped down into a vast room with French doors onto a terrace running its length—the *New York Post* had called the apartment her trophy. Twenty years her senior, Kathryn's ex left her for someone twenty years her junior. "My divorce," she once told me, "represented a complete failure of his imagination."

"Maya, Wynn," I prompted, "say hello to Ms. Stossel."

"Hello!" Wynn stuck out his hand to shake, and I squeezed his shoulder in pride.

"Do you have chocolate milk?" Maya continued with her agenda.

"Even better, we have chocolate croissant. Lachlan?" She summoned her fifteen-year-old son from a group of similarly cashmere-clad teens. "Would you escort these two to the pastry?" Confident and at ease to a degree that must obliterate girls his own age, Lachlan was the poster child for single motherdom. He led my kids away while Kathryn grabbed my elbow and steered me on a tour.

"Dining room, guest room." Kathryn continued at a steady clip. "And this is mine." She pulled the double doors shut behind us, blocking out the party chatter and jazz quartet.

"Jesus," I murmured as I took in the curtains. Only they weren't curtains, they were Grace Kelly in a Dior gown.

"Yes." She acknowledged the layers of swooping silk. "Sailcloth was having a moment—but Ikea is supposed to imitate us—not the other way around. Look, Rory, I need your help. I've gathered every major luxury brand in my living room. Pitch JeuneBug."

"Of course. For what?" Headwind, tailwind?

"Those girls think they're above advertisers because they're in the bassinet of flush funding." She picked an errant string off my dress and tucked it in the pocket of her camel slacks. "If Asher was managing our investment properly he'd be making these relationships so JeuneBug can diversify their revenue. That's not old thinking, it's solid thinking."

The doors cracked open and she spun around. "Oh, Kathryn, sorry." A man stuck his head in. "I lost Charlene."

"Bob, wait, this is Rory McGovern. Rory's with JeuneBug, the new endeavor I was telling you about," she said as she walked us both out. "Bob and his family are in from Dallas." That was all I was given to go on. I knew several major accounts were based out of Dallas—Audi, Lexus, DeBeers. Bob turned to me. I went blank.

"I—uh—do you run?" I managed to ask.

While he took me through his knee surgery I screamed something like a pep talk at myself. *Channel Taylor, channel Taylor, channel Taylor!*

"So . . . JeuneBug," he gave me another opening.

Deep breath. "It's unprecedented," I enthused. "JeuneBug's seeding brand loyalty at the ground floor. We're a digitally native business, a technology company that produces media instead of a media company that uses technology. Everything we're doing is optimized—" As I talked at every executive who crossed my path the Nigerians crossed the finish line below, the cheers and cowbells muffled by distance, but clanging just the same.

"I have to go poop." Maya brought me back to earth.

"So sorry, nature calls," I apologized to the account executive from Hermès Home and took Maya's hand.

"This way." She tugged me down a hall.

"You've already been?"

"With Claire. But for poop, I want you." We arrived outside the guest bathroom to find a woman whose hair cascaded so perfectly down her back that, had I seen it in tenth grade, I would have spent my Dairy Queen paycheck trying to achieve that wave.

Eyeing us, she leaned into the door. "Fly, are you done?"

"There's a fly in there?" Maya looked up at me.

"No!" a boy yelled back.

"It's just a boy, honey," I clarified.

"The boy's a bug?"

"You know what? I'm sure there's another bathroom—"

The paneled door swung open, and a boy Maya's age, ambitiously dressed in a long rock star sweater, stood with his skinny jeans around his motorcycle boots. "Wipe me."

"Fly." The woman wrinkled her tiny nose. "Can't you?"

"Consuela does it. Wipe me, Mommy."

She stepped inside.

"Don't close the door!" he ordered.

She bent down, her suede dress sliding up her toned thighs as she grabbed the toilet paper. It only had two squares left on the roll. "Ugh."

Swiping a box of tissues from a side table, I leaned in. "Here."

"Thanks." She took it from me. "So!" She pulled out a social smile as we found ourselves in this together. "Who are you here with?"

"JeuneBug."

"Oh, how's that going?"

"Fantastic."

"Mommy." Maya tugged my hand down with her full weight as if trying to make the rest of me ring.

"My husband mentioned it. You're ramping up, right?" She wrestled Fly's jeans back up. "You just got more capital."

"We did?" Seeing the toilet free, Maya shoved down her tights and grabbed the hem of her dress. "Well then assistants can't be far behind. Apologies, but this is happening." We switched places as Fly sat on the floor to watch.

"No, I need pwivathy," Maya said, and Fly slumped out. I closed the door.

As soon as we left the powder room, Maya skipped back to the kids, and Kathryn was suddenly at my side gripping my arm. "He's here," she said through a tight smile as she touched the flowers in the arrangement beside me. "Uninvited." I followed the other swiveling and straining heads to see Asher Hummel handing off his coat by the door.

Preternaturally tan, chin nearly tripled over his signature white collar, he smiled pleasantly. "He can't know that I know you," she whispered before gliding over to him. "Asher, lovely of you to come!"

"Seems I almost missed the fun." Asher let her kiss him on both cheeks.

"Isn't JeuneBug his daughter's company?" Bob, passing by me, mused as he looked on.

"Sorry?" I asked, distracted by the fact that the woman I'd just been talking to was taking Asher's hand proprietarily. Fly, a child with a shockingly unfortunate combination of their attributes, squeezed between them.

"JeuneBug." Bob dropped a handful of spiced nuts into his mouth. "Someone said it was Asher's daughter's site. The one from the first marriage: Taylor."

And all at once I placed the wide brow and the rounded lump that must have been the original provenance of Taylor's nose. No, I recalled Kathryn's initial concern, Asher *wasn't* thinking with his head. Oh my God.

Was I staking my family's solvency on some girl's graduation present?!

Kathryn met my eyes as she handed off the flutes, her telegraphed request reaching me as if our foreheads were connected by wire. Excusing myself, I quickly ducked into the kitchen where I wove around the caterers to the back door and slipped out.

"Kathryn Stossel sweats. I've learned so much today," Claire said as she handed over my coat a few minutes later in the lobby. I waved Wynn over from where he and Maya were circling the marble table with extended arms as if performing modern dance for the doormen.

"Of course she's sweating!" I took Wynn's hat from his pocket and handed it to him. "This whole time I'd stupidly assumed, regardless of where Kathryn's ego fell in this, that those girls must know what they're doing or they'd never have gotten the money. But they got the money because it's Daddy's."

"Easy, there." Claire attempted to rein me in. "It's not Daddy's; it's

Stellar's. Besides, build an eight-thousand dollar toddler bed and they will come. They *have* come. You've already proven that. Your vertical sold out, right?"

"Yes, but only mine." I wrestled my arm into my sleeve. "Claire, do I need a B plan to my B plan?"

"Can I talk to the chick who was selling the crap out of this site ten minutes ago? You have to trust yourself, Rory. Hey, guys, wasn't your mom awesome up there?"

"I didn't see you," Wynn answered. "Lachlan has crowntail Siamese fighting fish. That thing's so expensive they don't even have them at the zoo."

"Study hard," I instructed. "Get a good job, and buy one for yourself someday." I put my arm around him as Claire waved good-bye. "We're meeting Dad at the finish line," I said, hoping the kids couldn't read my nerves.

"Yay!" they cheered.

I felt like such a fool. What was that ad? In life there are drivers and there are passengers? I was a passenger. Wearing a blindfold. In the back of an unmarked van. In the Mojave.

I fixed my lipstick and then, holding their hands, we pushed through the crowd. I spotted Blake before the kids did. *Turn*, I thought. *See me.* Our eyes met, and his softened. I smiled. His hug was exactly what I needed to ground me.

"Hi!" I said as we reached him.

"Daddy!" Maya yelled, and he heaved her into his arms before we could connect.

"Dad, we could see, like, the whole park from the party. It was awesome," Wynn said as Blake hugged him. "And he had this fighter fish that kills any fish you put in the tank. It was the coolest."

"Is Daddy coming home tonight?" Maya asked as she climbed on his shoulders.

"Yeah, Dad, is your shoot done yet?"

Jostling strangers pushed us closer. "They're, uh, trying to figure out a new ending. We're in a holding pattern."

"But you want it to wrap up?" I sought his confirmation.

"We've put a lot into it. We just want it to be good, you know?"

And from what Blake had told me about his parents' divorce, this was where his mom would have started screaming until his dad ran off—all the way to Scottsdale to buy a condo with the hygienist. *You can't just—!* And, *How dare you?*

So I couldn't do that. But I had to do *something.* We were literally standing at the finish line for fuck's sake.

"Thanksgiving," I announced with the certainty I didn't remotely feel. Blake's eyes flew to mine. "Daddy's shoot will be done on Thanksgiving and we'll be eating turkey together at Grandma and Gramps." Heart pounding, I pivoted to clap for passing runners. He just needed to be invited back to the party. His own mother told me so. "You can do it!" I shouted into the crowd. "You can do it!"

It was written on Blake's shirt just as surely as the markered tanks of those limping past. If he couldn't see it, I would see it for both of us.

Chapter Nine

"Thanksgiving," I said to Jessica on the way into the office Monday morning. "Three weeks. I can do that."

"You can totally do that. In your sleep. They're calling my flight. I'll text you when I land." She hung up.

"Rory." Ginger caught me before I put my bag down. "Taylor wants you."

As I approached Taylor's door I overheard, "God, why does my stepmother have to be such a fucking round hairbrush in my asshole?" I paused.

"It's her life's purpose," Kimmy wheezed.

Had I Googled Taylor before taking the job, I would have known she was Asher's daughter from one of the four wives who had led him to the "bikini designer" I'd met in Kathryn's bathroom, who was—and I'm giving Taylor this—two years older than her. Was JeuneBug just Taylor's elaborate ploy to get back at Daddy for Fly?

"My dad doesn't even talk to her. They have dinner, like, once a month and between retching up her food in the bathroom, she tells him she heard at some party we're *understaffed?!* So now I—the one who runs an actual business, not just some fucking moleskin full of lame sketches of bathing suits—*I* have to waste time combing spread sheets like some fucking accountant. It's totally unfair."

"It is."

"Fucking. Hate. Her."

Shit, had Asher's wife figured out who I was? Had she shared *that* with Asher between her retches? And if she found out, would it reflect badly on Kathryn—or me? Girding myself, I stepped inside and found Taylor filling her PUSSY mug. I was starting to suspect she just liked pouring liquid from one container to another, like Maya in the bath.

"Good. You're here." She pressed her freshly glossed lips together and strutted to a side table that'd been liberated of its hot pink Buddha head. She gestured for me to take one of the three chairs that had been shoved around it.

Kimmy pulled out the chair abutting mine, where she was forced to swivel her knees to the wall. Was this Taylor's idea of a sit-down?

Tinkling sounds came from the hall, like a hundred knives clinking against a hundred glasses, insisting a groom kiss his bride. Taylor plopped in the chair beside us and eyed the doorway expectantly.

Silence.

Annoyed, Taylor breathed out, mouth closed, a Darth Vader sound, then called brightly, "Gavin?"

A young guy appeared in an expensively distressed leather coat, tucking his chin-length blond hair behind his ear. I knew him . . . from? From? From? Oh, no. "Cool if I come in?" I watched as the guy who wanted to be inside me on Halloween rolled in a luggage cart dangling crystal light fixtures.

"Um, yes?" Taylor said with the half-smile of a head cheerleader enduring the class nerd. "It's your meeting."

"Hey, Gav," Kimmy called.

"Hey, Kim."

Crap.

He shrugged his coat off and then took in the room. "Barbi-tastic. You made nice, Tay."

"Which you'd know if you ever came by, asshole." What *was* he to her? Roommate? Little brother? Little brother of an old roommate? "This is my boyfriend, Gavin Roth. Rory's the head of our Be vertical."

I stood as he came to shake my hand, our skin meeting at the tips of his fingerless gloves. "Great to meet you," he said, his eyes widening in recognition.

"Tell her," Taylor prompted impatiently, her tone like a tapping foot.

"Right. So . . ." He spun to his work, so thrown he looked like he'd never seen it before. "Um, yeah, so everything's hand-blown in Bushwick. And I, uh, found this artisanal sand in—"

"Not the boring creative bullshit. The stats," Taylor spat. He looked as endearingly confused as I would have been. "The stats. The stats!" It would never have occurred to me to talk to a guy like this. I couldn't have even imagined there was a bark-at-him-like-he's-a-fucking-idiot option on the Get Him to Love Me menu.

Taylor pushed back her chair, practically tipping the tiny table into Kimmy's lap. "Fine, I'll do it. Apple Paltrow Martin has one. Ivanka Trump hung one in her nursery and ABC Carpet is asking for samples. Gavin is *the* up-and-coming children's chandelier designer."

"Congratulations," I said, as it seemed in order. "Are there many of you?"

"He has interest in Dubai," Kimmy said flatly.

"We *have* to feature him," Taylor said. "It's done."

Okay, Asher's daughter, whose best friend is her CFO, let's feature your boyfriend. For someone so obsessed with reinvention, her management style was skewing pretty Borgia.

Gavin cleared his throat. "Yeah, um, I was inspired by Roald Dahl, you know? Quentin Blake?" The three of them watched me look at the spiky pieces. "All the shadow in his work. I wanted to explore the juxtaposition."

"Gavin's going to make a shit-ton," Taylor assessed.

He blushed. "Well—"

"If he doesn't smoke it first."

"Mm-hm," Kimmy agreed, but whether to Gavin's sales potential or drug consumption was unclear.

"I got inspired in Peru." Gavin explained—possibly both.

"Okay." Taylor climbed out of our Business Women Tableau. "I want these all over the next Be spread. We'll take our next call in Kimmy's office. Make a good impression, Gavin." Taylor waved Kimmy to the door before turning back. "My place tonight," she informed him.

I would have paid cash money to see Taylor's response when a guy pushed her head down to his crotch during a hookup. Cash. Money. On a scale of confidence, with zero being, "I'm a waste of space," Taylor was permanently set at ten. It was weirdly reassuring that I got the same version of her that her boyfriend, dry cleaner, and Chinese delivery guy got too.

"You're gonna be cool, right?" Gavin asked furtively once we were alone.

"I'm going to work something up and send it over to you." I had no intention of having that conversation.

"Just so you know, we've only been together a few months, like, maybe, six, tops so when you and I—" He stopped short as Taylor lapped in to pick up her phone, eye him, and leave.

"Let's not," I said, exactly as I had to Wynn when I'd found him typing *boobs* into Google. I took out my phone to get some photos of the lights. "These are great."

"You think so?"

"Yes. They're really amazing, actually."

He tilted his head, my compliment reigniting the cockiness that had pulled me to him on Halloween. "Look, I just hope you didn't get the wrong impression." Was this child trying to let me down? "I wouldn't want you to think—"

"Oh my God, I didn't *think* anything because I'm *married.*" I flittered my fingers Beyoncé-style. Now he looked confused. "We're just going through a thing. You were an oat. Something I would pour milk on. *If* I had taken you up on your offer, which, for future reference, *could* give a less married girl the wrong impression—this would be a different conversation."

He went to kiss me.

I jerked back, barely catching myself on the rack, which teetered precariously.

"Fuck." He steadied the lights. "You're just so—"

"Are you breaking them?" Taylor appeared.

"Just testing weight for the shoot." I made a show of lifting one. "Perfect. I'll start making calls and we'll go hell for leather in the opposite direction," I said to Gavin. "Don't want to repeat a single thing that's been done. Fresh start." I did an about-face and left.

≡

I'd like to say that having a hot guy make a pass at me while the gate-keeper to his "shit ton" was in the next room played no role in my restored confidence. I'd like to say a lot of things. But when I picked up the phone on Thanksgiving to tell Blake the car was packed for our annual trek to my parents and we'd be over shortly to collect him, it helped.

He looked cringingly uncertain when we pulled up outside Jack's, but then I tossed him his parka and offered the wheel and in no time we were listening to Wynn explain *The Hobbit*. It felt sur-prisingly good to clear the bridge and see the winter sky stretch out around us. Blake hummed along to the radio. Maya danced her stuffed rabbit to the beat. The McDonald's pit stop led to a game of guessing how many diapers we'd changed in its bathroom over the years. As we rounded the hill into Oneonta, the cluster of Victorians looked picturesque in the gently drifting snow. *Yes,* I thought, *let's be charming.*

The kids tumbled from the car as soon as we arrived, giddily aban-doning their nests of cracker crumbs and headphone wires to race up the walk. "Great driving." I dared to squeeze Blake's hand as he with-drew the key from the ignition. "You made great time."

"It's good to get out of the city," he said, looking down at where we'd touched.

"Um," I tentatively broached, "so I haven't said anything to my family about . . ."

He nodded.

It wasn't that I hadn't been tempted. When my mom called to ask how I was doing, obviously sensing not well, shame kept me from answering truthfully. From admitting my husband's defeat, but more so, mine. Perhaps it had been delusional—like hoping they wouldn't notice that the vase in the dining room was missing be-cause it was lying in shards under my bed, all attempts to reglue it by my then nine-year-old hands having failed miserably. *But,* I thought, as I unbuckled myself, *thank God,* because here we were, intact.

"Mom?" Wynn was back, rapping on my window. I opened the door. "Aunt Jen needs a gravy boat."

"What?"

"Hey, Rory! Hey, Blake!" My very pregnant sister-in-law came down the walk in my mother's Kiss the Accountant apron. "We're doing two gravies, and I'm parked in." She waved at where her minivan sat between the garage and my uncle's Honda. "Would you mind? My back door's open. Just grab it out of the china hutch."

"No prob." I hugged her and then turned to Blake. "You want to come?" A quickie in their game room?

"I'll go in and say hello, if that's cool." He got out to stretch.

"Of course! Grab yourself a beer. Back in a jiff."

Arriving at my brother's house at the end of the cul-de-sac, the one with the maple leaf wreath, I let myself in the back door. If, in ninth grade, you'd told me I was going to grow up to envy a woman her mudroom, I would never have believed you. But Jen's was something out of *Better Homes and Gardens,* complete with cubbies for each family member, a labeled sports equipment rack, and a framed chalkboard to jot such reminders as, "Start on stocking stuffers."

I once heard an organization guru advise working moms to stock a separate school backpack for every day of the week, prefilled on Sunday nights with each day's requirements to ensure that Little Johnny would never arrive at practice without his cleats. That would be ten backpacks for us Turners. For the cost of the square footage required to store them, we could hire a butler.

Stepping out of my boots I walked around the kitchen island that could have held my kitchen. In the basement, there was a room used only by my brother to watch football and another, used only by Jen, to scrapbook, and still another, where their kids had a stage to put on dress-up shows. There were no sounds of traffic to obscure the whir of the heat coming up through the vent or the wind rustling the branches of the fir tree outside. Was this what Blake and I needed— silence? Space? A place for him to retreat that was on-site? Did we have too much baggage—or were we just crammed unnaturally on top of each other without room to breathe?

My phone rang, startling me.

"Hey!" I answered, walking into the dining room and grabbing the gravy boat.

"Ror!" I was greeted with Blake's sitcom dad voice.

"What's wrong?"

"She found it!" he called to whomever was in the room with him. "Just making sure you didn't get lost, there."

"You okay?" I asked anxiously.

"In a minute, then! You too, bye!"

I hurried back, blasting the radio to calm my unease. Scrolling through the same stations I'd listened to while dreaming of being anywhere but there, I found the same songs playing as when I'd left town in the nineties. It was such a time warp that I half expected to find Chip Brown waiting to break up with me on the front lawn.

Making my way through an assembly line of McGovern hugs and hellos, I finally arrived in the kitchen, where my father was already carving the turkey and Blake was bookended by my mother's sisters, who were probably already on their second glasses of chablis. His eyes flashed to mine.

"There she is! Welcome, Victoria." Mom took the gravy boat before pulling me into her arms. "I'm so happy you're here! Can you tell the kids to wash up?"

"So, your movie. When will we see it in theaters?" my aunt asked Blake, her palm resting on her cheek. Shit.

"I'll tell all my friends to go see you," my other aunt added.

"Well . . ." He gripped his beer. "There's editing and we never know release dates for sure, but yes, thank you."

"Rory, you'll tell us when Blake's new movie comes out, won't you? You two are so modest. I mean, you're friends with the director and everything! It's like we don't even have a star in the family."

"Ah, ha-ha," I trilled, actually trilled, as I went to the den where the kids were watching a game of Monopoly their older cousins had started hours ago. "Let's wash up, guys. Grandma's getting food on the table."

The blessing bought us a few minutes of relief, but then my brother, Fred, who'd been glued to football for the initial inquisition, turned to Blake across the table. "So, big guy, what are you working on these days?" To their credit, Blake usually regaled us with behind-the-scenes vignettes about failed technical effects or directors acting like children. He liked to hold court, and I loved to sit back with my wine, the drive behind us and a lazy evening ahead, and watch Blake be Blake.

But now he could only gaze down at his plate. "Uh, well, I, uh," he stammered. "As I was telling these guys, I just finished an indie. It's, um, a great part, but, uh, hard to know what'll happen from here."

"When are you going to be on TV again?" Gus, my nephew, asked.

"I don't know."

"Pass me the creamed spinach," I jumped in. "Did our pies make it out of the trunk?"

"What about directing your own thing?" my dad's sister asked. "Like Costner did with *Dances with Wolves*?"

I could feel him choosing his words as everything I'd eaten hardened to a brick. "Yes, yes, I should do that."

"Because I checked the kids' 529s," Dad said, reaching for the potatoes. "You haven't put anything in to match our contributions. You gotta seed it early or the account's not gonna grow fast enough to cover even a year of college. For Wynn, it may already be too late."

"Dad," I suggested, "maybe we should get someone in the city to do our taxes?"

"That's ridiculous. Why would you waste the money? I know you don't have it to waste."

"Honey," my mother reached across the table with her voice, and my dad filled his mouth with Thanksgiving.

From that point on, Blake went stonily silent, until, as the pies that had gotten crushed under Blake's duffel were being picked over, he unexpectedly volunteered us for cleanup. "Rory and I've got it."

"Are you sure?" my mother asked. "All by yourselves?"

"Really, babe?" I asked. Didn't he just want to go lie down? I wanted him to go lie down.

"Yep!"

There were so many dishes it was like we were doing penance. When I took a break to put the kids to bed, we were still only halfway done.

"I needed silence," Blake whispered when I asked why he had rebuffed everyone's offers of help. "It was the only way to get a break."

"So go up to bed," I whispered back.

"I can't lie in the dark right now. I'll go crazy."

I turned the water back on while he dried. "Do you want to talk about it?" I tried, as most of the guests had left or were snoozing in front of *Independence Day* in the den.

"No, I don't. Please, Rory," he begged, looking utterly exhausted. I wanted to touch him.

My phone buzzed by his elbow and he glanced down, his expression shifting. "Who's Gavin Roth?"

"I'm styling his light fixtures for our next shoot." I put another casserole in the drying rack.

"I want to give you the right impression," he read.

I grabbed the phone from him. "He's my boss's boyfriend. It's about the shoot."

"In the middle of the night on a holiday?"

"You get calls at all hours from work. I'm sure if I just picked up your phone you've gotten a billion texts since we got here—" I did and then went cold. "You're on Tinder?"

He shrugged, his gaze dropping to his shoes.

"Oh my God, Blake, are you dating?"

"I'm not dating."

"Sorry, 'hooking up'? Do they even still call it that?" My uncle coughed in the next room. I stepped close, straining to keep my voice down. "I thought you just needed space. I *believed* that. How could you do this to me?"

"To you? To *you*?" he hissed. "Do you have any idea what you did to *me*? You gave up, Rory!"

"When?" I asked. "When did I give up? I've been fighting for us for months, but you had to retreat or whatever the fuck Weinstein called it—"

"You talked to my mother?"

"Of course I talked to your mother! You've been unavailable!"

He stepped closer so I was almost under his chin. "Look, you left me first. I got kicked in the balls harder than I ever have and you couldn't get me to give up what I've devoted my whole life to fast enough."

"Because we're out of money, you asshole!"

He grabbed my arm and for a split second I thought he was going to lift me onto the counter and fuck me. For a split second, I wanted him to. And then he splattered a fistful of mashed potatoes in my face.

I was stunned. And then I was furious. Blindly furious. I grabbed at whatever I could—turkey fat, breadcrumbs box, serving spoons—and hurled them at him. I lost time. It might have lasted hours or seconds. All I know is that my father screamed my name and we were covered in food, panting. My parents were standing in the doorway, horrified.

"What's going on?" My mother recovered her voice.

Blake slipped in the mess, holding on to the oven to steady himself as he caught his breath. "We're getting divorced."

Part II

Part II

Chapter Ten

There are things in my life I call the missables—moments I could have skipped, things I wish I could unknow: walking in on my brother with a *Penthouse*, waking up during my appendectomy (yes, that can happen), Demi Moore's performance in *The Scarlet Letter*.

I add to that list every excruciating minute between crawling into our bed—my bed—the Sunday night after we got back to the city and peeling myself out the next morning. With Blake officially living at Jack's, I lay there, curled on my side, salty eyes unfocused on the bureau, torturously awake. They say eventually you pass out from pain. But the hurt pinballing through my body was like amphetamines. It was like my bloodstream was the CERN superconductor and the atoms of anguish were flying around, trying to collide and blow me up.

"I just need to—I just need to—I just need to—" My brain started the sentence over and over again, but for the first time since I taped Blake's face to my social studies binder, I couldn't finish the sentence. I had done it. Loved him, blown him, given him children, given him space, and yet there I was, there we were.

I cried, deep, wracking, relentless sobs, only to find there was no relief when they subsided.

Hurt supplanted humiliation, which was immediately supplanted by disbelief. How could I have been so stupid not to understand since Labor Day that this was where we were headed? How could he be doing this? Weren't we worth fighting for?

Was I really getting dumped at forty-one?

The part of me that was a girl wanted to die right there in that bed rather than ever have to say out loud, *Blake left me*. Wanted the mass of pain in my chest cavity to press down harder until my ribs cracked like kindling, puncturing my lungs, ending it.

But, thankfully, the part of me that was a mom was louder. And she bellowed, *You are irrelevant*.

As the sun slumped into my room, I knew I had to get my shit together. I had to shower, have coffee, pack lunches, give hugs to our kids, give explanations, be warm, be reassuring, be *fine*.

"Come on, Rory," I whispered. "You can do this."

"Mommy?" Maya whispered back, wriggling under the covers. "Who are you talking to? Is Daddy here?"

"No, duckheart," I said, rolling over to spoon her. "Just myself." Her small back felt so good against the ache in my chest.

"Mommy." She interlaced her tiny fingers through mine.

"Yes?"

"When's Daddy coming back?"

We had sat them down at my parents, under the supportively dis-approving eye of my brother and sister-in-law. Blake and I did our best to waffle our way through every horrible cliché about how much we loved them and each other and how nothing would change.

Only we didn't love each other, or them, enough to stay together, and everything was about to change. I could see that's what Wynn was thinking, and I didn't know how to refute it. I would have given a limb to keep them from going through this, and yet—we were going through this.

"You are going to see Daddy all the time," I gave a non sequitur answer I suspected I was about to become highly adept at. "Every day, probably." I tried to reassure her from the certainty that he wanted to be in their life as much as possible and that I would never interfere with that. Of course, that was the same certainty from which I would have, until recently, said we were going to grow old together.

"Will he come to my birthday?"

"Of course. I can't believe you're going to be four in less than a month. Four years old, Maya! I'm going to order the decorations today. Have you made a final decision? *Frozen* or *Brave*?"

"Tangled!"

"Ooh, *Tangled*. I did not even know that was in the mix." And we talked in low voices about decorations until the alarm went off.

"I just feel like I'm supposed to be *doing* something," I said to Jessica over the phone as I arrived later that morning at the photo shoot for Gavin's chandeliers—which Taylor was insisting our copy refer to as "a child's first earrings."

"You're doing it. Breathing."

"It doesn't feel like enough."

"That's because you're a woman. We idle at 'not enough.' How's Wynn taking it?"

"He didn't look at me all morning, but he's entitled to be angry. I'm just giving him space," I said, taking another swig of my triple espresso. "You know, because that strategy's working so well for me." The crates of Gavin's chandeliers were on-set, but no sign of Gavin.

"How are you holding up?" she asked me.

"Blake was out of town that time both kids got Coxsackie and I have still never been this tired."

"Get a prescription for Ambien," she instructed.

"But how does it work if something happens in the middle of the night? Like Maya has a nightmare or something and I'm called into action?"

"Then start with Klonopin. You can wake up and wash barf out of sheets while on it; you'll just be super mellow."

"Okay." I nodded. "That sounds good. I cannot be plunged into single motherhood and sleep deprivation simultaneously. I'm amazed more moms don't show up in court saying, 'Here, take 'em.'"

"You do not need to be present for this experience. Use sedatives.

Drink caffeine. Eat circus peanuts for dinner. Whatever you need right now."

"I'm buying a flask," I decided.

"Do it."

A door to another studio down the hall opened. *"Have a holly jolly Christmas,"* came bouncing from their radio.

I rubbed my face. "Oh my God, Blake couldn't have waited until January?! When *everyone* is depressed? I'll call you when we break for lunch."

"Rory." She caught me as I was about to hang up.

"Yes?"

"*I* love you. 'Til death do us part. I will not lose interest in you sexually. Or have a midlife crisis. You are my one true one. And I think you're perfect."

"Thank you. I have to go cry in the bathroom now." My other line beeped. "Crying postponed—that's Kathryn."

"Cry to her—I'm sure she'd love it. Hang in there. Bye."

"Hello?" I answered, widening my eyes, as if my lids could yank the "on" chord to my brain.

"Rory, it's Kathryn. How was your Thanksgiving?"

Cataclysmic. "Good. Weird. Yours?"

"I love collective experiences. I don't know why. I just think it's fabulous that for no good reason, we've all agreed to eat the same meal once a year. I took my son and some of his friends to see *Hunger Games* after dinner, and I pointed, I said, look at that line for the next showing. You know what every person on it just ate—isn't that amazing?" It was so hard to imagine Kathryn doing anything as mundane as taking a bunch of teenagers to the movies. I knew that Lachlan was close to Wynn's age when she divorced and I should ask for advice. But I wasn't ready to package this to Kathryn Stossel, let alone myself.

"You should do a story on it," I suggested.

"Rory, I won't keep you. I need another favor. Asher won't give me any of JeuneBug's numbers. I think he's hiding something. Can you get me whatever revenue information you can before the break? I want to take it all with me to Santorini." Where did we even keep that information? "I really need it or I wouldn't ask."

"Sure." *Really, Rory, how?*

"JeuneBug's not going to collapse, is it?" I asked.

"Not if I can help it," she said. "But if Taylor wasn't his daughter, there would be serious oversight measures in place. It's worrisome, Rory. I'm not going to lie to you."

"I'll do my best."

"You always do. I know that about you."

I hung up and looked at the set. I was daunted. How was I going to get this all up by myself when it hurt to even move? How was I going to get through Christmas? How was I going to find JeuneBug's revenue information?

Rory! The mom voice that had appeared in my head overnight snapped at me. It sounded like it was clapping erasers. Right!

I'd been instructed by Gavin's team not to touch the chandeliers myself because I wasn't covered by their insurance. But there was still plenty of work to do. I put in my earbuds to drown out the holly and jolly, turned up the Stooges, shook my can of paint, slid down my mask, and sprayed and sprayed and sprayed. I layered red and green, gold and silver, writing *joy, cheer, noel,* then *Blake is a fucking asshole* and spraying over it, singing, *"Somebody gotta save my soul—"*

"Rory?"

I spun, finger on the trigger. "Oh, shit." I jumped back, hand over my mouth in mortified horror. I had nailed Gavin *right across the chest.* "I'm so sorry."

Arms raised like I was mugging him, he looked down at the wet black stripe across his bespoke shirt, stunned. Oh God, I was going to have to replace that shirt. It was worse than a parking ticket.

A slow smile spread from the corners of his thin lips. "I've been tagged."

"You're it," I tried gamely.

He raised his gaze to me, giving me full stare. Full hot stare. "Can I take off my shirt and we'll try this again?" he asked huskily. God, he was cute. "You look beautiful today."

"I've been up crying all night."

He put his palm on my cheek. "It suits you." *I'm fine, thank you for asking.*

"Gavin, people are going to walk through that door any second." Even as I said it, his assistant arrived, looking like she'd just taken first prize in a Robert Smith lookalike contest. Or perhaps she'd just hit a pothole.

"I haven't stopped thinking about you," he whispered.

"Gavin, your girlfriend is my boss. My boss. My *boss*," I hissed a third time because he was smiling at me how I used to smile at Wynn when he was first learning to talk, the meaning irrelevant, the attempt empirically endearing. "So you need to stop this because if she finds out, I will get fired. And I and my two destructive children will move in with you and your chandeliers."

Clip clop, clip clop, clip clop. Taylor appeared in poured-on shiny black pants and a fur jacket with an oversized ruff she could have hid in. "Oh my God, what the fuck is this?" Taylor's whole upper lip retracted in double-sided stink face. Then she spat a few times because her coat was shedding in her mouth.

He stepped back, red creeping up his cheeks. "Rory, here. It's Rory, right? She was just explaining the concept."

I had been wracking my brain for what could possibly top our Halloween shoot. I was starting to realize, after the toddler meditation room I created for Thanksgiving sold out in a matter of hours, that we were tapping into a bizarre but underserved clientele. "I wanted to set the chandeliers off, not compete with them." They took in the graffiti, the child-sized urinal, the band stickers I'd recreated while I waited for their verdict. "It's a kid's bathroom inspired by CBGB."

"Amazing," he whispered as she came to stand on the other side of me.

"Oh, good," I said. "I was worried you were too young to know what that was." And he swatted me on the ass. I whipped my eyes to Taylor, but thankfully she was still staring at my Keith Herring, mouth agape.

"Well?" I asked her, stepping away from Gavin. "Are we ready to shoot?"

"It doesn't feel on brand," Taylor grimaced.

"It will," I stated confidently. I was a forty-one-year-old woman in emotional free fall who had somewhere, somehow made a series of grievous missteps to land me here, but that this shoot would be on brand? Of that I was confident. "Once the chandeliers are up." Oh fuck, he was still staring at me. Mooning, technically. "That's your cue, Gavin."

"Oh, right, right." He finally hustled away.

"He's so brilliant," Taylor said to me wistfully, watching him wedge a crowbar into a crate.

"He has a vision," I agreed, slapping a Ramones sticker next to the little steel sink I had sprayed with brown water.

"The first time I saw his work, I thought, 'This guy is a fucking genius.' I really want to give him a platform, help him reach a wider clientele."

"Hmm," I said encouragingly. "So, uh, can I ask, um, where do we compile our stats? Like, revenue, and that kind of thing?"

Her romantic whist flew away like a silk parachute taken by the wind to reveal a tank. "We are not fucking giving out bonuses. Stop asking."

"Um, I didn't."

"Only our top vertical editor gets a bonus."

Which, I thought, as far as I knew, technically was me. "That's not why I was asking."

"Well, we guard our growth story very carefully, Rory."

"Right. Of course. But for potential investors, you know, do they get . . . a deck?" I was using it in a sentence!

She just narrowed her eyes. "Our pitch materials are baller. Gavin!" she called. "Need any help?"

And she teetered away to him, like a fur Popsicle on latex sticks.

That night I opened a bottle of wine after the kids went to sleep— Wynn in his bed, Maya in mine. And I called Blake. It went straight to voicemail.

"Hey, it's me," I said, walking around the dark living room in the sweatpants I had thrown on the second I got home. "So, uh, how does this work?" I took a deep swallow. "Do we meet up to buy the kids their presents?" I set the glass down on the coffee table. "Do we make a joint list over e-mail? Are we all going to the Dorans' caroling party?" I sighed to the ceiling. "How do we do Christmas?" I waited. But it was voicemail. It was not going to talk back. "Okay, call me, bye."

And I drank until I filled a tiny plunge pool of anesthesia inside myself and jumped in.

"So." I sidled up to Tim's desk the next morning, full of Advil. "I'm pulling some revenue stats. Where should I get the most recent ones?" I decided Tim, our programmer, was the safest person to ask because no one else there talked to him unless they absolutely had to and then they never stayed to listen to the answer. He'd be left at his desk, his voice growing smaller as he blew some salient detail at a departing exposed lower back like Milo in *The Phantom Toll-booth.*

"Yeah, Taylor and Kimmy guard their growth story pretty carefully."

I nodded. "Yeah."

"Yeah."

"So you don't, uh, have those?" I tried again.

"No." He pushed his glasses back up.

"Okay." We kept nodding like we'd come to a deep agreement. "Would you know who might?"

"Just T and K, man."

"Cool. The dude abides." I backed up as my phone buzzed—a text. From Blake. *"Let's just take this day by day, okay?"*

What?!

Sorry, kids, Santa didn't bring you anything this year because Daddy is starring in a one-man production of *Godspell.*

I threw my head back, a hard sigh erupting from my gut. There *had* to be a way to play this. I thought of sitting on the lawn at school, watching Blake a few blankets away with Condra on his lap. I studied her because she knew how to get him, how to keep him.

I wanted my family, my fully intact family, to celebrate Maya's birthday, get a tree, watch the ball drop.

What was the next step, goddammit?

My day planner told me it was attending a holiday party for the soccer team, an event I was having mixed feelings about for two reasons. First, we'd be attending as a threesome when we should have been a foursome. Birthday parties didn't count—they were always a tag-out, with one of us making small talk while the other stayed home to glue model trains or play princess. But holiday parties? It was going to be me and forty some-odd couples.

Second, it was being hosted by Josh and his wife. Josh, who was always so easygoing and unpretentious. He let Matt put his cleat right on this thigh to tie it. And though he made jokes at his own expense about the hours he worked, he had a great rapport with both boys. Not like those dads who were a little awkward when they stepped back into their families on the weekends, pushing a stroller they didn't quite know how to maneuver, comforting a child who wouldn't be comforted, a look of mild panic on their faces.

Josh had wipes in his breast pocket, snack bars in his jeans, and Band-Aids in his wallet. He told me when he messed up at work, when I had spanokopita in my teeth, and when he unintentionally insulted the plus-sized mom by saying he had a big fat headache. Hanging out with him two hours every weekend had been the highlight of my shitty fall. I would miss it.

And now I was going to see inside his perfect life. And meet his perfect wife. And I wanted to. And I didn't.

"How's this?" Wynn asked for the sixth time, coming out of his room in yet another variation on an Iron Man T-shirt and khakis.

"A collar. A collar. A collar. And brush your hair."

"Bu she ikes iuhn mah," he mumbled.

"What?"

"She likes Iron Man!" he shouted.

"Emily Strang?"

"Yes, okay! Yes!"

"Then when you see her, unbutton one button and tell her how lame I am that I made you cover it up!"

"Fine!" He slammed his door. I put my hand over my heart. He liked a girl.

Wynn ran off as soon as the greeter took our coats, Maya tentatively negotiated a détente with Dylan, and I pulled up that half-smile I'd perfected years ago in the playground that I hoped said, *I'm having a great time.*

I was surprised by the apartment. It was a four-bedroom facing the park, which was inherently impressive, but it didn't feel like Josh—or the woman I realized I had spent an inappropriate amount of time imagining. Though he'd never mentioned a dog, I expected one, the kind that sheds. I thought there'd be a lot of smushy sitting spots and a clear traffic path for three rambunctious boys, family photos, and kids' art.

Instead the decor was a look I call *interchangeable.* The same sunburst mirror over the same white marble mantel flanked by the same Mitchell and Gold side chairs over the same key-patterned Stark rug, in a building where men came home from the same bank to women wearing the same white blouse and halfheartedly fucked them in the same position. If they got off on seven instead of eight, no one would be the wiser.

Even the holiday decorations were uniform—silver bells, balls, and baubles. No baby shoes or hand-painted blobs of clay. No ice-skating mice or penguins in woolly scarves. But, I noticed, the curtains were hand-print-free, the mohair couch had not a trace of Gogurt, and there was nary a skateboard scuff on the baseboards.

I took another sip of my champagne. Maybe this was the kind of woman I needed to get to know and learn from. The one who married the Right Guy. Who knew how to keep her kids Away From The Furniture. Who was Pulling This Off.

I saw Emily arrive with her parents. She had curled her hair and was wearing a short-sleeve dress. She looked around nervously. "He's in the back!" I wanted to shout, but I played it cool.

Suddenly Stella's Mom was at my elbow again, staring down her nose at the peppermint bark. "It sucks that we're fattened like calves for a month and then thrust into bikinis. I should have picked skiing, but who has the energy?"

"Travel plans?" I asked my go-to.

"Peter's family's been going to this compound in the Bahamas for New Year's since the triangle trade. It is the stuffiest thing you can imagine. Old people sit in the dining room and audibly fart. It is so depressing. What do you guys do?"

We *did* take the kids to Jessica's Christmas Eve, let them stay up late, stay up even later assembling their toys, get up at five, do the whole Currier and Ives thing, eat bread pudding from a family recipe, then fall asleep by the tree.

"Do?" I repeated.

"Over the break?" We never traveled during high-priced blackout dates. But we took the kids ice-skating, we baked brownies, and we hit the museums. We blobbed around in our pajamas. We were a family.

"I just started a new job, so I drew the short straw to work over the holiday." I managed to retain my smile, applauding my facial muscles like a heeling dog.

"Oh." She had no idea what to say to that. Then her face brightened. "Have you met Gillian?"

"No—I—"

"Gillian, this is Rory, Wynn's mom." Dammit, she knows my name. "This is Gillian, our hostess."

"So lovely to meet you." With her corn silk hair and blue eyes, she was definitely attractive, but it really had more to do with her diamond earrings and sleeveless white cashmere packaging.

"You look fabulous," Stella's mom said to her. "On me winter white just looks blah."

"Have you reached out to my shopper?" Gillian asked like she was her boss following up on an overdue marketing report.

"Not yet," she admitted.

"She'll save you so much time. And I'll give you the name of my makeup person—she comes over with a steamer trunk. Every brand. Every product." She was describing a piñata for grown-ups, but she was all business. "She creates looks for whatever you want—then has it all sent to you with video tutorials for your phone." Gillian not only read Goop, she actually *did* all of it.

Looking around I saw that all of her friends were The Tense; women who had married in their mid-twenties when their hotness was on par with their husbands' salaries. Now, fifteen years later, his worth had only grown exponentially, while her value was waning. Hence the tension.

Then the sickening thought passed through me: If I was going to be single, if someone who had not put the babies in me was going to see me naked, I really had a *lot* to learn. Because I'd be competing with women like Gillian, women whose appearance was their full-time job.

And I did not want that to be true. Any of it.

"Does she do skin care too?" Stella's Mom asked.

"You *have* to go to a dermatologist, Polly." Polly! "Do not buy shit off a shelf."

"It's a wonderful party," I jumped in. "Don't you think, Polly?"

"We like to get everyone together at the holidays." Gillian cast a vague glance over the room, as if she were the first lady, and had gathered us here but had no idea who we actually were.

Which, in my case, was true. "Are you traveling over the holidays?" Orbitz should have given me a kickback.

"Josh likes to visit his family in Delaware. I mean, the house is fine. It's on the river. But, like, get some new sheets, Betty. Treat yourself. And I have to bring all my own food," Gillian explained. "And someone's always trying to get a football game going on the lawn. Then his dad organizes story time." She rolled her eyes. "That happens in the den with sherry. You can't have seltzer. You have to have the sherry." Sign. Me. Up.

Suddenly there was a waist-high blur as Dylan and his friends cut a racetrack through the living room, past the cookie table, and out. "Gotcha!" I heard and the next thing I saw, Dylan was upside down over Josh's shoulder in the double doorway to the dining room where the buffet was set up.

"Put. Him. Down." Gillian's biceps flexed. "What is this, a barn?" she asked scary brightly, like light glinting off ice. "Boys, there are snacks for you in the den. Please stay in there or Matt's room. Chris?" she called and a teenager turned away from his group of friends. He looked like his mother. "Can you keep an eye on them, please?"

He looked like he was going to get right on that.

Gillian turned back to us, her eyes pinched open. "It is just non-stop."

I simply couldn't picture her with Josh.

Suddenly "Joy to the World" came over speakers embedded discreetly into the gray grass cloth, and the room quickly rearranged itself. Song sheets appeared. Children flowed out from the back on cue, finding their family cluster like penguins returned from the coast.

Where were my children? Was I just going to be left singing alone like a sad aunt? I made my way to the other side of the apartment. "Maya? Wynn?" I whispered as I moved through empty bedrooms filled with custom-made bunk beds and turtle aquariums and field hockey gear. *Where were they?*

I opened a door to find Wynn and Emily watching *Elf* in the oldest son's room with some of the other kids. They had the love seat to themselves, but they were as far apart as humanly possible. I knew she would talk about this for weeks. "Wynn, where's Maya?"

"Making a gingerbread house with the little kids."

"Okay."

I doubled back up the hall, shimmied behind everyone caroling in the dining room, and from there through to the kitchen where the catering staff was in a black-tie frenzy.

Where, in this apartment, would you let a group of preschoolers use icing sugar?

I opened the door to a maid's room that had been converted into an office. And, pausing my quest, shut it behind me, momentarily appreciating that the center panel had been wallpapered in the matching bamboo-pattern as the custom shade and desk chair upholstery. Then I started sobbing.

The door cracked open. "Oh, God, sorry," Josh said.

"No, no, this is your house." I leaped up from the daybed. "I should not be hiding in it."

"Having the most wonderful time of the year?"

I ran my sleeve across my face.

"Wait, no, here, let me get you a Kleenex." He reached into the bathroom and pulled out a linen-covered box.

"Thanks."

He sat down next to me.

"I'm so sorry," I said. "Shouldn't you be out there falalalalaing?"

He raised his hand, then let it flop down in his lap. "I don't know why she throws this party every year. I mean, I don't know why it has to be such a big production. She gets so stressed she just screams at me and the boys starting around Thanksgiving."

"Merry Christmas."

"I'm Jewish."

"And there's that."

He laughed. I wanted to put my head on his shoulder. "I should go find the kids," I said.

"First you need to wash your face. Your makeup's in kind of a crisscrossed pattern."

"Note to self: not the time in life to be wearing statement eyes." And before I let anything else slip, I stood up.

"What's the statement?" he asked.

"Very tired raccoon."

He stood up too. "I'm sorry," he said simply. "Whatever you're going through, I'm sorry."

"Thank you."

"I'm going to miss soccer." He reached out and squeezed my hand, then turned to leave, his warm reassurance imprinted on my palm. "What's Wynn taking this winter?" he asked, half out the door.

"Karate at the Y." I sniffled.

"Is it too late to sign up?"

"I don't think so."

He turned back and smiled at me. "Merry Happy."

"Happy Merry."

And he left me in peace to put myself back together.

Chapter Eleven

As the elevator chugged up to JeuneBug in its ominous way Monday morning, I decided I had hit on a brilliant plan. I was going to call, pretending to be that woman from Audi I'd met at Kathryn's house, and ask Taylor for the revenue numbers. I was going to wear a false moustache, auto-tune my voice, and use Claire's phone, which came up blocked. I was going to move to Uruguay and open an ecohotel. No, not an ecohotel. A coffee farm? Like Karen Blixen? I was going to—

The door slid open to audible sobbing. *Oh good, audible sobbing. I can get in on that.*

I crept through the bullpen where everyone who had their headphones off was awkwardly frozen, while those around them tapped on obliviously.

Across from a stoic-looking Kimmy, Taylor sat at her desk, ugly crying.

"Can I help?" I asked. Because I was a mom. It was a reflex. Better than my old mom reflex, which would have been to shove my boob in her mouth.

"Gah—gah," Taylor spluttered.

"Gavin's in love with someone else," Kimmy said, passing over another tissue with a crown embossed on it.

"And she's, like, *forty!*" Taylor coughed out.

"It's repulsive," Kimmy agreed.

"Did he say who she was?" I asked, bracing myself for Taylor's stiletto through my forehead.

"No, just that she has kids," Taylor spat, a clump of false eyelashes dangling.

"It sounds awful," I said comfortingly. "I should get back to—" I pointed over my shoulder.

They both nodded.

At my desk I had improbably matching texts waiting for me, the same word from both Gavin and Kathryn:

"Well?"

The morning of Maya's Little Mermaid party (last-minute burst of preschooler inspiration), Claire came over early to help me set up. "You got highlights," was the first thing out of her mouth as she passed off the cake. "And your phone is in the fridge."

"I did. And it is."

"Because you are cheering yourself up—or because you want this turd burglar back?" she asked.

"He is the father of my children. He should be living here. Christmas is in ten days. I need to *do* something."

"Fair enough. But he will never again be good enough for you in my eyes." I knew she meant it lovingly, but I wasn't ready to take advice from the woman who knocked every potential suitor in the knees with a proverbial tire iron. "And your phone?"

"The airplane function is broken, and I needed a break."

"From?" she asked, unwrapping the goody bag packages and starting the assembly of every cheap piece of plastic shit with Ariel on it I could order.

"Corporate espionage and a one-sided torrid affair."

"You do move fast."

The doorbell rang. "That'll be my parents," I said.

"You want me to . . . ?" she asked.

"Pretend to be me? Yes, but no." I walked to the vestibule, took a deep, girding breath, and opened the door.

"Rory!" They both threw their arms around me.

Thanksgiving weekend they'd waited until Blake caught a cab to the bus station, then deluged me with logistical questions until I screamed, "I don't know, I don't know, I don't know!" and sunk to the floor with oven mitts over my ears.

"How are you?" Mom asked intently.

"Hanging in there," I lied. Because this was Not The Time. I had gotten it together and now I needed to Keep It Together.

"Dodi!" Maya called, running from the back in her mermaid costume and red wig so Mom could scoop her up. We collectively had no idea why she called my mother that. We expected, as she got older, it would morph into what she'd been trying, since eighteen months, to say. But no. Dodi it was. "I'm Ariel!"

"I see that."

My dad made fish faces at her as I heard the key in the lock. I tensed all my tense places. But then the key turned back because the lock was already unlocked—then to locked again—then unlocked—and . . .

"Val!" I greeted her. "I thought you might be Blake."

She wedged herself in the door, carrying her usual assortment of totes with one or two old Duane Reade plastic bags thrown in, even though she probably hadn't shopped at a Duane Reade in a dozen years.

"He said he'd meet me." She turned to Maya. "Are you Bette Midler?"

"I'm The Little Mermaid!"

"Oh, the one who has her tongue cut out in exchange for legs?"

"Yup," I answered, taking my dad's coat.

"They feel like walking on knives," Val mused. "I'll never forget that—that's the translation of the German original. Walking on knives."

"Val, why don't you throw your stuff on our bed and get yourself a soda?" I asked as my mom's eyes welled up because I'd said *our.* "Maya, show Grandma Val where your presents go." She skibbled off, and I grabbed my mom's arm. "This is a four-year-old's birthday party, not a funeral for my shitty life, got it?" She reached for a Flounder napkin and dabbed her eyes.

"Got it."

"And when Blake gets here, behave. *Please?* For Maya's sake."

My dad nodded. I imagined him slipping his brass knuckles off in his pants pocket.

In my mind I dared Blake, dared him to see our beautiful home, the one I had personally sanded; see our beautiful girl, the one I had personally birthed, wig askew, frosting on her fin; see our beautiful life; the relationships I had personally nurtured, friends packed into our living room; and not see we were worth digging in for.

Maybe he saw all of that—maybe none of that. It would be impossible for me to know because the apartment was so crowded by the time I saw the back of his head that he managed to stay out of my sight line for the entire hour. He may, in fact, have been in the linen closet.

I periodically shot my father warning glares, *donotdonotdonot*, and kept the games moving, my lash extensions batting unwitnessed. Until it was time to blow out the candles. I knew what I was going to wish.

"Happy Birthday to you, Happy Birthday to you—" I walked the flaming cake into the living room, past Val and my parents, past Jess and Claire, past Gavin—

"Whoa, there," Jess said, steadying me before I set the carpet alight.

"Happy Birthday, dear Maya!"

Gavin was carrying a large box and had the most—hopeful—look on his face. I started to sweat as I set the cake down. Oh my God, he was crazy. He was crazy, and in the box was a gun and he was going to mow down my daughter's fourth birthday party and we would be the cover of the *Post*, and Taylor would take a personal day.

"Yay!" Everyone was clapping. I tried to keep my eyes focused on Maya, who spat her wish all over the front half of the cake.

"Who's that?" Blake raised me by my elbow and asked through clenched teeth.

"A colleague." My hand was shaking. "I think he's making a delivery—"

"—dating Rory," Gavin was across the room, simultaneously explaining himself to Jess and everyone in earshot. "I brought Maya a gift. I make light fixtures for children."

"I think it's a little soon," Blake whispered angrily.

"I did not invite him." Maybe this was the thing. Maybe Blake would gallantly come to our rescue, like Cape Fear, and this would bring us back together.

"I would have brought Cecily." *Wait—what?*

I whipped back. "Who's Cecily?"

"Who's this guy?" Blake pointed.

"Possibly a stalker here to kill us all. Happy?"

"You know, Cecily wanted to come and meet the kids, but I—"

"Oh my God. I have a cake to cut. Twenty four-year-olds to entertain, small talk to make, a house to clean up, and I cannot be thinking about a Cecily right now."

"Rory!" Val was holding the landline. "It's for you—someone named Kathryn—says it's urgent."

"Where should I put this?" Gavin was suddenly beside me with his present.

"This is not cool," Blake added.

"Going to cut the cake!" I trilled, walking past everyone back to the kitchen, through the kitchen, out the back door and up the fire stairs, hoping I was luring Gavin out like the Pied Piper.

"Rory?" I heard him call.

"Up here!" I tried to remember if I took self-defense in college or only talked about it.

Looking remorseful, he climbed to the landing where I stood. "I'm sorry. This is bad."

"I didn't invite you."

"I overheard you ordering the balloons and I—I—I'm sorry, this was a super-dumb thing to do. It seemed, it seemed really not dumb this morning."

Okay. Not crazy. Just twenty-four. I sat down. He sat beside me.

"Gavin." I took his hands, thinking of Wynn picking out his shirt for Emily. "You're gorgeous and young and any girl would be thrilled to have you surprise her. But I'm a woman. And my life is complicated. Too complicated for—this."

He nodded, but held out the box to me anyway. "Will you at least open this? I made it for your daughter."

I thought a gemstone sconce was the last thing this kid needed but pried the top off nonetheless. "Oh, Gavin, it's lovely." It was a Hello Kitty nightlight made out of milk glass. "Really lovely. And she will adore it." I turned to him on the metal steps that hadn't been mopped in far too long.

"You're really pretty," he said dejectedly. "Couldn't we just have sex and kind of see where it goes?"

I had to laugh. "I've seen. Look, what you *really* want is to be a successful designer. I just look good right now because I'm easier to chase than a dream. This . . ." I twisted my wrist in the air between us, "is a distraction. Go be brilliant."

He reluctantly walked down the steps and pressed for the service elevator.

I followed him down. "And stay away from women like Taylor. They will chew you up." And fire my ass.

He shrugged. "I can't help it." He smiled as the elevator door opened. "My mom's a total bitch." He kissed me on the lips.

"Bye, Gavin."

"Rory?" Blake stuck his head out the back door as the elevator closed on Gavin.

"Welcome to my office. Has anyone noticed I'm gone?" I dusted off my butt.

"Are you kidding? No one's even talking. They're all too busy eating cake."

"That is my favorite five minutes of a party," I said.

"It's a great party." It was the first nice thing he'd said to me in months.

"Well, she's a great kid. She deserves it."

He walked up to me. "Look, I'm sorry to throw that Cecily thing at you." *Oh my God, it was working. The lashes were working.*

"No, that's okay," I said breezily, afraid to scare the deer with questions like, Who the fuck is Cecily?! "We're figuring this out," I offered. "Maybe seeing other people is what we needed—" He cut me off before I could finish with, *to figure out that we don't want to.*

"I'm glad you feel that way because I realized I shouldn't be paying two rents, so . . ."

"Wait—you're coming back?" I asked, confused, elated.

"No, I moved in with Cecily."

"What?!"

"Not like that. She keeps her band's recording equipment in the spare room and I can feed her cats when she tours so she's cutting me a deal. It's doable." Looking back into the kitchen he clasped his hands over his head and blew out his cheeks. "What's important is that I'm in new space right now."

"With band equipment and cats." That are preferable to me.

"I'm telling you because I'm not going to pay the rent anymore— since you're making more than me and all. I mean, I'll help out with the kids when I can." I was stunned.

"Mommy!"

"I'll be there in a minute!" I looked away from Blake. "Why don't you go see what she needs?"

He went back in and I stood out there, with the stinky garbage bins, and the dust-caked pipes, wanting to shout inside, *You know what, Dad? Go for it!*

He wanted to sleep in someone's spare room??? My whole life I had felt like less than a grown-up next to my family, but next to Blake? Since when were the responsibilities of adulthood optional?

And I decided that, come Monday, I was going to fulfill mine. Impeccably.

I walked into the offices through the bullpen without even stopping to unzip my parka, and right into Kimmy's office. "Kimmy," I said.

"Yes?"

"I need our revenue stats."

She sucked in hard with her mouth closed, making a rumble through her sinus cavity. "I can't e-mail them."

"Can you tell them to me?"

She clicked her mouse. "Pick them up at the printer." She audibly swallowed some phlegm. "We guard our growth story very carefully."

"Thank you. How are you feeling?"

"It's back in my head."

"I'm so sorry."

I rushed back to my desk with the contraband pages in my hand. I had done it, I had done it, I had—wait— *What* exactly was I doing?

I stood over my computer, overheating. Was there a reason they guarded their growth story so closely? Could sharing this somehow hurt JeuneBug? Should I not give Kathryn Stossel what she wanted?

I couldn't even finish the question. Which was why Kathryn was Kathryn. I bet when her husband left her, he bowed and scraped his way out of the apartment in a ball gag, tossing money in the air like *The Wolf of Wall Street*.

To survive short term, I had to stay employed. But to survive long term, I had to stay on Kathryn's good side.

"Messengering now," I texted.

"Thnx," she texted back. "You're a rock."

And having Kathryn Stossel telling you that you were a rock, rather than that you did rock, was the greatest compliment you could get.

So why did I still feel queasy?

Christmas Eve I took the kids to Jessica's. Then I dropped them off at Cecily's, a third-floor walk-up where I would have been thrilled to live—when I was nineteen. But Maya and Wynn were just happy to be there and, as much as I longed to perch on the counter and make the best of it with them, I wasn't invited to stay. Over Blake's shoulder I spotted the missing picture of the kids in the bath resting in the windowsill and he looked apologetic as he closed the door, which only made it worse. Like he'd gotten schoolyard dust on my new Chuck Taylors instead of detonating my whole life.

I went home, where Claire met me. This was the first Christmas where her mother's Alzheimer's had advanced to the point that the trek to Minneapolis no longer made sense. So we watched *It's a Wonderful Life*, smoked pot, drank vodka, and pretended we were still in college—that life was one great big exciting unknown—until we fell asleep.

≡

Here's what I learned the following week as we went ice-skating, saw the Rockefeller Center tree, and made snowmen. Blake was the fun one. I had Neosporin in my purse, but Blake was always ready to dangle someone by their ankles or burst into tag. I tried. I really tried. Until Wynn put his hand on my shoulder as I gripped my cramping side and said, "It's okay. You can stop trying, Mom."

And then I dropped them back off at Cecily's to drag myself to some New Year's party as Claire's plus one. Light eye, red lip. Because as far as I knew, no one had ever cried off their lipstick. The dress was a loaner. Chanel. The skirt made entirely of black feathers. I felt just like Holly Golightly, when she smashes everything and falls into bed hysterical with grief.

"You look amazing," Claire said as I approached her on the Tribeca sidewalk.

"Let's do this," I said, as if she was escorting me into the dentist, instead of a former carriage house our host had renovated into five stories of . . . total batshit.

The wallpaper covering the entire stairwell was a blow-up of a Peter Beard photo of Cindy Crawford's tits. Hands were chairs and animals were rugs and bowls were cups and each floor had its own DJ.

"Who is this guy?" I asked Claire as we walked through a stream of pulsing pink light. Every room was packed with a who's who of a top ten of a one to watch. *Taylor would give anything to be working this crowd,* I thought.

"His family builds low-income housing," she shouted in my ear.

"Gotcha. Do you ever just go to dinner parties?"

"Who," she asked, "has dinner parties anymore? Not my actual friends who have kids. My donors. My donors have fucking dinner parties. And they suck."

"Okay." She was feeling feisty. I reminded myself I was not the only one who couldn't quite believe this was how the year was ending. "Let's get drinks."

"Claire!" a handsome guy in a suit approached us, grinning, palms out.

"No, Drew, no." She shook her head, pushing him away. "I have not had anything to drink yet. Try back in a few hours."

He slumped off.

"What was that?" I asked as the top of his head disappeared down the stairwell past Cindy's umbrella-sized areola.

"Producer from Charlie Rose. Never married. We've fucked a few times, but it never goes anywhere."

"Maybe—"

"No," she cut me off. "No maybes. Maybes are for thirty-somethings. Maybes are the garbage cans you put your time in so it can be collected at the curb."

"Okay," I said. "He just—he seemed cute."

"Rory, if you are going to get out here and do this, you're going to need to toughen the fuck up."

"But I don't want to get out here."

"Well, no one does," she agreed, running a hand over her Halston jumpsuit.

Further demoralized than I thought possible, we separated and I left her to be swarmed by her fans and admirers, the donors, the marrieds, the singles-for-a-reason.

The floor of the guest bath off the screening room was clear Lucite, with a view down to the master bedroom. Some other female guest had already carefully arranged all the linen-monogrammed hand towels in a ring around the toilet as best she could.

"Help," the sound escaped my lips.

After washing my hands, I opened the door to find a guy waiting. "Is this the bathroom I've heard so much about?" he asked.

"I hope so."

He had thick white hair, but he couldn't have been much older than me. He was extremely good looking—and knew it.

"I've heard his parties are pretty out there," he said as we swiveled to switch places.

"Aren't we at one?"

"Oh, this is a family affair," he said, his eyes twinkling at me conspiratorially. "I mean his *other* parties."

"Ah," I said as it sunk in. "How French."

"I've been to an orgy," he revealed matter-of-factly.

"And?"

He considered for a moment. "You're never looking at what you hope you'll be looking at."

"That feels like the motto of a German porn site."

"I like you . . . ?" he asked.

"Rory."

"I like you, Rory." He gestured inside. "Care to join me in the bathroom?"

He'd signed a lease. He had Cecily.

"Okay." I walked back in and hopped up on the sink while he sat on the floor in his tuxedo and lit a joint.

"So, what do you do, Miss Rory?" he asked after he exhaled.

"I design kids," I said, distracted by the kissing couple climbing onto the master bed beneath us.

"For the future?"

"Yes. I'm figuring out how to rid us of the gene for whining."

"Your company is going to make a killing." He smiled, squinting through the smoke.

"Right?" I asked. He held it out to me. "I've drunk too much," I begged off.

"No such thing." He snuffed it out on the toilet seat.

"I hope I haven't offended you."

"Not at all." He waved his hand. "My ex felt the same way."

"Does everyone have one?" I slipped off the sink, landing hard on my heels.

"New to the club?" he asked, looking up, a feather from my hem grazing his face.

I nodded.

"Is that self-recrimination I sense?" he asked.

I nodded again, looking down, wondering if he could see up my skirt.

"Rory, are you still best friends with your first best friend?"

I thought back to kindergarten and shook my head.

"Do you still work at your first job?"

I shook my head.

"Life is about accumulated experience. Perspective." He reached for my hand and with a hard tug I had him on his feet. He unlocked the door and slipped a card out of his breast pocket. "Some day soon that will sink in for you. When it does, please call."

"Okay." I took it from him.

"Happy New Year, Rory." He walked away back into the pulsing lights.

I glanced down at the engraved card. "Happy New Year, James Stanhope."

And maybe it would be. Maybe, despite *everything*, it actually would be.

Chapter Twelve

I had never been a pioneer. When I was looking for my first rental, a broker steered me and my meager budget to the Tribeca waterfront. But I would've had to walk through blocks of abandoned lots to get home from late-night shoots. I said no thank you, preferring to live in a cubicle uptown than move somewhere sketchy, hoping bodegas and dry cleaners would follow. Of course, had I nut up, when that place eventually went co-op I could have bought at the insider price and ended up living next door to Matt Damon.

In Wynn's class, we would be the sixth family to get divorced; we would be the first in Maya's. I did not want to be inventing a new way of being or be the one to introduce this thorny topic into our community. Also, selfishly, I had no role models, no one close to me who could say, *Honey, I've been there, and here is how you're going to get through this.*

So in the absence of guidance, we were relying on an actor Blake had worked with a few times who seemed to have had the ideal divorce. To mark the signing of their dissolution papers, they threw a party to which she wore her wedding dress, cut short and dyed sunburst yellow. They got a DJ to play songs we'd danced to in college and kissed each other good-bye at midnight.

When Blake suggested we use their mediator, I was instantly on board. Especially if he came in a package deal with her tailor and their DJ.

I know it seems crazy, but I was still praying that Blake would come to, *Notebook* style, and remember me—the woman who'd spent months living with an unintelligible fiancé while he prepped for a theatrical adaptation of *Lock, Stock and Two Smoking Barrels*. Who birthed him two children and still found energy for late-night pep talks, witty midday texts, and the occasional crotchless panty. Sure, there were times I'd been self-pitying and spread thin. But supportive? In our first weeks of dating, I fell asleep cupping the man's balls. If I thought about it for more than a minute, I wanted to throw furniture out a window.

I'd assumed mediations took place in the same municipal warren as jury duty, but it turns out they can happen anywhere. Melvin the mediator worked out of an office building in Little Korea, just a few blocks from JeuneBug. The convenience and a dollar fifty barely covered a bubble tea.

When I got off the elevator for the first time, I discovered that at the far end of the hallway, past the periodontist and a CPA, sat a black-clad bouncer on a stool. A base beat thumped from the door beside him.

"Oh yeah," Jessica said later when I told her of the clandestine karaoke club. "Those places are open twenty-four seven."

"Who's having a karaoke emergency at one o'clock on a Tuesday?"

"Are you kidding?" she asked in disbelief. "For two dollars you can get your own room for an *entire hour*. To sing anything. All by yourself."

Which is maybe where Blake's friends got the idea for their divorce party.

They certainly weren't inspired by Melvin.

Melvin's office was piled with so many files and knickknacks— yellowing certificates, tarnished penholders, ashtrays brimming with paper clips, a kitten calendar circa 1981—that we had to zigzag the five feet just to reach the chairs across from his desk. I wondered if, like a zookeeper at the pool's edge, his secretary stood at the door to toss him the sandwiches that left his mouth dotted with mayonnaise.

But I quickly realized Melvin couldn't be bothered with his surroundings because his organizational genius was entirely devoted to the systematic disassembling of his clients' lives. As he clinically worked his way through ours, I found myself thinking about what it felt like to make chicken salad, ripping cold flesh from bones while flitting in and out of awareness that the carcass was once a breathing being. Melvin's questions were like impervious fingers jamming between Blake and me, breaking the filaments that had secured us.

"What's an equitable midpoint to split the photo albums? Your daughter's birth? Can these homemade drink coasters from the trunks of your Christmas trees be equated with the sentimental value of the ornaments? The plaster handprint was a Mother's Day gift?"

Most excruciating, sitting in the chair parallel to mine, Blake came to possess what in the monotonous parenting trenches I'd most longed for: otherness. There were nights when he'd reach for me and I'd try to actively conjure those days in college when I would have given a limb for so much as a glance. Over the years, inevitably, he'd become an appendage. I always knew when he'd kiss me next.

And now I didn't.

So I found myself agreeing to everything just to get out of there.

Thank God for JeuneBug. For the irrepressibly pink walls, for the kids worrying if Hello Giggles would take their blog post or their ironic bowling team's T-shirts would arrive. Nobody was married except maybe the girl with the barbed wire tattooed around her ring finger. But she also had a gun-toting vagina inked across her shoulders, so it was anyone's guess.

My colleagues were psyched because Taylor was psyched and Taylor was psyched because sales were picking up, and not just from my vertical. On the day earnings were posted, she actually brought in bite-sized cupcakes, exactly one per person. Kimmy washed down hers with Emergen-C. Merrill deliberated hers as if Stanford PhD candidates were testing delayed gratification. I ate mine while reading an e-mail from Kathryn inviting me to dinner at Jean-Georges. Were we becoming genuine friends? Did she want to reward our hard work?

Booking the sitter to come a luxurious fifteen minutes early, I gulped wine, blew out my hair, and otherwise prepared to celebrate like a woman for whom a mini-cupcake was not going to cut it.

≡

Pushing through the wind tunnel to the restaurant's entrance, I reluctantly handed my coat to the hostess and followed her to the back
room where the glass walls overlooked the bronze globe that marked
uptown's conclusion. Trump is rumored to have commissioned it
after hearing his gauche building, perceived by many as an architectural middle finger, emanated bad feng shui.

Kathryn was seated in a corner banquet, her mink smartly draped
about her hunched shoulders. "Miserable out there," she said, half-
standing to greet me for a cheek kiss. "The holiday decorations come
down, and then it's one long slog of bundling and unbundling until
May."

"This was definitely worth braving the elements for," I said as the
waiter pulled out my seat.

"Well, this place is the reason my fridge is empty." She brought her
full martini to her lips. "I haven't gotten them to run a tray over to
me yet, but I'm wearing Jean down." She smiled. "Did you want
something in particular? He'll prepare whatever you'd like."

"As long as we're not arguing about you swallowing SpongeBob
toothpaste, this is better than the prom." I lay my napkin in my lap.
"One of those, please." I pointed to her drink and settled back as the
waiter departed.

"So?" she asked, resting her elbow on the tablecloth and chin on
top of her hand in an uncharacteristic posture. "How are things?"

"Fantastic, as you've seen."

"Yes, the numbers are surprising."

"Every vertical," I marveled. "Except Cleanse." I took in the fish
laid like rose petals on the plate slid before me. "Poor Cleanse."

"The BluePrint partnership was inspired, but I think parents
still just hear 'juice' and shudder." She slid the stem of her glass
between her pointer and middle fingers as I began to eat. "And
how are you liking full-time? Your family's managing without
you?"

"Actually," I swallowed, hoping my professional success would blunt the pain of having to state personal failure, "we've been going through a transition, Blake and I."

"A transition?" Silverware continued to clink around us.

"We're getting separated. Divorced." There. I'd said it. And the globe did not come unhinged from its axis and roll a path of destruction down Broadway. I took a drink, the vodka hot in my throat.

"Oh." Kathryn took me in, her eyes softening. "Oh, Rory."

"Yes, Happy New Year!" I mugged, the last bite of fish losing flavor.

Her fingers brushed my wrist. "I've got the lawyer for you." I loved that she didn't pry, didn't need to ask a single question.

"Oh, thank you, but we've just started with a mediator—"

"A mediator," she repeated as if I'd said *outhouse*. "How's that going?"

"Amicably, which I now understand means not actually killing each other."

"Yes." She took a bite before returning her fork to signal the waiter that she was done. "When I think of the hours I spent in counseling getting blamed for everything short of the Gulf War. Those I'd like back."

"This isn't counseling. God, if only."

"I know what mediation is, Rory. It's why God invented litigators. I'll call him for you. I'm insisting."

"Thank you." I looked for the arrival of the next dish, hoping it might offer a change of topic.

She studied me. "That's an awful lot for you to be managing with work."

"Please, work's my saving grace. It's been invaluable to have something to throw myself into."

"Mort's retiring," she said abruptly. "Which, of course, we all knew. He's in his eighties. How long can you care about acquiring *Cat Fancy*?"

"What's going to happen?"

"He's naming his successor June first. If you'd seen Asher swagger out of Mort's office after *that* meeting—ugh—the man marries children because he *is* one. Stellar won't survive him."

"You have to admit, JeuneBug's turning out to be a decent invest-ment," I felt compelled to point out.

"It's only a matter of time before competition arrives."

"But their software's proprietary."

"So some Silicon Valley savant will come up with something bet-ter." She leaned in, further dropping her voice. "This corporation cannot be handed over to a man who's reduced his masthead to an Oscar party. Who publishes not one but *two* Marilyn Monroe covers a year. She was beautiful, a blank slate the world could project on like a golden retriever, but she is not, by any measure, *news*." Kathryn looked—she looked scared. For a moment. Then her fingers passed over her thick bangs and she steadied herself.

"Asher isn't going to be named CEO of Stellar," I assured her.

"Asher stuck his neck out for your employers, albeit for the wrong reasons. I lobbied against them. This company will be *the* most recent mark on Mort's tally sheet, and it will either be for or against me."

"I'm so sorry." I didn't know what else to say.

"I'm not asking for your sympathy." She took out her lipstick, re-freshing herself without a mirror. Our eyes met, and it was suddenly, nauseatingly clear. Somehow I was supposed to tip the tally in Kath-ryn's favor.

"Kathryn, I wouldn't know where to even begin—"

"I don't have an appetite this evening." She dropped her lipstick in her clutch and turned her attention to the waiter. "You don't mind if we skip dessert, do you?"

"What do think she's envisioning?" Jessica asked me after I got home so disappointingly early that I still had two bedtimes to get through.

"I have no idea," I said, gob-smacked. "Pull the fire alarm before the investors' meeting? Smoke-bomb the toilets?"

"If you're going to get into sabotage, you have to think bigger than *National Lampoon*. How's it going with the mediator?"

"Fine. Polite. It's not like we have any assets anyway. I almost became hysterical when he started itemizing the wedding presents from Val's friends. *"Blake, if you're taking the petrified wood bookends, I am definitely entitled to the amethyst ashtray."*

"Well, I'm glad you haven't lost your sense of humor. If he tries to take that, I'll kill him."

A week later I was waiting for the elevator when I heard, "Rory!" I spun around to see Taylor clicking toward me. "Where're you going?" She came to a stop, wrapping her fingers around where her blouse opened at her biceps.

"Just running to a showroom at the DDB before they close. Need something?"

"It's only, like, three o'clock."

"They close at four on Fridays."

"Of course they do," she scoffed.

"What can I do for you?" The elevator arrived, and I put my hand out to hold the door.

"I got you someone," she said so coyly I half-expected the wall to lift and Blake to step out with flowers. "An assistant. You still want one, don't you?"

"An assistant—yes. Great!"

"Ginger found her." She flitted her fingers to give Ginger, sitting behind us at the reception desk, credit.

"On InternQueen," Ginger filled me in. "Ruth something. She goes to NYU and wants to work here, like, really bad. It's cute."

"What graduate program is she in?" I asked.

"You're welcome," Taylor answered, flipping her hair to the front of her shoulders before walking off.

Ruth was not in a graduate program.

Ruth was all of twenty and, despite the frigid temperature, dripping hair put her just out of a shower. Her only concession to being in public was a thick streak of eyeliner clearly applied en route. And her sallow skin suggested she hadn't seen a vegetable in a long, long time. Simultaneously underwhelmed, wary and wound, she approached me like this was the first day of the rest of her life.

"I'm Ruth Yelczek." She thrust her hand out for me to shake.

"Rory. Hi," I said, signing us into the lobby guard's ledger. "Thanks for meeting me in midtown."

"No prob." She looked at me askance as I dug through my bag for my notebook. "So you're a . . . ?"

"Stylist," I answered, motioning for her to follow me into the elevator. "To orient you, our next shoot's for the Valentine's Day spread. Since the site's for kids, this one's not about romance so much as the cheerful iconography of the holiday. We'll be creating a playroom. South Beach via Diane Von Furstenberg. Glossy white walls set against a red lips swing. Like those phones in the eighties." I unbuttoned my coat. "Does that make sense?"

"The eighties?" she said dubiously.

"Right. You were . . ."

"Not born. But cool. That sounds cool. I mean, kind of unrealistic but . . ."

I pushed through the door into the showroom, which was dotted with Jeff Koon's–like upholstered pieces. I scanned for Jenny, the salesgirl and unwound my scarf. "Jenny, this is Ruth, my new assistant."

"People don't actually buy those, do they?" Ruth was pointing to the designer's signature ribbon chairs that, it's true, looked like dog poop pumped out of a frosting tube—and cost the equivalent of a year of Ruth's education.

Jenny laughed uncomfortably. "I have two lip chairs in stock and another I could get rushed from the workroom. But see if the size works for you first."

"Suspended from sailor's rope, they would be fantastic," I exclaimed, passing my measuring tape to Ruth as Jenny returned to her desk. "If you could get the depth on those, I'm going to grab the tear sheets. Sound good?"

"Can I just ask?" Ruth stopped me. "How do you feel about making children think this stuff is what they want? I mean, it's not like my name's going on it, but, just, what do you think of that?"

I blinked at her. "What attracted you to JeuneBug?"

"That they called me back," she said flatly. Which was true for both of us, I suppose. "Wait, so I'm just measuring this, I mean, that's all? I'm not writing?"

"Ruth, I'm not sure what Ginger told you, but this internship is focused on the shoots. It's more of a hands-on thing."

"Hands-on," she repeated, I'm sure she thought neutrally. But the disdain escaped her ferret features as she looked down at the chair. She had no idea what she was doing next in her life or how she was going to get there, but enduring me was another unfortunate requirement.

"Maybe it would be helpful to get a quick overview of your goals here," I said, eyeing the wall clock.

"Okay, I want to be a writer, like a contributing position, or a writing-heavy role at a zine—something more Gawker than BuzzFeed. As much fun as it is to look at lists of cute animals, I'm trying to avoid having to make them for a living." She looked around the showroom, including me in with her gaze. "No superficial shit." And it struck me that as the Older and Wiser Woman, I had some duty to warn her that working meant enthusiastically drinking the Kool-Aid offered by those cutting your check. But we had all of fourteen minutes before closing. And I sensed she'd just shrug me off.

Then I thought of Kathryn's reaction as I'd declined her lawyer.

It's so fucked up that we can't know how things work until we know.

Sitting across from Benjamin Stern of Stern and Associates in his penthouse office, all I could think of was planning my wedding. To hire Benjamin Stern would have been the equivalent of my having tried to get Vera Wang to design my wedding dress. Or Harry Winston to make my ring. Or the Pope to officiate. I didn't know why the analogies were all wedding related. Maybe because that was the last time defining our relationship required vendors on whom we could have gone broke.

Among the skyline view, the mounted stag head, and aged scotch, Benjamin and I were not a fit. Sure, I could have sold an organ and hired him to fight Blake. For the right price, I could also have had Blake killed. And Benjamin's tone implied I might need to. Tilting back in his chair, he stared down his suspenders and repeated his question. "He's in your house when you're *not there*?"

"With our children," I clarified. "Just when he's taking care of our children."

"That has to stop." His chair dropped, his forearms landing on his desk. "He'll take care of them at his residence, or your nanny will watch them," he decided.

"We don't have a nanny, and I really don't think that's—"

"Of course you're not keeping financial papers in your apartment." His monogrammed belt buckle peeked out from below his belly. "Bills, insurance forms, investments?"

"Well, they're not at our country house," I joked.

"Where is this country house?" he asked.

"In my imagination. Look, if we had an asset like that, I wouldn't be sitting here." How long did I have to stay to be polite?

"Victoria." He slapped the blotter.

"Rory."

"Rory, if you insist on making yourself vulnerable by allowing this man access, then you need to take all financial papers, every single one, his included, and you need to get them out of your house. Immediately. Take them to a trusted friend." He said it as if Trusted Friend was yet another service I needed to procure.

"I appreciate that some of your clients are probably in more acrimonious situations than we are, but Blake is really—"

"No longer your husband, partner, or friend. You're employed, correct?"

"Yes," I said, wishing I'd taken him up on that scotch.

"And this man is not. So he's eligible for alimony."

I balked. "Oh my God, my husband would rather step in traffic than take money from me."

"Regardless, his representation will advise him to paint you in the worst possible light."

"Blake doesn't have representation. He's in no position to hire anyone."

He tossed his fat hand at me. "A career-obsessed mother who collects expensive shoes—"

"These were a gift from a friend." I tucked the pumps Claire had gotten me for my fortieth under the chair, the irony that I'd worn them to seem Grown Up doing little to unknot my stomach.

"—who runs in certain circles."

"Well, I do run in circles."

"My point, Rory," Benjamin spoke over me, his enthusiasm, if that's what you'd call it, draining, "is that this man, whoever he was to you in the past, has one agenda now and that is to get as much as he possibly can from you. Period."

This man? It was one thing for Blake to become an "other" in a matter of weeks, but to suggest he was someone I couldn't even trust to have in my life?

I told myself that Benjamin Stern didn't know Blake—didn't know me. That he wanted money and the more Blake and I feared each other, the more he stood to bank. But as much as I wanted to tell Benjamin off, the ground I stood on was giving way. "I should really get back to work."

"You'll call when you're ready." He gestured to the kidskin tray of business cards. Did his wife pick out that tray? Was she his first marriage, or had some lawyer once bullied him?

"Definitely," I lied, automatically picking up a card, hating myself because I didn't have the courage—the *faith*—not to.

"Whether it's me or somebody else, don't let the timing become your ex's. This is your window," he said pointedly.

"Yes, thank you. You've given me so much to think about. I'll be in touch."

"Give my best to Kathryn."

"Of course." I swept my coat from the couch, balled my gloves, hat, and scarf under my arm, and made it down to the bracing cold of the street.

Where I couldn't seem to move.

"Rory?"

My eyes focused on one of the many businessmen coming and going around me. "Josh?"

"What brings you to midtown?" he asked, his collegiate scarf striking a boyish contrast against his dress coat.

"My divorce."

His smile faltered.

"Sorry, I'm . . ." *What must I look like?* I gazed down at my gathered things as if I'd escaped a fire.

"Here, let me." He helped me on with my parka.

"Just coming from a meeting with a horrible lawyer," I explained.

"I'm so sorry." He studied my face with concern. "Do you need a coffee? A whiskey?"

I could only nod.

"Okay, let's see, there's . . ." He spun on his heels. "Monkey Bar down a block for the hard stuff and a chopped salad place across the street."

I buttoned up. "I . . . I don't want to hijack your afternoon. I'm sure you're—"

"Leaving the world's most boring client lunch? All right, executive decision," he said, pointing to the bar and I followed him. It was empty, save two tourist couples at one of the red leather booths. He ordered our drinks before our coats were even off.

"Sorry to drop this on you," I said, regretting that I hadn't begged off.

"You're not," he said, loosening his tie. "*I* interrupted *you*."

"Freezing to death? Yes, you should really stop that." I tried to switch us to the weather. But I didn't want to talk about the weather.

"Look, we're grown-ups," he said as the Bushmills arrived at our table. "This is grown-up shit. One of my sisters just went through it. I know how ugly it can get."

"It's humiliating and heartbreaking, but it's not— Blake and I, we're not cruel. Blake's a lot of things, but he's not that. However he's feeling about me, he loves the hell out of our kids." I took a steadying sip of the whiskey. When I looked back, Josh was still silent.

"That's good." He cleared his throat. "I mean, it's great that you know that."

"What happened with your sister?" I asked.

"She moved to Boston for the guy. Hated it. He traveled all the time, and she was totally alone. Then had a hell of a time getting pregnant. One day, when their twins were seven months, he said he just didn't want to be married anymore. When she wanted to move back to Philly so my parents could help with the kids, he went for full custody."

"Shit. So what happened?"

"They have joint, and the kids spend the summers and holidays with him."

I let out a deep sigh. "I keep thinking of this dinner party years ago." I ran my fingers along the tablecloth. "It was right after Wynn was born. When we all were so shell-shocked by parenting, walking around like demoralized zombies from sleep deprivation. I was cornered with this couple. She was going on and on *and on* about how much her husband sucked. And he was standing right there. So I went into the kitchen to get away, and the hostess said, 'Rory, we're not all going to make it.' So matter-of-factly. Just, 'We're not all going to make it.' It took my breath away."

He stared at me. "What happened to them?"

"Oh, the guy got medicated, and the kid started sleeping in his own bed, and they're fine. They still fight at every New Year's party, culminating in one of them storming out, but you know, they're married—while *I* am in the process of not being. But I would never talk about Blake like that."

"Because, as we've established, you're not cruel." He gazed at his untouched glass. "Good for them for sticking it out."

"I don't know, honestly," I said uneasily. "I wouldn't call them happy."

"That's beside the point, right?" He balled up the embossed paper napkin. "They're parents." His voice tightened. "What Blake's done, what my brother-in-law did, it's unforgivable."

I sat forward. "Look, I don't know your brother-in-law, and if Blake had left me with infant twins, I would have beaten him with them, but as much as it sucks that Blake doesn't love me anymore, I still don't want my kids growing up thinking permanent emotional retreat is just what a marriage looks like."

His eyebrows lifted.

"I mean, do you?" I pressed.

He opened his mouth and then closed it, taking a swig of his drink rather than answer me. When he finally spoke his voice was quiet. "Lately I keep thinking of this trip we took when we were kids to Nova Scotia." He angled the glass on the table, watching the ice shift. "My great-grandmother lived there. My dad got a van, and we did this round-trip drive that took, like, three weeks. My brother had colic and would only let my mother hold him and my sister was still in shock at not being the baby anymore. Then all of us got the stomach flu, *all* of us. And the trip culminated at my grandparents' house in Maine where my grandfather was getting chemo. Which was the last time we saw him, actually."

"Sounds horrible."

"Right?" He smiled, thin lines crinkling around his eyes. "The thing is my parents have *great memories* of this trip. I've asked them, How did you not just turn the van around? Not just come home? And they say, 'Because we were with you. You kids were the party.'"

I smiled at him.

"But," he continued, not meeting my eyes, "I wonder, can that work if only one of you sees it that way?" The last of his usual warmth and humor drained away, leaving nothing but sadness writ on his features.

I reached out and squeezed his forearm. "I want the answer to be yes."

He raised his eyes to mine. If Blake's were a Liz Taylor sapphire, Josh's were a vintage leather club chair. I wanted to rest in the way he looked at me.

"I should get back," he said. "They're going to wonder where I've gone."

"They wonder about you?"

"Well, after a client lunch, they wonder about the client."

"Of course. I'll get this," I said, signaling for the waiter.

"No. I offered you a drink. Let me." He pulled two twenties from his wallet.

"Thank you, again." I stood and went to give him a quick hug. His arms slipped around my waist. He smelled of clean laundry and after-shave. A hint of stubble brushed my cheek as he pulled back. "I guess I'll see you Saturday?" I asked.

"Rory, I think . . . ." He took my hand for a moment. "I think you want your lawyer to be an asshole." And then he let me go.

Returning home that night reminded me of walking into my parents' house after a slumber party where I'd watched too many scary movies. An overdose of candy, a shortage of sleep, and enough information about the fate of horny teenagers to put you off orgasms forever. It was suddenly possible that, for no reason at all, someone would pop out of places a person would never have been before—like the tub drain—and try to kill you.

I kept hugging the kids, needing to reclaim a sense of ownership over our space and drown out Benjamin Stern's invocations. "Mom," Wynn said to me as he overheard me yawning my way through *Llama Llama Misses Mama*, "watch a show already."

The next day I sat in the chair across from Blake at Melvin's. The two men went back and forth about who would take what flatware, and I silently asked Blake, *Even if you could take it all, would you?*

Then, when the elevator door closed behind us, Blake absent-mindedly beat-boxed the base that had been thumping from the karaoke club. And I grinned. And he lifted a finger. And I lifted a finger, like we used to for our performance of the world's tiniest disco, and he laughed. And I laughed. Then he looked so sad it felt as if the weight of our loss could plunge us to Middle Earth.

But it was ours. Our loss. And Benjamin Stern could find someone else to freak out, thank you very much.

"Dad wants to know where the checkbook is."

"Wynn?" I asked, jerking to my feet from where I'd been showing Ruth how to lay out the ropes at the studio for the Valentine's shoot. Before which I'd shown her how to unpack the crate. Before which I'd shown her how to fit the crate into the back of a van.

"He wants the checkbook—"

"Ror?" Blake was suddenly on the line.

"You're over?" I asked, alarmed by my alarm. Of course he was over. He picked them up from school.

"On time, yes."

"That's not what I meant. Why aren't you on your way to ballet?" I asked.

"Maya, uh, forgot her tights," he said. But I was sure I'd put them in her bag that morning. "Look, I can stay late tonight if you want," he offered. "My thing got canceled."

"Why do you need the checkbook?" And why was he asking the kids about it?

"I was, uh, trying to remember what I paid the guy to retouch that head shot." He sounded sheepish. "I want him to work on a new one to take out with me to LA for pilots."

"You're going out for pilot season?" I asked.

"Of course I'm going out for pilot season."

"But you don't have an—"

"I have contacts," he cut me off. "I have thirty years in this business. I am liked and well respected."

"Sorry, I didn't mean—it's just, um, I have the checkbook with me," I lied. *Why did I lie? Why did he need a new head shot? This whole thing felt off. Or did it?* "Can't you just download the Chase app? I mean it's all online."

"I don't want to stand here and download an app, Rory." And then, as if challenging, he said, "Just read it to me."

Only I couldn't because it was at home in one of the wallpapered boxes over the TV. For once I thanked God that he didn't know which end was up with our bills. "It's at the office. In my desk. And I'm at a shoot. I'll get it and bring it home."

"Okay . . . I guess. I mean, that seems like a hassle, but if you're cool with that."

"Absolutely! No prob. You guys better hustle. You know how they are if you're late." Now I was the one using a sitcom voice. Did he notice? The line went dead.

"Ruth?" I summoned her.

She turned from her phone, no doubt tweeting my narration of how to do her job—sorry—*internship.*

"Road trip."

Ruth Yelczek wasn't the last person I'd have chosen to stand in my living room as I shoveled everything from our desk into two suitcases and a duffel bag as if a mob was storming the embassy, but she was close.

"So you really like Paris, huh?" She looked derisively at the prints I'd blown up from a shoot Blake had met me on years earlier. "You don't think the iconography is a little clichéd?"

"Ruth." I heaved the duffel onto my shoulder, bound for the security of Jessica's Brooklyn basement. "I like Paris. People like Paris. They write poems about it and songs about it and sell their souls to cram into economy just to visit it for a weekend. Paris is real." I wheeled a suitcase to her. "It's older than you, bigger than you, and more beautiful than anything you can dream up." I put her hand on the handle. "Someday you will go. You will remember asking if I liked it as if you were asking about hot sauce. And you will cringe. So in the interest of saving you from wasting time in Rodin's sculpture garden feeling like an asshole, no more talking until we're back on the island of Manhattan, 'kay?"

"What's with the puffy-faced girl?" Jessica asked thirty minutes later as she leaned out the doorway of her Cobble Hill brownstone to peer at the curb where Ruth was smoking her way through her Worst Day Ever. "I don't know if white slavery's the answer, Ror."

"If only she was worth selling. My intern. She's got a Working for Old Bitches checklist, and I'm helping her cross off every box." I exhaled, my breath visible in the cold air. "If Kathryn really wants to fuck JeuneBug, just lock Ruth in a room with Taylor and see which one's tone-deaf declaratives make the other's ears bleed first."

"How are you dealing with that? Fucking JeuneBug?"

"I'm not. Dealing, that is. So, both boys are sick?"

"Yes." She pushed her fists into her hoodie pockets and crossed the two sides in front of her. "And Miles is in Milwaukee for a conference and I have twelve posts to edit. God forbid I actually use the family sick leave my boss championed to the city council. There've been so many bodily fluids on me in the last twelve hours I have stopped changing my clothes, Rory. I stopped . . . changing . . . my clothes. Hey." She perked up. "Does your intern want to nanny? Want to sell her to me?"

"Thank you so much for taking these." I lifted the last suitcase over the threshold into her vestibule. "I have to get back to the shoot."

"Seems kind of extreme, doesn't it?" she asked. "Ror, unless Blake's gotten a quickie law degree, he's got nothing to fight you with," she said with all the authority of someone in a T-shirt crusted in vomit. "He can want *all* the things Benjamin Stern said he'd come for. He can *want* them, but, I mean, I'm sorry, Blake and what army?"

"Rory?" Ruth called.

"Yes, coming!" I shouted back.

"No, um, I have to go," she said, stubbing out her butt.

"What?" I asked.

"I have class." She peeled herself away from the Honda she'd been leaning against.

"Why didn't you tell me that?!" I demanded.

"I can help you tonight . . . maybe." She started to walk away to the train, not even waiting for a ride back to the city.

"Mommy?" Jessica's son, Henry, called from inside.

Jessica reached over our luggage to hug me. "Don't kill her," she whispered in my ear.

"There's poop on the floor!"

"Don't kill *them,*" I whispered back.

Chapter Thirteen

I thought I just needed some quiet time to catch up with myself and get a grip and waited eagerly for the day I'd take the kids to JFK to meet Val, who was flying them to meet Blake in LA for midwinter break.

They'd been wrestling over the headphones the whole cab ride, with Wynn taking Maya's fluffy pink ones just to torment her because he was sick of me asking him to behave like the older one and me thinking, *I cannot get you guys through security fast enough.* But as they disappeared into the long line, their laden backpacks sagging over their bums, whatever had been binding my heart together abruptly disintegrated.

I cried so hard that the cabdriver, stuck with me on the highway, kept warning that I "better not to throw up." Back in our apartment, I sat on their made beds in their silent rooms. *Come on, Freddy Krueger,* I thought, *climb out of a desk lamp and finish me.*

So I walked right back out. I couldn't be with Claire or Jessica, couldn't bear to talk about it. I tried sitting at a hotel bar, but it was so terribly wrong I left before the bartender delivered my order. I bought a movie ticket but couldn't make sense of what was happening on the screen.

I considered buying sneakers in which to roam the city for the next seven days. Maybe walk to the ocean, a pilgrimage to bring my family back. Standing outside the Runner's Shop wiping my nose with a Dunkin' Donuts napkin, my cell lit up with a number I didn't recognize.

"Rory McGovern?"

I caught myself midsob. "Yes?"

"Hey, it's James Stanhope. We met New Year's Eve. Remarkable bathroom, unremarkable party?"

My puffy eyes went round. Hot guy? With the business card? The business card I'd kissed, thanked, and tucked in my jewelry box next to the kids' baby teeth?

"Bad time?"

Ha. "Just leaving a late brunch, actually."

"So, your work's intriguing. Really smart stuff. You've got a great eye."

"Two of them, I've been told." I spun to my haggard reflection in the window. Had he tracked me down? Or stumbled on JeuneBug?

"As I recall, your attributes are many. Look, I'd love for you to come over."

"Oh?" I fought the temptation to grab a passing stranger and confirm she could hear him, too. That the Boston cream donut hadn't tipped me into dementia.

"Much as it pains me, my daughter's outgrowing her nursery," he explained. "I'd like your take."

Oh, this was for work. Back to sad—or not! I'd never been asked to design a space people actually lived in for someone other than a friend. "I see. How old is she?" I asked.

"Suki just turned four."

"My daughter's the same age. Let me guess. She's thinking something along the lines of Elsa's castle?"

"And me with my bachelor pad . . ."

"Elsa's castle as sublet to James Bond?" I suggested.

"Or vice versa." Was that the sun coming out? "When would work for you?" he asked.

Now. Right fucking now. "Normally I'm fully committed, but my children just left to see their father for the break. I have some flexibility."

"First trip?" he dropped his voice in concern. Oh please, no, not concern. Concern plus smoldering was going to make me run—in snowboots—to wherever he was.

I bit hard on the inside of my cheek. "Yep."

"Yeah, there's no comfortable chair, huh?"

"No." I managed a little laugh. "Doesn't seem to be."

"Well, Ms. McGovern, come over. We'll find you someplace to sit down."

It was so unfair. The homeless guy marinating in his own feces could have offered a hug and I would've accepted. But a full-blown—what were we calling it—consultation? Date? Booty call? Whatever it was, I was as vulnerable as Lindsay Lohan leaving rehab. My bed hadn't been covered with this many clothes since the upstairs neighbor's tub overflowed into our closet. Throwing on Blake's old cashmere V-neck that shifted to expose the lacy top of an uncomfortable bra, I tugged on skinny jeans and—because you can take the girl out of Oneonta—denied myself a hair-flattening hat.

James Stanhope lived in a double brownstone in the far West Village—one I had walked past many times over the years, and never failed to sigh with envy. The interior was everything I'd imagined it would be. A fire crackled in the living room. A bottle of wine sat uncorked in the kitchen. And James greeted me in a white dress shirt made to fit his muscular torso and jeans that grazed the tops of his tanned feet. *Unfair,* I wanted to cry. *Unfair, unfair, unfair.*

"So is this all you?" I asked instead, taking in how the back wall of the building had been replaced with glass overlooking the garden. A wonky snowman complete with earmuffs stood outside holding a martini glass in his branch arm. "The decor, I mean."

"The art's mine. The rest I can't take credit for."

"Not even Rat Pack Frosty? That's a shame." I took the wine from him in one of those stemless glasses. "What do you do professionally?"

"You didn't do your due diligence?" he asked.

"I'm old school. In it for the adventure."

He laughed. "I'm an investor. Start-ups predominantly." Okay, he must have stumbled across me on JeuneBug. This was definitely just a consultation. But then he asked, "You want to join me upstairs?"

I didn't look away. "You're always asking for company."

"Am I? Funny, I like being alone. Except when I don't."

"I can't imagine that's a challenge for you."

"Quality is always challenging." He set down his glass and lay his hands on the marble island across from me. "I can describe her room to you if you'd feel more comfortable. I don't mean to be pushy."

I wanted him to push, to pull, to bend me over the stone. "I like to lay eyes on the goods."

He walked a few feet ahead up the staircase, which curved against the wall, past darkened floors where I caught glimpses of art and sculpture illuminated by the street lamps. We arrived at the top, and he flicked a switch in Suki's pop art nursery. I took it in for a moment before stepping around him to the windows overlooking the ivy-covered walls abutting their yard. I could feel him watching me from the doorway. "There's the ICEHOTEL in Reykjavik," I mused. "I could conjure that. Pale blue lacquer walls, a clear acrylic princess bed and play table. And I could do laser-cut snowflakes to tumble down the windows. Modern, chic, and not a spec of glitter. Think your manhood could handle it?"

He grinned. "And I didn't even offer you a chair."

"I work fast." I walked back to him feeling . . . what was it . . . it was heady, unfamiliar . . .

"Good, more time for dinner."

Oh. Confidence.

Dinner was at the crowded bar of a cozy restaurant a few doors down. Sitting so close my knee pushed against his thigh, I debated going home with him after we were done. Three more glasses of wine didn't make him any less charming. Our hands brushed. He helped me on with my coat, and for a second I felt the length of him at my back.

"James," I said, slowing as we reached the corner, feeling I should give some speech, some warning. It took me a second to compute he was stepping forward to hold a cab from which someone was emerging. Thank God it was too dark for him to see me blush.

"Let's take advantage of this time," he said, as I pushed myself to get in, our faces inches apart.

"Yes, let's," I answered, not wanting to move. "It's the name of a theater improv game, I don't suppose you ever played it in college?"

He shook his head. "I went to St. Andrews in Scotland. Major in whiskey, minor in golf. Are you a fan?" he asked.

"Of which? Whiskey, golf, or Scotland?" I replied.

He grinned that grin. "Just lie to me."

"Fine. I want you."

His eyes widened, and I slipped in the cab and left.

For the next week, I planned outfits and drafted e-mails with such care that it made me wonder where the energy was coming from and if it had been there all along. Had this part of my brain shut down when I got married? When I got pregnant? Was it subverted into keeping homework on track and toothpaste in stock?

While my world at home shrank to a path from the TV to the fridge—with their doors closed, the kids might have simply been asleep—I lived to swing by James's place at the end of each day to manage the transformation of Suki's ice palace. Lacquer requires plastering and buffing and waxing, followed by layers and layers of rapidly applied paint. I had a crew going twenty-four seven.

"Honey, I'm home!" James called Friday evening as I heard him jog up the stairs. "Holy shit." He stood in the doorway. "This is amazing," he murmured. "I can practically see myself in the walls. Great blue."

"Thank you." I turned under the heat of the drying lamps. "It's gray actually. If we're splitting hairs."

"Is there an upcharge for that too?" He slipped his hands in his pants pockets as he strolled over. He hadn't even stopped to take off his coat.

"Want to see my design for the bed?"

"I've thought of nothing else," he joked.

I slid the schematics from my satchel and looked around for a clean surface, wondering if he really believed I wore four-inch heels to work. I went to lay them on the plastic-covered carpet, but he lifted me up by my forearm. "Downstairs, don't you think?"

"After you," I agreed.

He jogged down a floor to his study and flicked on the Eames desk lamp. I spread the papers in the pool of light, and we peered at them as if plotting our next battlefield maneuver. "Fantastic."

"Happy you like them," I found myself almost whispering in the stillness.

"No, I mean, seriously. These and the other sketches you sent me. I'd like to show them to a licensing agent, this friend of mine. Any interest in designing your own furniture line?" *My own furniture line? Hold my heels while I do a back flip!*

"I'd consider it."

"Great." He walked away, back into the shadows. "This is a pit stop, regrettably. I have to go back out for an opening."

I nodded, stuffing the designs in my bag, deciding he was just a flirt. "Have you read all of these, or are the spines chosen for their color?" I asked of the wall of artfully arranged books as I passed them.

"I just offered to make you a fortune, and you want to know if I read?" he balked.

"Due diligence. Trying to be a grown-up."

"Overrated," he said, stepping into my path, desire written on his features. I took a half-step back, my breath slowing. He reached out his finger and it landed, warm and curious, on my collarbone. Tracing downward as his eyes held mine, his palm spread over where my blouse opened. His pinky dipped into my bra, circling down to graze my nipple. I didn't move. Couldn't move.

Suddenly there was the clamor of painters returning downstairs.

He dropped his hand. "In case I haven't made myself clear," he said steadily, "I want you, too."

"Not just my furniture?" I managed.

"Do I have to choose?"

"Mrs. Rory?" the contractor was stepping onto the landing outside.

"Coming," I called.

"Count on it," he said, waving a hand gallantly toward the doorway.

Did working for James have my panties in a twist? Yes. Was it delicious? *Yes.* The answer had arrived! I could have my own career *and* a sexy rich husband! Did I accidentally give my furniture designs for Suki to Ruth along with the tear sheets to be copied? That too.

"What do you mean Kimmy took them?" I looked up to where Ruth stood over my desk, fussing with her chipped nails.

"She was at the sink by the copier doing something to her nose, which was kind of disgusting. Have you seen it? With a little pitcher? Water was going in and coming back out the other nostril and I didn't know that was possible. Did you?"

"Ruth."

"Yes."

"You were making copies and Kimmy took them away?"

"Just the ones of that plastic bed. And the other sketches. Um, I'm going to have to get you the research for the next shoot later. I didn't get to it."

"But I already gave you an extra day," I said, trying to imagine what Kimmy would want with my designs.

"I can do it tonight. Maybe."

"Rory?" Kimmy called from her office.

She was smiling. Kimmy was smiling.

"L-O-V-E, love." Taylor circled the chair where I sat in stunned silence.

"Um, thank you." I needed to get back to my desk if I was going to cover Ruth's work and get to James's to meet with the guy doing the snowflake installation.

"Of course, we have to watch our asses with Disney, but we'll call it something else."

"Snow Castle or something," Kimmy tossed out.

"A furniture line for JeuneBug. On. Fucking. Point." She clapped to emphasize each word.

"There seems to be some confusion," I tried. "These were just some ideas I was toying with for a pet project."

"What 'pet project?'"

"My daughter's room. I shouldn't have used the copier." I eyed where the sketches were held hostage on her desk.

"You should take another look at your contract, Rory," Taylor informed me. "In addition to a noncompete—"

"—JeuneBug owns everything you design while in our employment," Kimmy finished her thought. "Everything."

Two hours later, I was standing at the metal barricades outside Jet Blue security having a nice last hyperventilation while I waited for Wynn and Maya.

"Everything?" Jessica asked.

"Everything," I confirmed, having pulled up the e-mail with my contract from September, that, if memory served, I had signed by pressing it flat against a Dumpster while Wynn pulled Maya's hair and she bit his forearm.

"Forward it to me," Jessica urged. "Let me walk it down to Legal on sixteen and see if they can give me any advice for free."

"Show them some leg," I suggested.

"Yes, men go wild for broken capillaries."

"On the plus side, if Blake wants alimony, let's see, my base pay, after taxes, minus rent, minus after-school, minus groceries and utilities, yes, he is welcome to fifteen percent of my nothing."

I caught sight of Maya's pigtails swaying as she ran toward me. "Oh wow, there they are. I'll e-mail you the contract." I hung up and crouched to receive my girl, firecrackers of joy obliterating everything else. Wynn slammed around us, doubling my euphoria. I reached my arms around both of them, breathing them in, squeezing them close. As long as I had this in my life every day for as long as they were mine, I could get through anything. "Hi! Hi! Hi! Oh, I missed you! I missed you!"

"Mommy, Daddy got a job!" Maya held my face as I almost tipped back.

"What?"

"Yeah, it's really cool." Wynn lifted and dropped on his sneakers as if pumping out the information. "The guy who did the island show with the plane—"

"*Fantasy Island?*" I tried to get to my feet. Val arrived.

"*J. J. Abrams.*" She slapped an *Entertainment Weekly* into my hands. "He's starring—starring—in the most anticipated show of next season. It's going to be *huge.* Isn't it wonderful?"

Chapter Fourteen

And then I lost my mind.

I spent hours that night online, tumbling down the rabbit hole of *J. J. Abrams* fan sites, all of which were breathlessly tracking the shoot. The premise of the show was that it took place entirely in a futuristic New York high rise whose tenants were being held captive by an unknown malevolent force via the building's security system. Like *Lost* meets *Die Hard*. The show was going straight to series, and shooting was starting immediately.

There was already an entire blog devoted to the cast. How they would be doing their own stunts. Stunts! He'd be doing stunts. *Instead of just pulling them*, I thought, refilling my glass with more slosh than precision. On Blake's page, the blogger had posted picture after picture, going all the way back to *Cooties*. She'd even gotten ahold of his wardrobe shoot. There Blake was—covered in fake blood, in a suit and glasses, in paramilitary gear, eating cheesecake in a towel between outfits. I was in a poisonous cloud of jealousy—of his success, his freedom, his cheesecake—so I missed the most relevant piece in all of this.

When it suddenly penetrated, I called Jessica. "Rory, what's wrong?" she asked, with the fire alarm responsiveness of a mom who'd been asleep seconds ago.

"Blake has moved to LA," I said, my hands shaking. "Permanently. He's about to have more money than God. He can ask for anything. He could try to get full custody."

"That's crazy, Rory. He would never do that."

"He'll build Wynn a sports court and buy Maya a pony. They'll never want to come home."

"Rory." I could feel her searching for a way to spin this. "At least now *you'll* get child support, right? And he'll finally be happy—the kids will have two happy, successful parents."

"Could he maybe be so happy he wants to be married to me again?" My voice was small. Like Maya asking for a cookie before dinner.

"Okay, I'm on my way."

"No, no. Go back to sleep. Thank you. Thank you, Jess."

But in the morning, when I woke from dreaming about having sex with Blake in his trailer between takes I was even further from clear.

"Mom, you're late," Wynn grumbled when I shuffled to the table with my hair in a towel. "You never shower in the morning."

Well, sometimes moms need to cry where no one can hear them.

"You're trending," Ginger came by my desk to inform me later that morning.

"What?" I was horrified. "On Twitter?" #StalkerEx?

"Oh God, no." She pulled a face. "On Design Hub."

Taylor clopped into the office. In her Thierry Mugler pony-skin suit, the effect was not unlike WarHorse. "*Some-one*," she sang with pride as she passed me, "leaked the ice castle designs and we're already getting preorders."

"Really?" I asked.

"Neiman's wants a sit-down, but I told them JeuneBug's the exclusive retailer."

"We should at least hear them out," I said, standing to follow her. "They're not a brand you want to risk insulting. If nothing else, we can leverage their interest—"

"Neiman's can bite me," she said, passing through her doorway and pushing it shut with her heel.

Having repeatedly reread my contract in hopes that the words would magically rearrange themselves, I now knew that I'd forfeited not only recourse and recognition but remuneration. I didn't mention this to James when he told me Taylor, wasting no time after seeing his name on my sketches, tapped him to invest. As far as he was concerned, we were all going into business together. And whether he was kicking my tires professionally or romantically, the fact that I'd signed my share away against a Dumpster wasn't exactly a selling point.

"Congrats," Clark, the style vertical director, grunted at me from under his visor.

"Thanks," I said, uploading Design Hub on my computer, which is like Porn Hub, only with slightly fewer cunts. Yup, there it was: JeuneBug's new nursery line. Even though Taylor had only snapped the pics of my designs with her phone, the 3D renderings looked great. I felt a frisson of pride. I'd finally created something that would last longer than a shutter click. *If* Taylor and Kimmy didn't fuck it up.

Then my phone buzzed. From Kathryn: *"Really, Rory? Really?"*

Shit.

"How did Kathryn even know it was you?" Jessica asked over the phone at lunch.

"JeuneBug does a nursery line? Who would it be? Tim?"

"So what are you going to do?"

"About Kathryn being pissed at me?" I whispered.

"Yes."

"Or my kids spending every other weekend Lakers courtside with Blake and Miranda Kerr?"

"Both things."

"Sit here and eat this cupcake until the lambs stop screaming." It was actually my second cupcake of three I had lined up on my desk.

"He's not going to make you fly your children across the country every other weekend," Jessica said practically.

"Remember when Ellen Barkin auctioned all that jewelry— millions and millions of dollars' worth of precious stones. Which somehow under the pre-nup were hers to keep, although she left with nothing else?"

"Yes."

"And it was a bitter, acrimonious bloodletting that went on for years?"

"Yes," she said through a mouthful of salad.

"Well, once upon a time, Ron Perelman came home from work with tens of millions of dollars for her in a velvet box. Just because it was a Tuesday."

"So?"

"No one sees it coming. The I-could-murder-you part. The get-your-ass-out-of-Mara-Lago part. Now that Blake's bankrolled, we don't know what I'm in for."

"Oh, Rory," she said. "I just want to hide you in my Kangapouch until this is over."

"You'd get frosting on your fur." I reached for a napkin.

"I'm coming over after work, and you can't stop me."

"Wasn't going to try."

Two nights later Blake still hadn't returned my voicemails. Nor had I heard any more from Kathryn—and the anticipation was getting to me. Not that Kathryn didn't have a million more important things on her radar, but still, there'd been stories. One about a mutinous editor who'd resurfaced as a dog walker. Another about a defiant designer spotted working at a Baltimore Home Depot.

I turned out the bathroom light, jumping when my phone rang.

James.

I hadn't had the bandwidth to volley back his I-want-you serve since that night in his library.

"How do you feel about being whisked?" he asked as a hello.

"And then folded lightly into the flour mixture?" I leaned against the doorway, inviting him to flood my rattled brain with a tsunami of sex and hope.

"Off your feet," he clarified.

"How far?" I walked to the bed.

"Milan."

"For?"

"The design expo. You can help me pick up-and-comers. Tell me where to invest." I sat on the duvet. The one I'd been putting off dry cleaning because it still smelled faintly of Blake.

"Be your consultant?" I asked.

"Exactly. Consultant with benefits," he added.

"Ah. Well, I charge more for that."

"So I can send you a ticket?"

I sighed. I wanted to tell him the truth. That my children's father had unceremoniously moved to LA and I didn't think Wynn and Maya could handle another parent gallivanting off to pursue some postmarital adventure. Instead I said, "With the nursery line, it's all hands on deck." Taylor's hands deleting e-mails from Neiman's. Mine not choking her. "You should appreciate that, Mr. Investor. How about we meet at an Italian restaurant and I bring my iPad? We can watch the live stream?"

"Yes, that's just the same."

I was not picking up what he was putting down. Was I scared? I was scared. No one but Blake and my obstetrician had seen me naked in over a decade. I wasn't ready. "I promise I'll make you feel just like we're in Milan. I'll sit way too close, smoke in your face, and charge you double for dinner."

"Saturday?" he suggested. *Eek. Too soon. Too soon.*

"A week from Saturday?" I bargained.

"It's a date."

I began doing lunges as I hung up the phone.

"Two words," Claire said to me as I finished tying Wynn's karate jacket closed that Saturday and waved him into class. "Spray tan. It hides myriad sins."

"My boobs could be neon blue—they'd still feel like empty soup bags," I whispered as Wynn ran into class. "If men woke up when their kid was six months to discover their penises were one inch long, postnatal plastic surgery would be a fucking birthright."

"I bet boob jobs are socialized in Europe," she shot back.

"Yet another thing I'll be missing out on."

"Go to Milan!"

"I can't." I sat down on the bench in the reception area. "Who knows what Blake's cooking up? It could be considered abandonment."

"You're showing such restraint."

"He's still their father. And I look awful in orange."

"Spin class starting. I love you."

"Have fun." I dropped my phone in my coat pocket.

Maya was at a play date, and I had forty-five whole minutes to read the paper. But I kept looking up expecting to see Josh. I hoped he could be a sounding board for this nursery line situation. Class started, and the other parents peeled out to grab coffee, but there was no sign of him. Shit, was he avoiding me? Had I overshared at Monkey Bar? Or maybe Matt was just sick.

But I couldn't let go of the feeling that I'd soured things. I started to replay our conversation, but then gave myself a mental *hiy-ah!* I had an actual soon-to-be ex-husband, and our relationship had in fact soured. I had a pseudo-suitor who seemed to really want to see me naked. And there was Kathryn.

I slouched under a poster of Bruce Lee, realizing I had always done this. I had first seen Blake on campus during those initial weeks when I was discovering I didn't want to be a performing arts major and was scrambling to get transferred to the design program. I had real things to do, real paperwork that needed to be filed, real coursework to make up, but all I could wonder was, *If Blake and I married, would I wear a dress with obvious bra cups like Cindy Crawford?*

I guess my crush on Blake had always been a kind of distraction. So what had my marriage to him been?

"Hi, Rory," Matt said, rushing past me into class, his jacket still flapping open. Gillian strolled in a few beats behind in a Canada Goose coat over yoga clothes. She looked up at the clock.

"Five minutes late," she observed with a shrug.

"Not so bad," I said.

She sat down next to me. "I guess they'll make him do push-ups on his knuckles again." She pulled the spring fashion issue of *Vogue* out of her Mulberry tote. I wondered which weighed more—the magazine or the bag.

"One of those mornings?" I asked. She didn't answer. "I personally hate weekend classes," I continued, "because it drags that whole weekday *can we make it out of the house* pressure into Saturday and I can't take the suspense."

She took me in for a moment. "My husband thinks you're *hilarious*."

"Pardon?"

"He's always quoting you. Rory said this. Rory said that." She glanced down at my left hand. I hadn't removed my rings yet—neither the gold band that had been Blake's grandmother's nor the diamond he splurged on because he'd just booked a razor commercial in Asia. I just wasn't ready to walk the world without my shield. *My hair is dirty? My skirt has a stain? Yeah, well, somebody has chosen to spend the rest of his life with this stain.*

"I'm flattered he even finds me intelligible before coffee," I deflected.

"Your husband doesn't do the weekends?" she asked. "I don't think Josh has ever met him."

"No, he's an actor." I tried to infuse the word with as much success and hotness as I could. "So he spends a lot of time with the kids when he's not on set, but, like, right now he's in LA on this new J. J. Abrams show, so . . ."

"God, that must be so hard. Not knowing when the break's going to come. I mean, I'm basically a single mom Monday to Friday, but I know come Saturday morning, it's me, my green drink, my hot yoga. Peace and quiet until Monday."

"That sounds like heaven," I said, but thought, *You still have a family, enjoy it.*

"Josh keeps wanting to get rid of our live-in, but I said, well, you're not the one coordinating babysitters, so you don't get a vote."

"Is he sick?" I ventured. "So many people have this flu that's going around.

"Oh no," she said. "He was all ready to head out the door in his Malo sweater, the one that brings out his eyes. And I said, honey, why don't I take karate from now on?" Oh. *Oh.*

Whatever she was imagining, he would never, I would never, we would *never.*

"That's great," I said, setting down my paper. "Everyone I work with is twenty. I am starved for some good mom conversation."

"Hmm," she said. "Me too." And opened her *Vogue*.

Monday, after a protein shake lunch that left me hungry for lunch, I sat at my desk, cooling down from taking the stairs. Jessica had assured me that leading experts in mom fitness, an oxymoron if ever there was one, extolled the virtue of small changes leading to big results. What small change was going to reattach my stomach skin to my abdominal wall I was not sure, but taking the stairs was in my grasp.

Just as my heart rate was starting to come down, a parade of buyers got off the elevators and marched toward Capri. How did I know they were buyers? Because it was either that or we were being audited. I'd only gone to a handful of design shows in my life, but I knew that unwavering look of stony disapproval. I had frequently tried to imagine buyers in their own homes. Did he look like that when his child fingerpainted a butterfly? Was that her expression when her spouse proposed intercourse?

"What's going on?" I asked Merrill. She just shrugged and replaced her headphones. Through the glass wall I saw Kimmy and Taylor standing at the head of the table. My cell rang. "Hello?"

"Rory, it's Melvin."

"Hi." He'd never called me before. I wasn't even sure he was allowed to. "Is everything all right?"

"I'm sorry to bother you, but Blake's attorney just reached out to me."

"His *what*?" I asked as my mouth dried. Okay, fine, *hit me,* I thought, *hit me and get it over with*.

"Apparently he's retained a lawyer who threw out a new parameter and wanted to see if we could fold it into our agreement." I could feel a thudding under my ribs.

"Which is?" Taylor was making a presentation in front of two easels. Stony faces. Stony faces.

"Their argument is that Blake's income is linked to his employment. You can work anywhere. He wants a full fifty/fifty custody split so he's insisting you move there."

"He's insisting *I* move to LA?" I sputtered. "I thought he'd want—Wait, can he do that? Can he insist that I move?"

"Rory, the point is that we're outside the bounds of mediation—"

"No. I can't be a single mother without any support, any infra-structure. I have a job in New York. My friends, my family, his mother, our lives: they're here."

"In that case you'll need a litigating attorney."

"To stay in my own life?" I asked.

"Yes."

I dug my nails into my palm and asked, "How much will that cost?"

"Assuming this is the only dispute. Seventy, eighty thousand."

A sound escaped me like I was being strangled. I looked up from my phone to see Taylor, with as much grace as she could muster, pull the cloths off the easels to reveal my work. I wasn't even invited to the meeting I insisted she take? "I have to call you back." I walked to the doorway of the conference room in a fugue state, like Bette Midler in *Stella Dallas* just trying to get a glimpse of her daughter's wedding.

Taylor shot me a warning look of pure venom. I spun on my heels. *I should be presenting that line. I should be leaving Blake, telling* him *where to live, making* him *throw up in his mouth. I'm forty-one, dammit! I should be setting the sky on fire and making my mark!!*

"Where're you going?" Ginger asked as I headed to the stairwell, bag and coat over my arm.

"To get a spray tan."

"Well, this *is* an unexpected treat," James said a few hours later as I sat across the table from him at Circo. I was freshly waxed, newly bronzed, and the girl from Agent Provocateur had been very helpful in selecting alluring undergarments that obscured my tummy and lifted my boobs. I was ready.

"I'm sorry to be meeting so ungodly early, but—" if we're going to get back to your place to have sex, "my sitter has to leave by ten."

"You look terrific," he said, opening the napkin swaddling the bread. A puff of steam escaped. "Have you been on vacation? Is that why you haven't been by?"

"Oh, no." I looked down demurely. "Just in the park with the kids, you know."

"Suki won't go outside if it drops below forty."

"Oh, Maya is pure Irish. Even as a baby, she boiled over. I'd have her out, completely underdressed, getting the dirtiest looks. But she never gets sick so, I figure, what's the harm?"

"Her room is fantastic, by the way." He looked past me for the server. "Only she's now insisting I call her Queen Suki. You haven't seen it yet?"

"I've been firing on all cylinders since the kids are back." Was this weird? Unsexy? Talking about our children? I should have read a book on how to do this. Or looked it up on YouTube.

"I hope you don't mind," he said as the waiter arrived, "but I know what to order here. You like truffles?"

I nodded, just as happy not to have to think about food on top of everything else. Like, was Wynn finishing his homework? And did I have a small glob of wax stuck to my inner thigh?

He ordered champagne and the $200 pasta with fresh truffles.

"Is this how you whisk Stateside?" I asked. I was teasing him, but I was also deliciously aware that I was being wined and dined by a guy and didn't think I ever had been. In my twenties I was lucky when someone bought me a drink—or a taco. In my thirties, a joint bank account really took the romance out of Blake "buying me" anything.

"Oh, you have no idea," James said.

After two decades fighting for a seat on the subway, fighting the rent-control board, fighting the school board, fighting gravity, I wanted to. I really wanted to.

He had a town car waiting as we stepped onto the sidewalk. I was trying to steady my ankles against a champagne and chocolateganache-induced wobble. The driver opened the door, and James raised an eyebrow. Was my getting in even in question?

Inside I crossed my perfectly tanned legs, the champagne making me feel twenty-five. Was I really going to do this?

Part of me was damned if I was going to get hit by a bus and have Blake be the last person who was inside me.

Part of me still felt like I was cheating.

Okay, okay, I said to that part as James put his hand on my thigh. Could I decide that I was cheating and just let that be . . . hot?

He took my chin gently in his left hand and tipped my face to his. His lips found mine, gently at first, then hungrily, his tongue sliding between my teeth. He tasted like dessert.

Yes, I answered. *Yes I could.*

Here's what I learned: even with the lights on, if you stay on your back your stomach looks great. If you keep your bra on, your boobs don't fall into your armpits. *Sex and the City* sex suddenly made so much more sense.

James was unlike anyone I had ever been with before. He was what romance novelists were thinking of when they described masterful lovers. Just as in design, James had a vision. He was not a member of the *GIRLS* generation. He was not going to ask me how it felt or what I liked. He had been doing this for twenty-five years and he knew, goddammit. Or at least he thought he did.

Since having Maya, I didn't like nipple play like I used to. The skin was still overly sensitive, and it got ouchy before it got erotic. I almost came when he was going down on me, but then he pulled away to penetrate me swiftly. And I didn't.

I tried not to compare him to Blake, but it was inevitable. After ten years, of course, it was sexier. I was wetter. Like a teenager. But Blake also knew to avoid my nipples and that I liked him to slide into me slowly at the beginning.

I knew what I needed to do was speak up. But *I* also wasn't part of the *GIRLS* generation. I knew how to talk to Blake about sex because I could talk to Blake about anything (except Blake).

So I was content to lie against James's sweaty body, unorgasmic, but having crossed a significant milestone: I'd ripped the Band-Aid off my vagina.

In yet another important way, I was no longer married to Blake Turner.

Chapter Fifteen

"I have to go," I whispered a few minutes later, attempting to make a sexy exit. I sat upright, trying, and failing, to get my breasts back into the tiny balconette bra cups. But before I could slip out of bed, he grabbed my wrist.

"Wait," he said, "don't go." I wasn't sure if he meant it, or it was just a safe thing to say to a woman who had kids to get home to. I turned back to give him an alluringly aloof protest—

"Aaaah!" He leaped up.

"What, what, what?" I screamed. "A mouse? A waterbug?"

The sheets. Were. Brown.

"I—I—" was horrified.

"What the fuck is that?" he asked. His Frette looked as if it'd been used to catch a pig.

"I got a spray tan," I said meekly. I wanted to be swallowed by his cowhide rug.

"When?" he demanded.

"A few hours ago?"

"And you haven't showered?"

"Was I supposed to?"

"Before you got into bed? Yes." He looked as indignant as a man wearing a condom on his flaccid penis could.

"I didn't know," I said. "I've never done it before. Here, let me strip the bed." I bent at the waist to pull the sheets off, not my best look. Now we were two adults, streaked brown and white like zebras, our genitals hanging out.

"No, no, don't be silly. I'll sleep in the guest room. My house-keeper will be here in the morning."

"At least send me the cleaning bill." It was like we were at the worst cocktail party ever.

"Of course not."

"These sheets are a fortune," I pressed.

"I'll tie-dye them."

I burst out laughing. "Something you learned at summer camp?"

"It'll be a fun project with Suki."

And suddenly we were comfortable naked. Nice naked.

"You might want to take that off before it leaks," I said.

"Thanks. I've never used one before and wasn't sure how long to leave it on."

I blushed. "I'm going to find my clothes."

"Don't. You look great like that. I think they're out there." He gestured to the stairs.

"Thanks."

"Will I see you again?" he asked. "Like this."

"Oh, sure," I said as I backed out of the room. "I've got my eye on that white chaise in your living room. Next time I'm bringing red wine."

When I got home and the hilarity had worn off, I cried for half an hour. But that's to be expected, right?

"If you marry him, are you going to get a facelift?" Jessica asked over the phone the following morning as I waited for the office elevator.

"I love how your journalistic brain gets right to the important question. Look, if he didn't talk about his daughter in such an endearing way, I wouldn't even take him seriously. But there seems to be a part of him that's craving something real."

"You are real, baby," she said.

"So real."

For the first time in months, I was actually feeling something approaching human when I stepped into JeuneBug. That god-awful

Peaches song was playing in my head, and I wondered if she was right, if you could fuck the pain away.

Then I saw Asher Hummell and a severe woman I didn't recognize sitting stone-faced in the conference room. Taylor and Kimmy crossed to join them from their offices, looking scared. Had Stellar come to shut us down?

I flashed to all those articles from 2008 about the bankers who had to yank their kids out of private school, sell their apartments. Only my kids already *were* in public school and I didn't own shit.

Then I flashed to my friend, Tony, whom I met when I got to the city. We were regulars at the same East Village bar. She was putting herself through the MBA program at Stern selling her used panties. Now this was before the Internet, so we are talking about a serious trailblazer. She would mail each of her clients a pair of used underwear in one of those pretty Chinese food containers, wrapped in patterned tissue paper, with a handwritten note saying what she'd been doing when she wore them. It was fucking genius. No human contact. And she put herself through business school. I wondered where she was now. Probably running Google.

But these days, you could get worn panties out of a vending machine. And I was too old to be a high-paid hooker. I'd just have to head to the West Side Highway with the trannies and hope for the best—

"Rory!" Ginger snapped me back. "You're in Capri."

"I'm what?"

"Asher Hummell is here," she said like a House Bunny informing me that Heff was in residence.

"To see *me*?" I asked.

"Yes." Ginger, having shared the excitement, shifted back into her default mode: Moderately Annoyed.

What in God's name did they want with me?

"Is this her?" Asher asked gruffly as I took a seat and pulled off my coat. I tried not to audibly gulp.

He was talking to a woman in a tight black suit with exaggerated puffs at the shoulder, like a 1930s cartoon villain. And he had a newly pierced ear. Oh, Asher.

"Rory," Taylor said from where she sat at the other side of the table. I had never seen Taylor sit *at* this table. "This is my father, Asher Hummell, and this is Sage Porter, the head of Stellar's PR."

"It's a pleasure to meet you," Sage addressed me, glancing at the wall where, in lieu of the wallpaper that had yet to arrive, I had been putting up screen grabs of my work. "This is all from your vertical, right?"

"Yes, it's great to meet you both—"

"Sorry, Sage," Taylor cut me off. "I'm still unclear why our Be editor needs to be here for this."

Sage crossed her fingers and shifted her fist left, while she leaned right as if she was trying to see over someone's shoulder. Her Veronica Lake hair cascaded onto the table. "I've asked everyone here today because we're still not getting any publicity traction. And I've gotten the feedback that it's because of our story."

"Our story?" Kimmy asked.

"I can't sell a site about kids—"

"High-end *lifestyle*," Taylor interjected. "Kids' high-end lifestyle."

"A site about kids created by people with no kids," Sage pressed on. "There's nothing to fill copy; there's no connection with the consumer."

Taylor's tiny rib cage flared just as everyone's eyes went behind me. I turned to see Kathryn walking in. "Hope I'm not too late." She dropped her fawn-colored Birkin on the table.

"I don't believe you were on the memo," Asher said with obvious irritation. "I'm assuming your mole tipped you off?" I became acutely aware of sweating into my blouse.

"Asher, don't be paranoid, you know how Sage relies on me," she tsked, sitting in the chair next to mine. "Kathryn Stossel," she said to me in her warmest icy tone, not to be confused with her icily warm tone. Her manners had more shades from red to blue than a Pantone wheel. "Rory McGovern, right? You've styled for *World of Decor*? I don't believe we've met."

"Yes," I managed. "Now I'm the Be vertical director. It's a pleasure."

"Can we just please get to the point?" Taylor addressed Sage.

"Yes," Sage continued. "It's been decided that we're going to recede you as the face of the company."

Taylor blanched beneath her tan, her forehead turning a mustard yellow, then her cheeks, then her neck. We heard the thumps of her shoes falling off her feet.

Unable to face Kathryn, I looked to Kimmy, but she had slipped her hair out of its bun and was pulling it across her face as if trying to fashion an emergency mask.

"No one cares about J. Crew's founders," Sage continued. "They care about the color the creative director paints her son's toenails. I'm told you have kids?" I realized she was asking me.

I swallowed, trying to wet my mouth. "A ten-year-old boy, a four-year-old girl."

"Perfect. That hits all my boxes." I wanted to call Blake and tell him the upside of our lack of family planning was two kids who hit all Sage's boxes. "After this, you and I are going to debrief."

"About what?" I asked, still not understanding.

"I'm putting together a new press kit for JeuneBug with you as the story."

Taylor half-lifted out of her chair, spluttering, "You can't just—I won't let—it's not fair—"

"Tay-lor," Asher cut her off, admonishing like she was about to squeeze out too much ketchup.

Taylor just stared at her father, audibly panting, her expression readable to any parent. It was one I would do anything to avoid ever seeing on Wynn's face—even, I realized as I sat there, put them on a bimonthly plane to Los Angeles. *I hate you,* it said. *Deeply hate you. In ways you will never be able to make up for.*

"I have a conference call." She pushed back and hastily exited, shoeless. Dropped six inches, she looked like a scrawny teenager, two angry blotches on her cheeks telegraphing that most likely the washroom was her actual destination. At Jessica's office, there is a space everyone calls the crying kitchen. JeuneBug needed a crying kitchen.

Kimmy made apologetic squirrel noises and hustled out behind her. I had no idea what to do. I needed money. If I helped the company become more successful but Taylor hated me, I'd remain in a precarious position. If I begged off to please Taylor but we went belly-up, well, that was an even more precarious position.

"I'm going to return some calls," Sage said. "I'll be right back."

Asher stood as Sage left and straightened his tie. Which was a funny expression of attention when his white hair was spraying out from the base of his bald head and his gut was straining the placket of his custom shirt. He looked over us as he spoke as if addressing a packed room: "The thing about building an empire is that the whole time someone's ramming you in the balls." And he left.

"That could be where his parenting philosophy went awry," Kathryn said as she stood in her bouclé Chanel the color of a latte. "I'm sure Sage will understand that this proposal doesn't suit you."

"Asher isn't going to replace you," I said intently.

"If Mort picks him to run Stellar, Asher will have me out before lunch." She slipped the bag over her elbow and crooked her arm. "And there is nowhere to go but down. Tina Brown is one start-up away from running a hot dog cart."

"What would my reason even be?"

She looked at me, lifting her glasses. "That you're a woman who values her privacy. And given your tenuous situation with your husband, the privacy of your family." She crossed to the doorway.

"I mean, he has an earring, for God's sake," I said. "Mort would never put him in charge."

She held the door for a second. "Mort thinks Asher is the future."

"Of the eighties?"

She allowed herself a hint of a smile as the door swung shut.

I begged off from meeting with Sage, claiming a family emergency, which was legit. That night, I waited until the kids were asleep, and I was on my third glass of wine, to dial Blake's number, against the advice of Jessica, Kathryn's lawyer, and the online tarot site I visited while Maya was in the tub.

He picked up: "Hey."

"Oh my God, you answered." The monologue I'd planned went pouf out of my head.

"I'm on break. With all these action sequences the set-ups take for-ev-er. And there're no stunt doubles, so yesterday I actually rappeled down the side of a building. The insurance alone must be insane." His voice sounded different, buoyant, like how I remembered it from long ago. I realized it had so gradually leaked its sense of purpose that I hadn't even noticed it happening. "How are you doing, Rory?"

Clawing my way back to functional. "Good, except for this whole aborting mediation thing. What happened? I thought we were figuring this out."

"Now that I'm on the show J.J. just didn't want me to agree to anything without having a lawyer look at it." *J.J.?*

"Kathryn didn't want me to either," I tossed back. *Who were we?*

"Okay, good. I'll have my lawyer draft something, and yours can take a look at it."

"But, Blake," I tried to pull him back from his new craft-services lifestyle, remind him of life back here on Val's worn afghan. "The reason we're doing mediation is it's way cheaper. I'm thrilled for you, but I don't have $80,000."

He sighed angrily. "I'm going to be based here for the next seven years at least. It takes nine months to shoot a season. I can't be away from the kids for that long." I had already become an annoyance, the ex-wife who wouldn't fall in line.

I drained my glass. "So I'm just supposed to pick everything up and move to LA?"

"LA?" he balked. "We're not in LA. Well, I mean, we are, but the state."

"What?" I asked, not following.

"For the tax breaks. Belcher, Louisiana. With the rice paddies and swamps here, we can—"

"Swamps?" My arm hit the lampshade.

"Looks just like Southeast Asia for the subplot. They can conjure a ton of locations inside of, like, five miles."

"You're demanding I move to Belcher, Louisiana?" I could not even see out.

"Rory, I'm working, I have a job—"

"And I'm thrilled for you, I am, but I have things going on here."
I tried to straighten the lamp. "JeuneBug's building a whole campaign
around me."

"What? You're breaking up."

"I'm not your appendage."

"I gotta jump, Ror." When we first started dating he bought me a
pair of leopard-print knickers. When I looked horrified he said,
"Roar, get it?" "I know you'll do what's best for Wynn and Maya."

He hung up, and I scrambled for my laptop. Google maps pixilated
Belcher into view. It was a strip of trailers on a dusty stretch of road
miles and miles and miles from anywhere. Two hundred and seventy-
two people currently lived there, over half of whom, Wikipedia
thought it important to note, were in families. Only 10 percent of
those remaining were between the ages of twenty-five and forty-
four. My chances of employment, of friends, of meeting an eligible
man were nil.

I went to the front hall and upended my purse on the floor, digging through everything until, almost panting, I found Benjamin
Stern's card.

"You sold your engagement ring on Forty-Seventh Street?" Jessica
asked, half-horrified, half-impressed as she sat across the kitchen floor
from me the following night. "God, I wish we could have a fund-
raiser. Can we Kickstart your divorce?"

"Lemonade stand?" I asked.

"Car wash?" she volleyed, waving her ice cream spoon. "You know
I got a press release today saying you're co-chairing the Moms for
Change event at the end of the month."

"I'm *what*?" It was an annual fund-raiser that anchored the New
York City spring calendar. Kelly Ripa and Tina Fey eating cotton
candy alongside Park Avenue mothers and their seersucker-clad off-
spring. I had never been, of course, not having a spare thousand dollars to attend the Big Apple Circus, but apparently now I was the
co-chair.

"Look." She pulled the e-mail up on her phone.

"This is crazy." I took it from her to read. *'Come meet Rory Turner, new face of JeuneBug.com.'* When were they going to tell me? Oh, I see. Asher's wife is on the committee." Stellar was one of the sponsors, so adding me was within Sage's powers. As was, I would guess, holding a hamster and being able to drain it of its youth with her eyes. "I can't be in the same room with his wife again," I said. "What if she places me from Kathryn's bathroom?"

"Women like that can't pick out their own gyno from a lineup. You'll be fine," she tried to reassure me while digging out all the chocolate-coated pretzels.

"Right, how bad could this be? I have to sit on some bleachers for a couple of hours and eat cotton candy. And if I get overwhelmed, I'll just say Maya's tired and beat a hasty retreat."

"You're a lady with a plan," she said, nodding.

"And then I'm going to break into the raffle box and steal $80,000."

"Just don't let Jessica Seinfeld catch you. She will cut a bitch."

The one thing I did know was that this was the perfect opportunity to return some of James's generosity. It was like having front row seats to Aerosmith in high school, only in this case it was sitting on a stretch of bleacher near Madonna. And it would give James and me the chance to meet each other's kids in a low-key way they wouldn't really notice. Something parenting based, but with a thick varnish of glamour on top.

Which was sorely needed, I thought as I tried to get ready and finish Wynn's volcano at the same time. Why, you might ask, was I trying to finish a volcano and get everyone ready for the most exciting thing that had happened to me in ages? Because Friday night, after French horn practice, Wynn had karate, Saturday morning they both had birthday parties, Saturday night he had a sleepover, Sunday morning I collected him late because Maya wanted to know what would happen if she poured orange juice down her play sink and then we had to buy the supplies. Now here we were, doing something I thought sitcoms had invented. But no, he had a volcano due Monday morning, and it was 20 percent of his grade.

We were still waiting to hear if he'd get into the performing arts middle school at Lincoln Center (do-able) or the one on Coney Island (IhavenospaceIhavenospaceIhavenospace).

After coaxing Maya into finishing her lunch while calling out directions to Wynn from my iPad while a hairstylist and makeup artist tried to make me look like—like someone who didn't have a bathtub full of homemade lava (for the record I asked if we could just eBay one of those chocolate fountains they have at weddings and cover it in papier-mâché and got a resounding No!)—I discarded the bathrobe protecting my outfit. Sage's stylist had selected J Brand riding pants, striped tee, and fur vest.

"Maya, dressed, check! Wynn, dressed, check! Me, looking better than I did at my wedding, check! Team, move out!" I called, only ten minutes behind schedule.

"Mom, Mom, Mom!" Wynn cried from the living room, where he couldn't pry himself away from the mountain. "Wait, wait, I think I've got it!"

"No, Wynn, not n—"

Boom.

It was like when James Dean strikes oil in *Giant*. And for a second all I thought was, *Wow, you really look like your father. You're going to break some hearts.*

And then I thought, #$%^&*, but all I could say was, "Frogballs! *Frogballs!* FROGBALLS!!!"

Miraculously we were only thirty minutes late. And if you didn't get close enough to Wynn to smell him, you would never have guessed that the pomade slicking his hair back was a science experiment. But who would notice in the throngs of insanely well-dressed people making their way into the Big Top? Already the sound level was approaching nightclub decibel.

"*Here!*" I texted Sage.

"*Thnk Gd,*" she texted back. After years in New York media, I was used to the hysteria, the urgency. Until I finished plumping the pillows and rotating the urns, everyone on set treated me like a neonatal oncologist. *"Sndg vus 2 u."*

It was all a license plate to me. *"?"* I texted back.

"K?" she replied. I gave up.

I craned my neck in the madding crowd, looking for James, who was also running late because Suki couldn't find her magic wand. I felt her pain.

"Rory!" If he turned heads on an average morning walking down the street, James holding Suki on his hip was causing all the moms in his vicinity to shift in their tight pants. Actual ovulation was happening.

"Hi!" We elbowed our way to each other. Suki was burrowing her face into his shoulder.

"This is Suki," he said.

"Hello, Suki. This is Wynn." He gave a curt wave. I think his scalp was starting to itch. And he was still put out that we were taking James and Suki instead of Emily and his friend Peter. I couldn't explain that Mommy had a few short months to dramatically make over her life so she wouldn't be a tragic ex-wife slowly going up sizes in pajama jeans. (Yes, that's a thing.) "And Maya." Maya was holding my hand and pressing herself against my leg as if it was going to open and make a space for her like the fairy nook in Val's oak tree. "Let's find our seats."

They were not hard to spot. Front row. Center ring.

"Well, you're clearly very important," James said as we sat down. And I got that little shiver right below my belly button. The tiny upside to being upended? The shiver. The point scored. The laugh earned. The look. He's intrigued. He's in. It had been years since I'd tried to get any of those things.

"Only in the Big Top." I smiled and leaned in, over Maya's head, lowering my voice. "I can tame lions."

"Do you have a whip?" he asked.

"On order. And I ride the horses. Bareback."

"I'd like to see that." And it was his turn to shift in his seat.

"Excuse me, excuse me," a man in a leather jacket boomed, in that way that meant, *Excuse you for living and occupying space I should be occupying.* And then a few things arrived in my consciousness simultaneously, as if getting off a very packed elevator.

- It was Asher.
- With his wife and their son, Fly.
- They were sitting next to us.
- Fly shoved Wynn over very hard.
- Wynn sent Maya's popcorn airborne.
- Maya leaped up, making Suki drop her ice pop.
- Both girls burst into projectile sobs.
- I caught myself with my right hand, squarely in James's crotch.

"Oh," Asher's wife said flatly. "Sorry."

"That's all right," I said, because that's what we say to other parents, even when their child has just beaned our child with our own child's truck and then made off with it, laughing maniacally. We still smile, like their child isn't a sociopath, and say, *That's all right.*

I kept my head down as I tried to comfort Maya, salvage the popcorn, and retrieve the ice pop, my blown-out hair forming a curtain between me and Asher's wife.

The spotlights started swinging in figure eights. An announcer welcomed us. A woman in suede pants made a speech about underserved children. The adults clapped. The kids threatened mutiny.

Finally, with the thunder of hooves and the lighting of hoops, the show started. *"u rdy?"* Sage asked.

"4 wt?" I texted back.

Suddenly a woman in Lisa Loeb glasses was crouching at my knees. "Hi, I'm Sarah Glassman from the *Times*," she shouted. "We were supposed to talk before the show!"

"Oh, right, of course."

"How has mother . . . influenced your fline erk?"

"What?" I shouted.

"How has motherhood . . . uence . . . design work?"

"Um," I said, "should we do this at the dinner after? This seems counterproductive!"

Using my knees as leverage, she lifted herself to kind of take my ear in her mouth. "I can't stay. I have to file my copy by eight. What about your life is aspirational?"

"Aspirational?"

"How is your aspirational life the genesis for JeuneBug?" She'd had sausage.

"I'm raising my kids to be citizens of a very sophisticated city!"

"What exactly are you doing for them that's sophisticated?"

Asher leaned over the kids' heads. "This is very annoying," he huffed, and I could sense that James was starting to get equally put out by our guest, but I didn't know how to answer these questions. What had I been thinking? There was no way to talk about a lifestyle site for kids without coming off as an asshole.

"Okay!" I said. "Let's go out to the lobby." I started to get up.

"I want to go with you!" Maya shouted.

"Maya, you're going to stay with Wynn and Suki and watch the show."

"No!"

"Lady, we can't see!"

"Fine, come with me." I started to try to shimmy past Asher, holding Maya's hand, head down, hair still veiling my face.

The little hand darted out so fast I didn't register. "Aah!" I bolted upright. Fly had dropped a handful of blue slushie down my pants.

"Oh," his mother said again. "Sorry."

"Lady, move!" I tried to get past her and Asher as fast as possible, tugging Maya. I was losing my balance.

"Oh wait, Ashie, this is the woman I told you about, from Kathryn's."

He looked at me harder, his glare twisting my ankle. "You're the fucking mole?"

"We, uh, we, uh—" and I fell right into the ring.

Chapter Sixteen

If I had ever dreamed that the answer to my problem was running away to join the circus, my performance in the Big Top put a swift end to that. The clown car that nearly ran me over made Maya cry. The swelling ankle that forced us to leave enraged Wynn. Sage fool-heartedly demanding that my fall be omitted from the story annoyed the reporter. And that I apparently needed to work on the distinction between being "accessible" and "retarded" was very "concerning" to Sage. Sour faces all around.

Except one.

Later that night, after dropping Suki at her mother's house, James surprised me by slipping in our back door as if it were high school and we couldn't wake my parents. He brought absinthe to ease my pain, taking a long swig from the bottle before passing it over. Then, wordlessly, he lifted me onto the kitchen counter, spread my legs, and sunk to his knees between them. He didn't come any farther into the apartment, didn't come at all, just told me to be a good little patient and get myself to bed.

Trying to remember the last time I'd pulled the duvet over limp thighs, I fell asleep. Asher who?

Here is a Parenting Truth: your kids don't care what your night was like. Food poisoning, insomnia, burst pipe, sick sibling—doesn't matter. The next morning, at 6:43 a.m., Maya resumed her bedtime mission with the subtlety of a radio blaring on after the electricity's restored. "Whereth my chocolate clown?" she demanded, marching into my room.

"Good morning to you too." I blinked awake. Jesus. Absinthe. Evil. "How's my girl?"

"My chocolate clown, Mommy. I can't find it anywhere, and you thaid I could have it today. Help. *Pleathe.* Pleathe, I thaid!"

"Your chocolate clown, let's see . . ." As I swung a throbbing foot to the floor, the pain bookended in my skull.

"From my gift bag! From the circuth!"

"Next to the cookie jar. But that's a special treat. You can have a little bit of it tonight if you eat a good dinner and do listening and cooperating."

"It'th not there! Where ith it? Where?"

"Okay." I used the headboard to get myself to my feet as Maya tugged her nightgown in distress. I put treats by the cookie jar because that's where they went. Had I not put it there? Absinthe! Evil! "How 'bout we do a fun breakfast—"

"I don't want a fun breakfatht! I want my chocolate clown!"

"Do you know how Dad's getting to the karate thing today?" Wynn appeared at the door, a crust of drool at the side of his mouth. "In the bus with me or taking the train?"

"Um." Walking was excruciating. "Babe, I don't think he's going."

"He *is*," Wynn insisted, his shoulders rounding. "He's coming to see me in the exhibition match."

"He's flying in today for the Up Fronts," I reminded him.

"What's Up Fronts?" Maya asked.

"It's where all the TV channels get together in a ballroom," I stated to see if I could put a Disney spin on this, "to share their new shows and find out what commercials will run with them." Nope. "I'm sorry, honey, there's no good explanation. It's a grown-up thing. Wynn, I'm sure he'll call me when he lands and we can figure out a time this week to—"

"He landed last night," Wynn interrupted, my ignorance counting against me.

"Right, okay. You guys aren't leaving for the match until 3:00, right?"

Wynn twisted his fists into his pajama top. "He's been gone all season. He hasn't seen me spar or anything."

"We'll figure it out," I reassured him. "As soon as he texts. And I go to the bathroom. Let's get dressed."

Wynn stepped into my path. "If he can't go with me, then I want to go to his hotel after school."

"After school you have your karate trip that you've been talking about for weeks."

"I'll skip it."

"Wynn, for all we know Dad has a thing tonight."

"He *doesn't,* so why are you making me go to this stupid ass—"

"Hey," I said sharply. "We don't talk like that."

"I want my chocolate clown!" Maya pushed between us, sending me onto my ankle.

"Please," I gasped. "Please be careful of Mommy's feet."

"I *ate* your chocolate clown," Wynn declared with a vengeance that stunned us. Maya sucked in air for the wail to follow while he stared at me defiantly.

In the cornucopia of challenging parenting moments, this was among the ones I hated most. When your child's gone farther than he wanted and you can't help him return, your only option is to come down on what he just did and you both know it.

"Why would you eat her candy?" I demanded.

"Why won't you let me see Dad?" he leveled back, the thin vein distinct at his temple.

"I *am* letting you see Dad. I just think it's important for you to do the thing you wanted to do! Aren't you going to see black belts from Beijing? Your whole karate class is going to be there. And Dad's here all week. Now apologize to Maya."

Wynn shrugged aggressively, imitating a much older kid, a kid capable of screeching out of the driveway in the family car. "No."

"Apologize, Wynn."

"I'm not apologizing because I'm not sorry."

"You're not sorry? She's sobbing." I went to lift her but couldn't. Trying to embrace her while ballasting myself with a hand to the floor, I was blinded with rage. *When* he deigned to call, Blake would show our kids his hotel swimming pool, complimentary video games, and room service that probably prepared chocolate clowns to order.

Meanwhile, I was the barrier. In addition to body piercing, motorcy-cles, and Big Gulps, I now stood between them and Daddy. "Apolo-gize now."

"No."

"Apologize so I can go to the bathroom, get everyone dressed, and track down your fucking father!"

Maya whimpered. Wynn receded behind flattening eyes, a response so evocative of Blake it turned my stomach.

"Please, I just have to go to the bathroom and my ankle is really hurting. I didn't mean to swear. That was bad. I'll call Dad. We'll get you guys together as soon as he can see you, I promise." I reached out to draw Wynn to us. To start the day over as they deserved—with a mother not hook-up hung-over and publicity-hobbled.

Refusing me, he hurried from the room.

"I." Sniff. "Want." Sniff. "Chocolate."

"Yes, Maya." I let her help me up. "Waffles with chocolate sauce for everyone."

Scoring a Percocet that could have been a Tic-Tac for the potency it'd lost in an old makeup bag, I somehow got them to school. And despite my screaming ankle and silent son, Wynn's volcano made it intact.

Sage was waiting with her glam squad when I limped off the ele-vator at JeuneBug. I'd planned to set up camp in the conference room and crank out set pieces for the Fabergé nursery. Much to Ginger's annoyance, boxes containing giant Styrofoam eggs were lin-ing the hall, awaiting my brush and glaze. "Did I miss an e-mail?" I asked as I dug for my phone. "I have to prep for the Easter shoot tomorrow."

"Change of plans," Sage chirped tensely, wearing the smile I used when I needed to sell Maya on a canceled play date. "Okay, so you fell into the center ring and it's on YouTube. It's a setback for the face of a luxury site, sure, but not a death sentence. I managed to rustle up a full day of opportunities so let's work extra *extra* hard, okay? We'll stick together and ensure this story stays on track."

Feeling as if I'd been set on fire, I excused myself to the kitchenette where I filled a bag with ice and took a second to catch my breath. In the first moment of stillness since I'd awoke, I identified a third source of pain. Between my legs.

Sad.

Just seeing James on his knees, wanting me like that, had gotten me off, despite his aggressive execution. But today—ow. His technique was to burrow. When he finally stood, I half-expected to see a scuba mask–shaped suction mark on his face.

Joining Sage in Capri, I took a seat in front of the makeup woman, propped my foot on a chair, rested one cold pack on my purple ankle, a second on my lower lap, and texted Ruth. *"SOS. Any chance you can come earlier today?"*

Sage began pacing back and forth behind the makeup artist. "Okay, my fault for not being clearer with the mandate. You are a working mom. I mean, obviously, we can't get around that. But a *chic* working mom. You live the lifestyle you're selling. You're someone we want to go yachting with."

"Someone who needs an aspirin?" I asked, spotting an array of heels presented for Sage's selection. "There is no way I can walk in those today."

"Please?" She pointed to a pair of python Laboutins.

"I need a wheelchair as it is."

"Oh, no, no, no. What you need . . ." She paused for dramatic effect. *A co-parent? The robot nanny from* The Jetsons? *A vacation?* ". . . is a steroid shot."

A steroid shot! That's what this party had been missing. Within an hour of the doctor's arrival, it was like the night before had never happened. I wanted to rip open my blouse and point to my heart: *Here. Stick me here.*

If there was a press opportunity to be had on the island of Manhattan that day, Sage had set it up: go-sees with the luxury magazine editors, a ribbon cutting of the new Gehry building's playroom with Kelly Rutherford, and a guest spot touring the Guggenheim's Children's

Museum with The Real Housewives. At every stop I clucked about "children's lifestyle" until I could return to our town car, where I barked instructions at Ruth, who, in exchange for dropping her *Flight of the Concords* binge, I promised to introduce to a *Daily Show* contact.

Nine hours into the day, here's what I discovered: those stilettos they sell at Bergdorf's for $1,800? They're for women *with drivers* (and probably steroid shots).

Also, doll-sized portions of food are served at these things because the ladies attending them make a day of it—like the traveling dinner parties our parents tried in the eighties, only without the fat. Strips of crudités are served at one event; a platter of chicken skewers circulated at another. Lemon squares the size of a stamp are offered at the next. By the fourth place you'd eaten sort of a meal.

On our way to the Time Warner Center for after-work cocktails with media moms, which Sage promised was the last stop, a text came through from my sitter: *"Maya coughing a ton—feels really hot."*

"Work on saying 'I,'" Sage instructed from the seat beside me.

"Can you take her temp?" I typed back. *"Thermometer on top shelf of medicine cabinet."*

"You keep saying 'we' or 'JeuneBug,'" Sage critiqued. "Connote more ownership. 'I.' Let's hear it."

The sitter wrote back, *"100.2. Snuffling. What should I do?"*

"Children's Tylenol," I typed quickly, even though technically I knew fevers are a body's best friend. But not when your mom's out and your dad moved to Louisiana and your big brother ate your clown. *"On second shelf. She gets—"*

"You're losing focus." Sage dug in her bag. "Here, take a sublingual vitamin B."

"No, I'm— My daughter's coming down with something. Just need a minute." *"—1.5 milligrams. Put on movie. She can watch in my bed. Done soon. I'll call when I'm on my way."* This last event was thankfully spitting distance from my apartment.

"So, Rory, where did you get the idea?" Sage asked.

"Will do," the sitter responded. *"FYI after this you're out of Tylenol."*

"The idea, Rory?"

"Maya's eyes were glassy this morning, but I thought it was the circus excitement." I dropped my head, felled by a Failure Wave. "I gave her chocolate for breakfast."

"For JeuneBug," Sage pressed.

"Oh. Um, we—"

"I," she corrected.

"I—sorry, do you have a pen?" I asked. She slid a gold stylus from her bag and I scrawled "t" on the inside of my palm. *Tylenol. Buy Tylenol. Buy Tylenol buy Tylenol buy Tylenol.*

My phone buzzed. Ruth. *"I couldn't find the gray decals so I improvised."*

Good, I thought, sitting back. *She was catching up, taking initiative, maturing— Wait, what??*

"Gray decals?" I typed back.

"For the words."

"What words???"

"image copyr"

"One more minute," I begged off from Sage, then hit Call. "Where do you see those words?"

"Seriously?" Ruth asked like I was an idiot. "They're really big on the layout you gave me. I mean, they go across all the gold bunnies. I couldn't find them so I got a gray paint pen and did it by hand."

"The light gray letters? Is that what you mean?"

"I guess they're kind of light," she acknowledged.

"Ruth." I bolted up, the seat belt restraining me. "That's just the watermark from the photo I used! You wrote that across all the gold leaf?" Those bunnies cost $10,000 each.

"I mean it's on the plan you gave me. Also, I IMDB'd your friend and he hasn't had any credits in, like, five years. Are you sure he's still at the *Daily Show*?"

"Rory," Sage commanded as the car pulled up to the Time Warner Center and we got out. *"Rory,"* she repeated as she pushed through the revolving doors. "Remember, 'I.'"

"Don't touch anything, Ruth." A hundred thousand dollars of

borrowed bunnies. Ruined. "Not one thing. Just sit tight. Can you do that?"

"But—"

Sage waved impatiently from the elevator.

"Please," I implored. "Can you? Please, just say yes."

"Fine, yes."

"Thank you." The doors slid closed, and I scrolled for the number of a decorative painter who owed me a favor, my one shot at fixing this. All those *bunnies* had to sell now.

"Heads up," Sage called, pointedly dropping her phone in her bag and leading me into the bar. Women milled about in expensive suits, gulping their wine and nibbling their bites. Sage began crisscrossing the room, striding past me as if spotting a friend, only to pause at my back and whisper someone's pertinent stats like I was running for office. "Marcy Price, she's this evening's chairwoman." Sage leaned behind my ear. "Hedge fund partner. Breast cancer survivor."

Stymied for a cancer sequitur, I thanked Marcy for being included and then tried to pinpoint where the servers were entering so I could actually eat.

Sage pivoted me toward a tired-looking woman holding court nearby. "Dana Kensington. Exec producer, GMA. Three kids. And Rory, *nothing* about Israel." As if I hadn't shut up about it.

But before I could introduce myself, someone broke into the song "Tomorrow" from *Annie*. I stood up on the tips of my evil shoes to see a young woman dressed as Dora the Explorer clutching a sign that read *Dora Explores Your Broadway Birthday!* "I just stick up my chin! And grin!" No one stopped chatting. "And sayyyyyy—" As if a gong was hit, a lady in a sheath dress and headset abruptly ushered Dora away.

"*What* is this?" I asked Sage.

"Marcy's brainchild," she filled me in. "Vendors get sixty seconds to display their service to elite industry moms. It's a different theme every month. Holiday toys, bar mitzvah tutors, summer camps. Genius."

A man with a thin mustache darted into Dora's place. He had a banjo strapped to his back and a puppet on each hand. "Monsier Renard!" he screeched in a Monty Python voice, waving the duck at the fox. "*C'est votre anniversaire aujourd'hui, n'est ce pas?*"

"*Ouais, mais mon gateau au chocolate a disparu!*" the fox bemoaned ten registers deeper. "*Nous devons le trouver!*" The animals were flung off, the guitar was swung around, and *We're Going on Une Gateau Hunt* was sung—until the lady in the shift reappeared and he raised his "Celebrate with Pierre the Puppet Man!" sign with molecular desperation before being seen out.

Two people jogged in wearing clown suits, juggling toy cars, whooping and hollering like the whole room was in on the fun. It was not.

"Oh, the tiny car guys," a woman nearby observed in a nasal drawl. "I've heard good things."

"Justine got them for the twins' second," the woman told her friend. "Eight hundred for a half-hour. Not bad."

My phone buzzed with a text. "*Maya says her stomach's feeling funny.*"

"Sage." I turned to her. "Goodnight, I need to get home."

"And you will just as soon as— What's *she* doing here?" I followed Sage's gaze to where Taylor stood at the door, livid, eyes locked on mine. She strode over, grabbed my arm, and tugged me.

"Taylor." I pulled back.

Sage puffed up her hundred pounds to obscure us from the room. "Taylor, Rory will be finished in five," she said through clenched teeth. "You can speak then."

"Right now," Taylor growled. "Or I swear to God I'm going to fucking hit you both."

"*Go.*" Sage handed me off and I followed Taylor out a side door—inexplicably. Except that I came up in a time and place where you did what your boss asked of you, even if it meant staying all night with no overtime, and following her, even if you knew you were about to get reamed.

The small room was lined with people waiting to go on, the air dense with sweat and the specter of student loans. My phone rang.

"I fucking hate you," Taylor started in as I silenced it.

"Excuse me?"

"*Hate* you. *Every fucking thing about you.* How you move, speak, think—so fucking slowly! I hate that I have to explain every fucking thing to you with time I don't even have! And that pen you put through your hair! How you label your shit in the fridge! Your clothes! Your hat! How you send an e-mail for *every fucking thing* like it's four hundred fucking years ago! Working with you is like, like having a babysitter—no—it's like having my *mother* in my office. And now, after dealing with you every day, after letting you get all the press for *my* working my ass off, I find out you're a fucking *plant?*"

The last veil of my absinthe hangover cleared, leaving me staring into Asher's eyes as I tumbled ass over tits.

"It's not that dramatic," I said as my phone rang again.

"Don't you dare—you're—you work for *me*! Me! I *own* you. I can take your name and stick it on dog shit if I want to. Do you *get* that?"

"You're upset," I tried.

"Don't you tell me how I feel! How can you even look in the mirror?" she sneered. "How can you look your own kids in the face—"

I answered my phone so I wouldn't beat her with it. "Yes?" I twisted away.

"Rory, it's Josh."

"Josh?"

"Ex-*cuse* me?!" Taylor thrust her face into mine.

"The boys got a little overzealous after watching the black belts," he said urgently, "and we've had an accident. We're at Westchester General with Wynn—"

"What?!"

"He's okay," he said quickly. "Everything's all right, but it's a compound fracture of his left tibia."

"Mort picked my dad," Taylor continued over my shoulder, trying to pull my attention back. "Kathryn doesn't even know yet, but she'll be out by the end of the month."

"He was pretty freaked out by the blood," Josh admitted, "but he's asleep now."

"Oh my God." I felt hot. And light.

"Hang up, Rory," Taylor seethed.

"Can I talk to him?" I asked.

"They're prepping him for surgery."

"Surgery?"

"Just get yourself here. I'll stay with him."

"Thank you. Thank you, Josh. I'm on my way." I hung up to spin in search of an exit sign.

"Are you seriously leaving right now?!" Taylor exploded.

"Taylor, my son is hurt. I can call you later or we can continue this in the morning, but I have to go."

"Absolutely not!" She was at my heels. "We're having a discussion. You don't just walk away from me!"

"Taylor, you don't know this yet, but sometimes in life you have to pause things you *desperately* want to resolve."

I found the door, took off the shoes, and ran.

Chapter Seventeen

This is the downside of a steroid shot: something very bad happened to my ankle between the back door of the bar and the front door of my building. I called Blake's cell and, miraculously, after dodging me all day about the karate trip, he answered. "Can I call you back? I'm getting ready for a—"

"Wynn has a compound fracture." I started to cry. "He's at Westchester General with his karate class, and I don't know how to get to him."

"Where are you?" he asked.

"In our lobby, but I've fucked up my ankle and I have to get to the train and I don't know how I'm going to—"

"I'll get Jack's car. Give me thirty."

Pounding the elevator button, I nodded, even though he couldn't see me, and as I got on, texted Claire to see if she could spend the night.

The sitter swung open the door and Maya raced to me, clutching her worn bunny. I dropped my things to take her into my arms where she slumped like a wool blanket pulled from boiling water.

In her bed, I curled around her and whispered stories about stuffed animals until, wrung out, she finally fell asleep.

I hobbled to get the sitter cash and then opened the door—to James—with an Agent Provacateur shopping bag in hand, the luxury lingerie designer that specializes in $600 takes on the naughty nurse and sexy secretary.

"What's happened here?" he asked, taking me in.

"Maya has the stomach flu." I leaned my weight into the knob. "And Wynn's got a compound fracture in Westchester."

"So it's a perfect time." He lifted an eyebrow.

"Blake's on his way to pick me up so we can get to Wynn." I tried to pull my brain from the four tracks of logistics it was mapping. "And I still need to change and get things together." We both looked down at my lame foot.

"Here." He hoisted me into his arms Scarlett O'Hara–style as our sitter tried to tiptoe unobtrusively past. Through her eyes, this was ridiculous. Or it was just ridiculous. I didn't have the bandwidth to judge.

Shutting my bedroom door with his loafer, he set me on the bed, his debonair dropping as the smell hit us.

"Maya was in here," I explained as I pushed up to stand. "I'll open a window."

"Let me." He lifted one as far as it would go and cool air gusted in.

"I really need to be ready when Blake gets here." I limped to the closet.

But, instead of taking my cue, James cleared a stack of laundry from the bench, and sat down. "I saw the preorders today. Looking good. Soon you'll have your own driver."

Keeping my ass facing the closet I pulled off my dress. "You know, James, I'm not actually getting a cut from this line you're investing in." I zipped up a sweatshirt over my bra. "And if I leave, which I have to, I'll need you to advise me on how to take something with me or start my own—"

He frowned as I tugged on my jeans. "I couldn't be party to your leaving. They'd have a case for tortious interference."

"But you're the lead investor, you could pressure them to pay me."

He opened his hands. "Can't, unfortunately."

"So you're not going to help me?" I hopped back to the bedroom door to retrieve my sneakers. *Okay, I had to pack a bag for Wynn and call Val and my parents so someone could stay with Maya tomorrow—*

He walked over to me. "It doesn't mean we can't find something else to do down the road. Or now." His hands slipped around my waist, his pelvis pressing into mine. He bent to kiss me, but his spicy cologne and pricey whiskey breath were suddenly a little much for the here and now. "I like seeing what's behind your curtain," he said as if the chaos was a set of lingerie I'd donned for his amusement. "Ugh!" he jerked his hand out. "What's this?"

"Vomit."

I heard the front door open. "Rory?" Claire called.

"In here." I pushed him away as the buzzer also rang, meaning Blake was downstairs.

"Thank you for coming to get me," I said as I looked between the map on my phone and passing road signs.

"Of course," Blake said.

"I mean, I'm sure you could have choppered there or whatever."

"They offered me a car, but I couldn't deal with someone else driving right now."

"I'm glad you're the one driving," I said. I was. No one else in the world cared about Wynn as much as I did. No one else ever would, not in a parental way. We would be forever united by this. "I mean, for what it's worth."

The song on the radio ended, and Blake turned up the volume on the news. *"Now entering day two of the crisis. Engineers are working around the clock in the luxury high rise to override the security system, which has shut in approximately seventy residents and building staff."*

"So, what's happening?" I asked.

"It's amazing. You know that super lux new tower that just opened on Fifty-Seventh Street?"

"The one blocking the sunshine in Central Park?"

"Yeah. It has this, like, Pentagon-level security system."

"Because the owners are all from Russia and Qatar?" I asked.

"Yep. So, anyway, yesterday morning it got triggered by some glitch, and went into lockdown. No one can get in. No one can get out. I feel bad for them, but the timing for Up Fronts couldn't be better. Our show isn't just cutting edge, it's, like, psychic. So what was this thing that Wynn was at?"

"Karate exhibition. He really wanted you there," I dared.

"I know. I hate being so far away from you guys," he said miserably.

My phone buzzed with a text from Claire. *"Her fever is up to 101. What should I give her?"* Looking down at my left hand, where my wedding band caught the light of the passing streetlamps, I saw the smudged "t." *Tylenol. Shit.*

"There," he said, pointing to the red glowing word in the distance. Emergency.

Blake dropped me off to park and I made my way along the hospital walls, following the colored arrows to recovery, my ankle forcing me to move much more slowly than I wanted to. I remembered when Blake brought me in to St. Luke's to have Wynn. Despite my relentless contractions, we were twice sent away because I wasn't dilating. As per the doctor's instructions, Blake walked me all over midtown at the pace I was currently hobbling. He was amazing, letting me grip his shoulders, drop my head to his chest, and scream as needed. Wynn's birth was so hard and so long I dreaded Maya's, but her labor was ninety minutes start to finish. I had never known what to expect.

When I limped in and saw Wynn hooked up to a monitor and IV, my heart twisted in on itself. He looked so much smaller than he had in my bedroom doorway that morning—too little to be here. "Hey, baby," I said, tearing up as I went to take his hand. He shifted in my direction but didn't wake. "I'm so sorry. I'm here now."

"They have him on a morphine drip so he's pretty zonked." I turned to see Josh stretching up from a chair. He opened his arms, and I slumped against him.

"Thank you for being here. I don't even know what to say."

He dropped his chin to my head. "He's a tough little guy."

"I was so horrible to him this morning, Josh. To both of them. He just wanted to know where his dad was and I totally lost it."

"Hey, now," he said gently, sweeping my hair from my forehead.

"He doesn't deserve any of this."

"Neither do you." It was the kindest thing anyone could have said. His embrace tightened around me, just enough to make me give over my weight.

"Oh, Jesus," Blake murmured as he walked in and Josh jerked back.

"Josh, this is Blake," I said. "He drove me up," I added although I wasn't sure why.

"Hey," Blake said. "From soccer, right?"

"Josh's been with Wynn all evening," I told him.

"Thanks, man. So what happened?" Blake asked.

Josh seemed to remind himself to keep talking. "The kids were worked up from the demonstrations, and the next thing we knew, Wynn climbed on a post in the parking lot. The doctor can fill you in on everything, but Wynn's okay."

Blake put his arm around me.

"Well, you're here, so I should go," Josh said.

"You must be exhausted," I answered. "I'm sure you just want to get home."

"I don't, actually," he said quietly, the revelation seeming to sur-prise him as much as it did me.

"Well," I said quickly, "thank you so much." I glanced at Blake. "Can we give you a ride to the train?"

"Oh, no. No, I'll order a car." He busied himself with his jacket and checked his pocket for his phone. "Okay then. Glad you're here."

Blake nodded, gripping my hand, looking down at our sleeping son.

"Good luck." Pausing in the doorway, Josh glanced back over his shoulder. And through the mesh curtain I could see it written on his face. This hadn't been the act of a concerned parent or even a con-cerned friend. This was something else—something neither of us could let ourselves want.

A nurse took pity on me and bandaged my ankle, and then Blake and I took turns trying to sleep in the reclining chairs while they came in and out, monitoring Wynn's vitals.

"Okay," the resident said after giving him morphine at 2:00 a.m. "I'm going to let you guys get some rest for a few hours." I watched Wynn's features finally relax into a place beyond the pain.

I felt tears breaking.

"What's going on?" Blake asked gently, pushing the door in to follow me into the bathroom.

"What's going on is that when I found out my son broke his leg, I forgot to grab Tylenol on the two-block run from getting reamed out by my boss. Maya's fever worsened and she was without me, and without you, or her brother, and crying." My cheeks wet as the day caught up with me. "So while you were dozing, I downloaded the Taskrabbit app on my phone; then I uploaded the task; then some nice kid from Fordham brought Claire the Tylenol for $15."

"You did it," he said gently. "Why are you crying?"

Because I couldn't do this alone anymore.

Blake slid down the tile wall, reached out, took me by my waist, and lowered me into his lap, curling around me. It was quiet save the swooshing of cars passing on the road outside. I gave in to the black pull of exhaustion.

"Remember with Wynn," he said quietly, "how those assholes wouldn't give us a bed?"

"Mm-hm," I murmured as he rubbed my back, my tears dampening his shirt. "Was thinking about it earlier."

"That's the night I knew there was nothing I could do."

"What?" I opened my eyes. "What do you mean?"

"I mean you made him and then you nearly tore yourself in half to get him out for me. How could I top that?"

"*We* made him." I pulled back to look at him. "Both of us. And nobody expected you to top it."

He stared intently into my eyes. "I wish . . ." He shook his head, unable to finish the thought.

"What?" I asked. "You wish what?"

He searched for the words. "I wish it could be like when he was born. When we thought that the hardest thing could just be behind us."

I nodded.

His palm cupped my cheek and then he kissed me, really kissed me, with lips that knew mine. Our tongues coordinated effortlessly. I raised up on my knees and he unzipped my sweatshirt. He pulled back to look at me, really look at me. I loved him, had always loved him. James was an SNL sketch next to what was between us.

"Is this okay?" he asked.

"Yes." I nodded. "Please."

He kissed my throat. I found the back of his neck where my hand fit perfectly. I tugged his head back to gently bite his earlobe; then all the rage, the hurt, everything erupted as we pushed against and gripped each other. I didn't care about any part of me that hurt. I just wanted him inside, wanted our faces a breath apart. Tugging at each other's pants, he lifted me onto the windowsill. And then he was in me, and we moved together in a rhythm perfected from years in which children could interrupt at any moment. For months, I'd felt like a released balloon, but Blake caught me firmly in his grasp. We came within seconds of each other. And with a last kiss, we collapsed.

It was my phone that woke me as the dawn was coming through the blinds. "Claire?" I answered, sitting up on the reclined chair in the mess of hospital sheets.

"No, Ruth."

"Ruth?"

"Yes. I have something to say to you."

I listened for the shower, but it wasn't on. Had he gone to get coffee?

"I think you should know that you can't just treat people like this. And I'm sorry, but you really need to know that."

I spotted Blake's note on the dry erase board. *"Early call. Big presentation today! Arranged for car to pick you up at hospital. Mom will be at hotel waiting for Wynn, and I'll be with him tonight. Take care today and time for yourself, seriously.* ♥ "

". . . and then I waited until midnight for you to call me back. And it's just really, really disrespectful. You act like you're this nice woman, but you did that. You did that to me. My time is valuable, too, you know. And the thing is that you need to think about what you're modeling. Or, like, not, okay? On top of this internship I work at Cluck U *and* at the library. I live with seven other people in a two bedroom in Bushwick where I have been mugged—twice. My loans kick in next January—twelve hundred dollars a month. And all you care about is gold bunnies for, like, evil, *evil* people. I did not spend two weeks in a tent on Wall Street for this."

"Uh . . . thank you for that."

"You're welcome. Good-bye."

Maya, thank God, rose with a voracious hunger and song in her step, as only a four-year-old can. Claire took her to school and accepted my eternal gratitude.

Wynn was so groggy that he slept all the way back to the city while I held his hand as he hadn't let me since he was seven. It was the first blindingly sunny spring day after the April rains had lingered, and I hadn't thought to bring my sunglasses. Eyes closed, I found myself thinking about Ruth and my own twenties. Although it wasn't Bushwick, I was living in a walk-up with a toilet that never stopped running. And I battled perpetual terror that my part-time gigs, short-term leases, and three-week boyfriends might never gel into a Life. Ruth was doing the best she could at a time when every box is nauseatingly unchecked. Some women find that freedom exhilarating, but for the ambitious, like me—like Ruth—it feels like waiting for your parachute to open.

I couldn't help but wrestle with her indictment.

Two decades later, was I trying to be a model? And for whom?

My kids. Just my kids.

And how was that working out? What exactly was Maya supposed to take from my example these days?

I'd just wanted them to have everything I didn't. Culture, diversity, food trucks. I thought of our friends who'd decamped years earlier for the husband's midwestern hometown. The wife, a banker and mother of three, said to me, "If you have a plate full of meatballs and you keep adding meatballs, at some point meatballs are going to start falling off the plate. My meatballs are falling off my plate."

My meatballs were falling off my plate.

I wanted easier. Blake wanted easier.

Wynn lolled his head to rest against my shoulder. His other hand hooked around my arm. Nothing was more important than this. I didn't need to show the Ruths of the world how to grow up. Maybe I didn't even have to figure it out myself. Maybe I just had to move with Blake somewhere that didn't require an app package for survival—where, whatever it lacked, life would at long last be manageable and we'd be living it together.

Blake's suite overlooking Central Park South was a far cry from Westchester General. Val helped me tuck Wynn beneath a billowing duvet and then saw me to the door. "Blake should be back in an hour or two. I *was* in the middle of a silent retreat," she muttered. But not even Val's narcissism could wind me.

Glimpsing the king bed in the master, I was inspired. "I'll be back as soon as I'm done with my shoot," I offered. "I'll bring Maya and we'll surprise Blake." I kissed her on the cheek and pulled the door shut before she could dissuade me.

The car then took me straight to the studio. I could have just not shown up. Taylor certainly had it coming. But I was forty-one. I didn't need to set things on fire or educate anyone. I needed to finish the project as I'd started it—without any assistance or assistants—and then get us the hell out.

We were done by five. Eager to get home so I could shower before picking up Maya and taking her to the hotel, I flagged a cab. My phone rang as we pulled in front of my building.

"Have you heard?" Jessica asked.

"Can I call you back, actually?"

"No, you need to hear this. I can't even do it justice, I'm putting on our entertainment reporter. Johnny! Come in here. Tell my friend what just went down at the Up Fronts." There was a shuffle as the phone was passed. I paid the driver and got out.

"Uh, hey, it's Johnny."

"Hi, Johnny." I tried not to sound impatient.

"Tell her," I heard Jessica prompt in the background.

"Yeah, so the J. J. Abrams presentation was a bit of a shit show—"

"Mrs. Turner, you cannot go in there," the doorman said over him.

"What?" I asked.

"Mr. Turner upstairs. Said you cannot go up."

"Oh, is he surprising me?" I kept walking, thinking whatever romance Blake had in store could wait until I got out of these gold-leaf-speckled clothes. "What do you mean a shit show?" I asked as I pressed for the elevator while the doorman looked on helplessly.

"Since that guy died last night," Johnny said.

"What guy?" I asked.

"One of the Russians in the malfunctioning building on Fifty-Seventh. Haven't you been following this?"

"A little?"

"The security system freaked out and trapped everyone in their apartments—no food, no water, no septic system, no air, it was like, well over a hundred degrees in there. Apparently feces were literally leaking through the walls. So this guy finally tried to make a dash for the stairwell, but he got sprayed with toxic foam and his airways shut down." Johnny's voice crackled as I rose to my floor. "Anyway, when ABC played the clip from *High Fall,* the audience was horrified. Not one bid for the advertising, and ABC immediately pulled the show with an apology to the family."

As I fished out my keys, I wasn't even fully processing it. *Blake's show pulled? What did that mean?*

The elevator door opened, and the answer was immediate.

There were no rose petals, no Al Green playing from beyond the door. Nowhere to even insert my key. Where my simple lock had been there was now a meatloaf-sized bronze key pad and a little pyramid of metal dust on the floor beneath it.

He had locked me out.

Chapter Eighteen

I leaned hard into the bell. "Blake?"

The door swung open and Val greeted me with her finger to her lips. Then she pointed to the couch, where Wynn was dozing under the afghan. "He had some Jell-O at the hotel," Val whispered as I followed her into the dining room, like this was any other day. "And pineapple because the bromelain is good for ligaments and red meat to rebuild his qi. I had my herbalist make him a formula." She started rummaging through her totes. "You can send me a check."

"Val, why is the lock changed?"

"Blake was kicked out of the hotel today. So rude." She found her bag of herbs. "Tea?" She walked away into the kitchen, forcing me to limp after her.

"What does that have to do with me?"

"My therapist explained it all to me. When your tax returns are filed, the rent control board will see your income is too high and we'll lose my apartment."

"Your apartment?" The room was starting to spin like Ichabod Crane having a panic attack.

"The plan was always when I get too old to drive, I'd move back here and you'd take care of me." Had Blake told me that six months ago, I'd have granted him a divorce on the spot.

"This is ridiculous." I didn't know why I was even talking to her. I called Blake.

And heard his phone ringing in our bedroom.

I ran back there on my crap ankle and found him curled in a ball in the middle of our bed. "Blake?"

He just stared at the wall with flattened eyes.

"Withdrawing," Val said in a stage whisper from the doorway.

"Blake," I said, bending to try to get him to look at me. I'd never seen him like this. "I'm so sorry this happened. I understand you're devastated, but your mom is trying to evict me. I need you to sit up."

He reached up, grabbed a pillow, and pulled it over his head.

"Blake."

He began to moan.

"Rory, there's no point talking to him when he gets like this."

"Your son is in a ball," I said to her, emphasizing each word as if translating. "Crying into a pillow." No impact.

Blake was heaving silently, looking headless. Oh my God, this was happening. It was really happening. "Blake, you have to do something," I tried one last time. "Blake?" My mind raced through every worst-case scenario Benjamin Stern had thrown at me. "Okay, fine. But I'm not setting one foot outside until Blake's lawyer agrees, in writing, that my departure in no way affects the custody discussion."

Thirty minutes later, I'd numbly lined the vestibule hallway with duffel bags and was waiting for an affidavit from the lawyer while literally holding one foot in my front door. My cell rang.

"We good?" Val asked from the foyer. "That everything?"

"It's the lawyer. Hold on." I pivoted for a second to answer it, and the door shut.

"Val!" I called. "Hello?"

She cracked it open with the chain on.

"Rory, hi," the lawyer greeted me with his gravely voice. "I have your affidavit all ready to e-mail over. As per your request, I'm confirming that your moving out tonight in no way implies that you are relinquishing custody."

"Thank you."

"And that you are agreeing to pay Blake a lump sum of eighty-thousand dollars."

"What?!" I looked through the gap at Val's rainbow-rimmed bifocals.

"Eighty-thousand dollars," the lawyer said again as Claire and Jessica got off the elevator, slightly out of breath from running over from their respective offices.

"American?" I asked.

"Yes," he confirmed hesitantly, probably quickly calculating if accepting the payment in Australian dollars would yield Blake a profit.

"Where on earth do you think I am going to pull eighty-thousand dollars from?!"

"*Blake wants eighty-thousand dollars?*" Jessica asked incredulously over my shoulder.

Claire's eyes went black. "I'm going to kill him. I am going to fucking kill him."

Val shut the door. I put the lawyer on speakerphone as he continued: "The option of paying him alimony indefinitely is still on the table."

"How can you live with yourselves?" I shouted at the peeling door. "This is *pathetic*."

The lawyer made a little cough he probably used to stretch billable hours. He'd probably racked up hundreds of thousands with that cough. "The legal industry has been doing a lot to combat reverse sexism." My blood was vibrating. "I strongly advise you to accept his terms or face a protracted legal battle—"

I hung up. I couldn't—I just couldn't—not one more word of it. I pressed for the elevator and we shoved the overflowing bags inside.

"Oh my God." I put my hand to my forehead as the door slid shut. "I married the wrong guy." It was humiliatingly official. "Blake is just a shitty, shitty human being. That I *chose*."

"I'm the parenting expert with no time to parent," Jessica offered, patting my shoulder. "My kids are probably going to grow up to write memoirs about how much I suck."

"I gave up on myself and took a soul-deadening job flattering rich people," Claire joined us.

"Being forty-one sucks," I added.

The door opened in the lobby, but nobody moved, we were stuck.

"Okay, now *this* is pathetic." Claire pushed herself to unload the bags.

"I thought we were just getting rolling," Jessica said brightly. "I haven't even started in on my body and my sex drive and my eyesight."

"Look," Claire said, slicing the air with her hand. "You'll stay with me. We'll get online tonight. It's almost the first of the month. We'll find you a place to live and you'll be reunited with the kids inside ten days. I'll loan you the money for the broker's fee and security deposit."

"But how will I pay you back?" I asked.

"We don't get to choose if we get older or not," she cut me off. "We don't get to choose if we have to start holding menus out to read them, or if our knees make a sound like a coffin lid every time we go down stairs. We don't get to." She was whipping the bags out of the elevator. "When it comes to life, we are offered one choice. One: stay in or get out. And I choose to stay in. Without the right guy, or the right job, or the right expression of my talents, and I was fucking talented." Her voice caught. "And I miss it." She looked from Jessica's face to mine. "I thought if I spent my time raising money to house other people's art, while I talked about other people's art, with other people who like art, it would be the same. But it's not. I need to paint. I'll move to Bay Ridge and give up my health insurance. I'll dog walk, I'll cat sit, but my life has to have meaning."

I actually started clapping.

"Sorry, sorry," Claire said, coming back to herself. "We're supposed to be focused on killing Blake."

"No. No, we're not," I said.

"You're not going to fuck him again, are you?" Jessica asked, alarmed.

"Oh God, no, not if we ended up at the last old age home on earth." I shuddered.

"Then," she asked, "where are you going to get $80,000?"

Not from JeuneBug, but I was obligated to show up there the next morning anyway. Sitting at my desk, rolling out the cricks in my back from sleeping on Claire's couch, and waiting for $80,000 to walk through the door felt like being stuck at the wrong party when I was single—*the first time*. One of those cocktail-party-rapidly-devolving-into-a-gay-orgy things thrown by a colleague where, inevitably, no one wanted to talk to me. And all I could think was that my soulmate was not about to come out of that fuchsia bathroom wearing a mesh T-shirt.

Now I silently chanted *eighty thousand, eighty thousand, eighty thousand*. I Googled, *price for a kidney* and *oldest living porn star*.

"Rory!"

I jumped up, winced, and dropped back down again. "Yes?"

Ginger pointed to the conference room, where the other editors were already assembled. "Staff meeting," she said.

By the time I limped in, Taylor was already standing at the head of the table, arms crossed. "I want everyone to tell me where we are with graduation," she instructed.

Clark spoke first. "This year we're pushing classics. We're seeing the graduate in seersucker, pinstripes. The story for girls is about a crino-lined 1950s Sally Draper thing."

I leaned in and whispered to Merrill, "Graduation from . . . ?"

The travel editor jumped in. "He wants to take the summer off. He's looking for less structured time. Starting kindergarten can be stressful, so we're telling a beach story rather than being enrichment focused." She tapped her stylus against her tablet. "We killed the piece on India."

"Gifts?" Kimmy rasped. She was objectively gray. And had a crust around her eyes.

"A Koons balloon puppy is evergreen," Merrill answered.

"Kwiat is doing a diamond Peppa Pig that's kind of fabulous. Apple stock."

"Love," Kimmy mouthed.

"And Be?" Taylor asked, glaring at me, full-well knowing I had nothing prepared. *Oh, you want to play, Taylor?*

"Our graduate," I began, taking a breath, buying time, shrinking Aerin Lauder to three-feet high, "wants a fresh start. She's left behind a key stage in life, and redecorating is first and foremost on her mind. My shoot is focused on what she'll need for fall. Shagreen desk, Louis Vuitton iPad dock, DSM wall unit. For him, I'm seeing a stitched pigskin beanbag for reading and a vintage meat hook for his back-pack."

"That's sounds fine," Taylor answered tightly. "And, Clark, where are we with the lobster shoes?"

"McQueen sent them over. We uploaded the video and the photos onto the site this morning."

I coughed up my tea. "You didn't actually photograph toddlers walking on jewel-encrusted claw heels, did you?"

"He's launching a kid's line," Taylor said, like that was the last word on that.

"Lady Gaga could barely walk in them! Kids will twist their ankles and break their arms," said the lady who had twisted her ankle in flats. I don't know why, of every insane thing that had been discussed in this room, this was the thing I had to push back on, but I couldn't stop seeing Wynn in his cast. "We can't endorse that."

"Endorse it?" Taylor asked incredulously as Clark spun his iPad to the table and pressed play.

"This is the raw footage," he said, "just to give you a sense."

There they were, four-year-olds in leotards with spikes launching from them like porcupine quills trying to balance on shoes nearly as big as they were.

"Elody, stand up straight," her mother chided, shifting her lime green Michael Kors bag to her other elbow. But poor Elody was just trying not to keel over.

"Okay, let's go!" The director clapped, startling the girls, who fell over in one unit like a tipped cow.

"This is inhumane," I said, looking at all the other directors. "You have to take it down."

"Oh, but they're balancing in the final cut," Clark tried to assure me.

"I don't care. Suri's one-inch heels were controversial. We're about to launch a nursery line; we don't need controversy. New mothers think everything is out to strangle, smother, and suffocate as it is. Let's not seem to be blasé about safety. Discretionary income, yes; safety, no."

Taylor just looked at me like if she could have pulled a Taser out of her purse she would have. "Do you think the beauty mags cared when they told everyone to get formaldehyde blow-outs?" Taylor asked. "Shut up, Rory."

I spent the day doing what adults sometimes have to do: their jobs—to a quiet inner mantra of, *Go me, making money, doing something I'm qualified to do, that I can find the upside in, because I like food and shelter.* I was just looking at the clock to see when I could break away to check out some rentals in outer boroughs that cost more than I made in a month when Tim, the tech guy, called out in the quietest way you can call out, "Guys? Guys? Something's happening?"

"Yeah," another director echoed. "Something is definitely happening!"

Ginger came running past and flung herself into the doorway of Taylor's office, catching her elbows on the frame so she bowed like a sail. "Our numbers are going through the roof."

"Victoria Beckham finally retweeted me!" Taylor gasped.

"This feels bigger than that," Merrill muttered, looking at her iPad.

"Bigger than that?" I whispered to Clark.

Taylor came out to the bullpen clapping her palms, her fingers splayed away from each other. "It's happening! It's happening!"

Everyone looked at her, no one daring to ask what "it" was.

"Check sales!" Taylor shouted. "Sales are going to put us in the black today!"

We manned our screens, waiting, watching, the plants leaning toward us, hoping someone might exhale some carbon dioxide. *Was this it? Was the site going viral? Were we going to go public? Would I be the next Sean Parker? Could I hire Blake to live in the linen closet and perform "Beowulf" on command?*

Across the floor one of the editors sprang up and away from her iMac like she'd just found anthrax on it. Kimmy touched Taylor's shoulder and pointed at their troops, clustered in shock.

The headline on Jezebel read, "WHY JEUNEBUG IS ONE OF THE SIGNS OF THE APOCALYPSE."

"It's been shared over ten thousand times," Merrill warbled from the back.

"#PetiteAssh★les is trending," someone else added.

"The Onion just mocked up our home page."

"Look," Taylor cut in, "it's a day. A cycle of haha at our expense. Goop went through it. It's just jealousy. Ignore it."

"But shouldn't we—"

"Ignore it!"

I got her impulse. If Taylor's future husband ever sued her for alimony and custody of her enamel baby shoe charm collection, ignoring would go a long way toward Zen. But this felt a tad more ostrich than Buddha.

"For every ten Target shoppers laughing at us, we'll pick up a new client who's been craving for someone to aggregate this marketplace. You'll see. Our numbers are going to climb. Think Goop!"

They went home, thinking *Goop*, thinking *fuck*, thinking a lot of things. I took two Advil and went to see a beautiful two-bedroom in Park Slope, which was only in my price range because, I discovered, the previous tenants had let their cats use it as a litter box. The entire twelve hundred square feet of floors would have to be ripped out. And the landlord was looking for someone who would shoulder the expense themselves, which was another seven grand I didn't have. From there I hoofed it back to Columbus Circle and the kids. I had two hours with them while Blake and Val were at a movie.

I made them dinner in the kitchen she was single-handedly wrecking one melted spatula at a time and reassured them this was only temporary until I signed a lease on someplace they would love.

Oh God, I wondered as I took the bus up to Claire's. *Would I not find anything that I could pay for on my own? Would I end up having to leave the kids with Blake?* I got back online and looked for one bedrooms. *I could take the couch and they could share for a couple more years, right? When did boys start masturbating constantly? Twelve? Thirteen?* I'd get Wynn his own iPad with a waterproof cover and a lock on the bathroom.

Assuming I still had a job.

After midnight I powered down Claire's laptop, pulled the covers over me, and took stock. I was forty-one years old. I was sleeping on a friend's couch with a sprained ankle. I had momentarily lost, if not legal custody, then custodial duties of my children. My job, which had been the rope out of the quicksand of my industry, was fraying. And my soon-to-be-ex-husband, whom I was apparently *never* going to be able to read right, had decided to have good-bye sex with me in a hospital bathroom.

And my last thought as I fell asleep? I was now no longer even qualified to get a summer job at my parents' bank.

I wanted a do-over.

Chapter Nineteen

"Rory, get in here," Claire called from her bedroom where she was painting at her easel early the next morning.

"Claire, this is awethome," I said, admiring her work, toothbrush in hand, mouth full of foam.

"No, no, no," she said, pointing my attention to the TV, where JeuneBug's home page was floating behind Joe Scarborough's head.

"Why is he talking about uth?" I asked, looking around for somewhere to spit.

"It's something about banks funneling money to Iran." She handed me her coffee cup.

"JeuneBug's not funneling money," I said, wiping my mouth with the back of my hand.

"Are health care costs spiraling?" she added, piecing it together.

"The company's on Stellar's insurance plan."

"And more people have fallen below the poverty line in the previous month than any other since 2008," she tried to follow Scarborough's thread.

"What?" I asked.

"Oh," she said, slapping her forehead. "You're evil! That's the story. JeuneBug represents everything that's wrong with the one percent."

"Well, yes." I waved my toothbrush. "So do a lot of things! I don't manufacture sharkskin wipe dispensers. I just feature them."

"Well, technically, that's not true." And there, on CNN, were my designs. "Chris Cuomo just said your snowflake bed retails for $15,000."

"It does?" I was stunned. Pricing hadn't exactly been under my supervision.

"What I'm interested in," the commentator was saying, "is how this reflects on Asher Hummell. The CEO is his daughter, right? Was there any oversight? Was she just given the keys to the Ferrari? And where was Mort Studecker in all this? What does a toddler in lobster shoes say about America?"

"Nothing," I shouted at the TV. "The shoes are French. And nobody lost dialysis coverage because of them."

"Rory, you don't even like JeuneBug," Claire reminded me, taking her paints to the kitchen.

"But this is a bad moment for America to agree with me. I need money. Desperately. I can't be without a job for even one minute. If JeuneBug's getting demolished, I have to be the rat that rides out on the wrecking ball."

"Then do me a favor," she said, raising an eyebrow.

"Hit me."

"Take my old crutches today. *Please*."

What is it scientists warn about before hives collapse? Chaos in the hive? We had chaos in the hive. As I got off the elevator, people were dashing from one terminal to the other, as if doing their jobs at manic speed might help us outrun the deluge of vitriol being heaped on us. Not since Octomom had a national news story about, really, let's face it, nothing, invited such universal condemnation.

I could see Taylor on the phone in her office. Kimmy was holding up a yellow pad on which she'd just scrawled a solitary "FUCK." I powered up my desktop, praying my e-mail opened to reveal messages my phone had yet to deliver. Between Sage's showboating and the sales spurred by my vertical, companies had begun wooing me for placement. Only yesterday a nursery muralist had sent a flower bouquet made from paint tubes and now . . . radio silence. Not one vendor had responded about the graduation shoot. An e-mail appeared from the custom-embroidered bedding company who'd become my go-to. In one legally delicate sentence, they informed me they were "putting a pause" on "any further exposure" with JeuneBug.

In a few strides I was at Taylor's doorway. Kimmy swung her bat-wing sleeve to block my entrance. "Taylor, let me help," I said over her arm. "We have to say something to the press or at least to our vendors—"

"We have this covered."

"I have curated the most profitable vertical on this site." I stood my ground. "And my vendors—our vendors—are bailing. We have to pivot and then we have to get the word out. Immediately. If Sage won't give us talking points, we'll craft our own. What are we telling people?"

"'People?'" she mimicked. "Tell your Facebook friends we're getting slaughtered and Mort Studecker's coming in for a front row seat at five. I swear to God, Rory." Taylor was shaking. "If you don't get out of here right now, I'm going *to kill you*," she bellowed, tears springing from her eyes as she charged forward. The door slammed, causing the glass wall to undulate in one massive, unsettling wave. And for a split second, the bullpen was still. Just one. But in that time, I managed to ask myself the question I hadn't asked in I didn't know how long. The voice came clear and sharp into my ear, *What do you want, Rory?* And when the answer shot back I knew exactly where I needed to go.

Kathryn's assistant was waiting to usher me inside her office, which was piled waist-high with design books and boxes of samples awaiting her verdict. The desk was vintage Knoll, the Chesterfield uphol-stered in raw silk, but the focal point of the room, the anchor piece, was the woman herself.

"Rory." Greeting me, Kathryn pulled off her glasses and came around to give me a kiss on the cheek. "It should be noted I'm tearing myself away," she said, tossing her hand at her computer.

"Can I get you something? Espresso? Pellegrino? Marshmallows to roast?"

"No, thank you," I said, not sitting down.

She nodded to dismiss her assistant and I waited for the door to click shut.

"It's time to do something." I put my bag on the couch. I wasn't carrying a burned broom, but I was ready to have my request granted.

She leaned back against her desk and crossed her arms. "No, it's time to do *nothing*. Asher dug his own grave with his little sausage fingers."

"There's a grave," I countered. "But we don't know who's going in it."

She cocked her head. "What does that mean?"

"Mort's already decided on Asher. You're out, Kathryn. Taylor told me."

"Oh, Taylor," she scoffed, retreating to her desk chair and putting her glasses back on.

"We need to move. Mort's shutting Jeunebug down at four o'clock. Announcing his successor can't be far behind." I dug my hands into my pockets, grabbing the business cards I'd been given by those blue chip companies I'd chatted up at her marathon party. I came around, dropped them on her blotter, and crouched so we were eye to eye. "Get on the phone. Call every one of these guys and anyone else you can think of. Offer them free ads on JeuneBug for the next month, or three months—whatever it takes to get them onboard. They'll do it if you ask them to; you know they will. They'd strip naked in Times Square if you say so. Call in your favors. It's time."

"To say what?"

"That my vertical has consistently sold out. There are waiting lists for almost every item I've featured."

"For that to have any weight, they'd need a commitment that you're staying."

I wasn't ready to play that card. I stood back and crossed my arms.

"Tell them that despite the smug press for the site, our sales are strong and our customers loyal."

"How does this help the company—help me?"

"It will stabilize the losses and buy time to keep the revenue growing; then you can talk them into buying ads at full value in the fall. And *you* can be the person who not only didn't gamble Mort's $5 million; you rescued it."

She nodded, knowing I was right. If she was going to beat Asher, she was going to need this insurance policy. As I picked up my bag, she raised her eyes to me. "I've never said this before, but I'm going to owe you."

I reached for the door. "I know." And I knew exactly what I was going to ask for. "But first save yourself."

Arriving back at JeuneBug, waiting for word from Kathryn, breath held, I stepped off the elevator to see Ginger tearfully trimming her bangs at the reception desk with a pair of fabric sheers. She pointed the blades toward the conference room.

Mort.

Was already there.

Shit. Shitshitshit. I texted Kathryn, *"MORT MEETING RIGHT NOW!"*

As I slipped in behind her, Taylor was talking very quickly: "A blip, that's all. We just have to wait this out. Goop rebounded and so will we." Overnight someone had put up the long-awaited wallpaper—a photomural of Kimmy and Taylor stretched out on Asher's yacht, toasting champagne bottles at some club, leaning into each other on skis. "We can absolutely sustain this," she continued emphatically. "Our revenue's climbing, and we're on target to be profitable by next year."

"Next year?" Mort wheezed. "At this rate, you don't have an hour. I'm not throwing good money after bad."

"You are being totally shortsighted," Taylor spit.

"Enough," Asher admonished. "The decision's been made."

"And you're siding with *him*?"

Pointedly ignoring her, Asher stood. "Sorry to disrupt your day, Mort. I wish you'd let me take care of this."

"Hold on." I stepped around Taylor, who was wild-eyed but didn't stop me. "Despite this not being her blunder, Kathryn Stossel's been on the phone all morning, offering her advertisers free banners on JeuneBug—"

"Free?" Asher scoffed.

"Free until we *stabilize*," I finished. "These are personal relation-ships she's leveraging on our behalf."

"Uh-uh. No way." Taylor shook her head. "I swore we wouldn't do ads. We're not going backward."

"What brands?" Asher demanded. "Name one deal."

I gripped my phone with its unhelpful black screen. Fuck me. "I'd be happy to." I stalled. "Let me just pull it up."

"Would somebody tell me who this is?" Mort asked the room.

"Rory McGovern, sir." I walked to him with my hand extended. "I'm the director of the Be vertical, which has been selling out since launch."

"And you work for Kathryn?" Mort tried to piece it together.

"*With* her," I corrected him. "I'm working *with* her."

"This is bullshit." Asher stared me down. "Even the mighty Stossel couldn't pull that off."

"We have deals, Asher," I told him. "Yes, we do. I wouldn't just barge in here if we didn't."

"With who?" Kimmy genuinely asked.

"Yeah, who?" Mort turned to me.

"And I will tell you. Here I go . . . I'm going to . . ." Sing the three verses of "Bye Bye Miss American Pie" I can remember from choir. My phone buzzed, and I whipped it up—almost kissing it when I read the word. "Cartier!" I proclaimed. "Cartier will be placing an ad with us." My phone buzzed again. "And Armani Casa. Armani Casa's in too. And that's just the beginning."

Asher scowled, the bronzed folds of his face layering like a shar-pei.

Taylor shoved back her chair. "With ads this just becomes every other site!"

Mort stood and was not much taller than when he'd been sitting. "If Kathryn can see the way, so be it. I have a lot to think about. And I have a lunch." As he shuffled his way clear of the door, Asher gripped the table as if the room was spinning.

"Sorry!" Just then Ginger was standing in the doorway, trying to octopus herself across it to bar . . . Gavin, pushing past her into the conference room.

"Hey, like, dude," he said, "No one's answering my calls and I had five orders through your spread. Am I still filling them? Cuz your vendor portal crashed and—Oh, hey—" he said, stopping short at the sight of me, his whole face smiling broadly, sexily. Taylor saw and her eyes narrowed to murderous slits.

And I shrugged.

Because she got me, finally—the one who was, like, forty.

As I rolled into our building an hour later with a locksmith and dared the staff to call the police, it dawned on me that Blake was right all those months ago. I had been waiting, but not for rescue. I'd been waiting for something, someone to make the life I'd built feel legit. I'd been scanning the horizon for endorsement. And I thought being chosen by Blake Turner was as close as a girl could get.

Now there he was, standing in our foyer in his boxers, the man who had unchosen me. "You're going to have to fix that," he greeted me, pointing at the hole in the door. "I have a guest com-ing."

"A guest?" I dropped my bag at my feet, the dislodged lock on top of it.

"I put an ad on Airbnb. I'm going to share with Wynn for a while." He held up the pad where he was making notes. "Just while I get myself together."

"No." I crossed my arms, shaking my head, letting that "no" fill up my whole body. "Not only would that give me grounds to sue you for sole custody. But, no. No rotating cast of strangers sleeping down the hall from my kids."

"*Our* kids."

"Have you noticed how everything is ours when it suits you, yours when that's more convenient?" I asked, hearing it plainly for the first time myself.

"Rory, you can't just—"

"Blake," I cut him off. "For the last nine months, you've thrown me for one loop after another while I accommodated and accommodated and accommodated. I've explained the unexplainable, accepted the unacceptable, and pulled a career out of the fucking ether. I've learned the scoring system in karate, solved new math, and fixed doll furniture with gum. I've stood through three-hour soccer matches in the rain with the flu, sent work e-mails while cleaning vomit out of grout, and gotten Wynn into middle school. And all of it, *all of it*, I have done without you."

"You're capable, Rory," he sneered, his eyes flashing. "I get it."

"But *I* didn't. The tasks required to keep our family running, the things that take stupid amounts of time and energy and figuring out—nobody claps, nobody reads about them in *Entertainment Weekly*."

"Okay, look—"

"Nope. Can't. No more looking. You chose to end our marriage. That's it. That's the choice you get. Now *I* choose how it goes down."

"Rory."

"This is my apartment. My name's on the lease. *My* name. And I'm going to live here, with our children, until I find the perfect place for them. Then, and only then, will we move out. You have a day to get yourself a room somewhere and start over or whatever the hell you are doing and then I am coming home. Are we clear?"

"You know this couldn't be a worse time for me."

"Oh, Blake." I looked into his eyes. "You still don't get it, do you? You got fired. And that's a heartbreaking blow. But you did not invent this experience." I took a deep breath. With or without his ring, I had a family, a career, the ability to love deeply and be loved back. "And neither did I."

Although I know we didn't move out until weeks later, in my memory, when I closed the severed door on him that afternoon, that's when I left.

Epilogue

The Friday before Labor Day weekend, Manhattan slims down; the lucky head to their country houses, the lucky-adjacent stay with family and friends who own them, and the lucky-aspiring quadruple up in shares nearby.

This year I'm a different kind of lucky.

"Small chocolate cone, please," I order, anticipating walking up Sixth Avenue and eating an ice cream without looking down the whole time to see if someone is wearing theirs.

As I got dressed this morning in my new apartment, I was so keenly aware of how good it feels to be coming out of months where my focus shrunk to everything I was losing. Now I'm solely grateful for everything I have: the kids most nights, and a two bedroom in Morningside Heights with a sunken living room and views of the George Washington Bridge. I have air in my lungs and a heart that is finding a steady rhythm again.

I also have my furniture line back. Once JeuneBug stabilized, I asked the new executive director of Stellar, and she had to say yes.

So, have I really missed those two weeks up in Woodstock? No, I have not.

It's given me the freedom to work long hours. And since I was wrapping up my work at JeuneBug *and* overseeing the launch of Rory M Designs, it was much appreciated.

We already have orders from Beverly Hills to Savannah; now the focus is on quality control and production costs. I never could have imagined I would enjoy the business side of a business so much. Maybe it's because this company is finally something wholly mine or, I'm willing to concede, something from my time with Taylor seeped into me indelibly. RM Designs is a paper-free office, and not only can I now force-rank a deck for optimal ad click-rev with the best of them, but Taylor is still the person I channel when I'm facing the buyers—and it works. I heard she's developing an app that helps you pick a plastic surgeon. I truly hope, for her peace of mind, that it's a hit.

JeuneBug closed for the holiday weekend at lunchtime. They had a little farewell party for me (Cushbars for everyone!) and, after hugging Ginger and Merrill good-bye, I found myself walking uptown, knowing, and denying, where I was headed.

The kids are at Val's through Monday night. At first Blake was reluctant to join them because he can't legally sublet on Airbnb if he's not in residence and the Turners still live in fear of losing their rent control status.

Oh, I think as I finish my ice cream cone and cross Forty-Seventh Street, *it's so nice not to be a Turner anymore.*

Once his J. J. Abrams lawyer was gone, Blake was consigned to return to mediation, where we finished working out what was best for the kids (Airbnb *only* when they're not in residence; half the revenue goes to their support). Blake is still committed to eking out an acting career, apparently content to share a bathroom and refrigerator with a changing cast of adults, happy to live out of his childhood bedroom, happy to be whatever character he's prepping for that week. Lately I wonder if I was trying so hard to make a three-dimensional life with someone who would have been perfectly happy with two. I guess the point is that I wouldn't have been.

I still get that electrical storm feeling when I see him, but it's not one of need so much as poignancy. And when the car pulls out with the kids waving good-bye and I'm not in it, I still have to walk for a while and breathe through the plunger suck of sadness. But I'm learning it abates within hours instead of days. I hear at some point the hours will be minutes and eventually, to paraphrase Toni Morrison, it will just be the weather.

But I also know that on this anniversary of sorts, I need to have a destination.

Fanning the top of my sundress from where it clings to my chest, I cross from the shaded side of the street to stand under the sun-washed stretch of sidewalk in front of Josh's office building. I've written him a thousand e-mails in my head, but this wasn't something I was going to write. So I'm just going to go in and have the guard call up. Just like that. Just . . . go.

I smooth down my skirt. Blot the sweat off my forehead. Fix my ponytail. And stand there.

"Rory?"

I look up and all at once there he is, in a khaki suit and tanned. Lighting strikes below my belly button.

"How are you?" He gives me a quick hug. I smell a second of him.

"I'm good," I say. "How are you?"

"Sweltering."

"Yes," I say nodding, sweating, smiling.

"Are you on your way . . . ?" He looks uncertain.

"To see you." God, I am ridiculously nervous. He seems surprised and then a little frozen. "I'm sure you guys are heading out for the weekend, but I was wondering if you have a minute—"

"I was just grabbing a soda, actually." He nods to indicate the deli across the street.

"Can I walk with you?" I ask.

"Please," he says and we turn, waiting for the cars to stop.

"Josh—"

"No," he warns, pulling me back as a taxi races past. "Okay, now." He motions that it's safe to cross and I follow him into the store and down the narrow linoleum aisle to the refrigerators. He pulls out a bottle of Mexican Coke. "The one thing they do not stock in the machines upstairs. Want one?"

"Please."

He reaches into the case.

"I'm just going to talk at you for a second," I say quickly while he's not looking at me. "While we're here and it's cold."

"Rory, you don't have to—"

"No, I do. I'm so sorry that I never reached out. I mean, you stayed with my son for hours. That was such a graceless moment in my life and, honestly, I didn't know if it would be appropriate to call and say thank you."

He lifts his eyes from the bottles to me and I can barely look in them. The energy between us is as I remembered it and there's nothing to be done about that. "I don't know if we should even be talking or if it's weird or gross for me to say any of this out loud—"

"Rory—"

"But there've been so many endings in my life lately, and as I was tallying things up, I just didn't want the last time I talked to you to be while I was standing in a hospital room holding my ex-husband's hand. You deserve better than that. What you were to me deserves better than that."

"Were?"

"You did a really great thing that you didn't have to do. And I know it's not cool for us to be friends anymore, but I just needed you to know that you were a bright spot in a very, very dark year. And that's how I'm going to remember you, okay?"

He looks down at me, into me, and I want to do things right here up against that chilled door that you cannot do to another woman's husband. That I wouldn't.

I start to back away.

He clears his throat. "Where do you live now?"

"Morningside Heights," I answer. "It's a bit of a trek, but it's leafy."

He nods before saying, "I live on Second and Seventy-Third."

"What," I ask stunned. "You sold that apartment? But it was gorgeous—"

"No, I mean, we're—I'm—separated. Still getting used to saying that." He shifts and I feel my heart do the same on its axis.

"Oh. Oh! I'm so sorry. And here I'm only offering you a soda. I should be buying you the hard stuff."

We can't take our eyes off each other.

"Would you prefer a cocktail?" I venture.

He shakes his head.

"A beer?"

"No."

God, I'm misreading this.

"I'd prefer," he says in a low voice, "to kiss you." He steps in and leans down. "We can do that?" he asks so close his lips are almost grazing mine. "Can't we?"

"Yes," I whisper, rising to meet him. "We can."

At my age it's so nice to know that just when it feels like all your firsts are behind you, you couldn't be more wrong.

Acknowledgments

Emma wishes to thank:

My mother, Joan, who broke her finger, found her glasses, and packed up the car more than any girl should have to. And never once lost her sense of humor.

My godmother, Carolyn, for teaching her, and by proxy me, how to pull up one's socks. My godfather, Jacoby, who made Being a Grown-Up seem a lovely and worthwhile pursuit. And to you both, for doing the same for Being Married.

My father, John, for being right about life coming down to who has the best stories to tell. And my stepmother, Janet, for loving him as much in the silence as the telling.

My husband, Joel, for keeping the Body of Work torch—and my heart—lit, no matter the weather.

And finally Nicki for each of our girls, including Lola. Especially Lola.

After the near million words we've strung together, it turns out none do justice to my feelings for you.

You are my one true one.

Nicola wishes to thank:

Emma, my love, you have walked in lockstep with me for fifteen years, and together we have co-created ten wonderful children. We have had success beyond our wildest dreams, failures that put us in great company, and met Madonna. We've hidden in bathrooms together, taken turns making amazing social gaffes, and gotten better all the while. 25 to 40. Man, we have grown up together. And raised each other. Since the day we met you have been on an inspiring quest to become the best version of yourself, and I have been privileged to have a front row seat. So if this is a senior yearbook of sorts, let me end by saying . . . *because I knew you I have been changed for good*.

P.S. I'll talk to you in five minutes.

About the Authors

Emma and Nicola have been writing together for fifteen years, longer than most marriages, and hope to feel grown-up any day now. They are also the co-founders of the creative coaching firm TheFinishedThought.com, where they help aspiring authors become published writers. They love to answer writing questions, so please find them @nannydairies, on Instagram as therealnannydiaries, and through their site.